HOWL AT THE MOON

Christine Warren

St. Martin's Paperbacks

This is a work of fiction. All of the characters, organizations, and events portrayed in this novel are either products of the author's imagination or are used fictitiously.

HOWL AT THE MOON

For information address St. Martin's Press, 175 Fifth Avenue, New York, NY 10010.

ISBN: 0-312-94790-9
EAN: 978-0-312-94790-3

Printed in the United States of America

St. Martin's Paperbacks edition / November 2007

St. Martin's Paperbacks are published by St. Martin's Press, 175 Fifth Avenue, New York, NY 10010.

10 9 8 7 6 5 4 3

CHAPTER 1

S eriously, there's this thing called 'the sun,' and it gives off this stuff called 'sunlight' that it's important to have occasional contact with."

"Uh-huh."

Samantha Carstairs narrowed her eyes and glared over her left shoulder at her best friend. Annie clearly wasn't paying any attention, which, though annoying, wasn't exactly unusual.

"Without this 'sunlight' stuff, your body can't make any vitamin D."

"Yeah."

"And if your body doesn't make enough vitamin D . . ." Sam barely blinked as the phlebotomy needle bit into her skin. She was too busy trying to figure out if her friend remembered that more than just her forearm and veins was still in the room. ". . . your tail is going to shrivel up and drop off."

"It would not. At most, if the tailbones softened that badly, I might develop a slight curve." Annie Cryer untied the rubber tourniquet around Sam's bicep and dropped it onto the stainless-steel laboratory counter.

"Open and close your fist a few times. Your veins are being stingy today for some reason."

"Maybe because you've already sucked more blood from me than a vampire with an iron deficiency," Sam grumbled, but she made the fist obediently. She had this routine down after the last eight months of regular withdrawals. The only thing she didn't have a handle on at the moment was what had added the barely perceptible sharpness of nerves to the other woman's scent.

Annie looked up from the slowly filling vial of blood and frowned. "Have you been feeling light-headed? Damn it, Sam, I told you to let me know if you started to not feel well after the donations. I'll stop collecting from you. I've got a couple of vials left from last time. Those would last me a few more weeks, if I just cut down on the number of tests I'm running in each batch."

"It's fine, Annie. I feel fine," Sam sighed. Not because she was lying, but because it was so like Annie for the subtle approach to go flying over her head without even slowing down. Not that subtlety happened to be one of Sam's specialties. "You're the one I'm worried about. You need to get out of this building before your muscles atrophy. Have you even been back to your apartment in the past week?"

Annie shrugged and efficiently switched out vials. "There's a sofa in my office. And I can shower in the doctors' lounge."

"Not my point. You're a werewolf, An, remember? You need to get outside."

Sam knew the truth of that better than most. After

all, she was a werewolf, too, a member of the same pack. In fact, her mother and Annie's mother had given birth within a few weeks of each other, and the girls had been raised as littermates from the age of four. They had, literally, grown up together.

"I'm fine."

"Sure, the way Victor Frankenstein was fine," Samantha retorted. "I'm starting to worry about leaving you alone during electrical storms."

That was only a slight exaggeration. Before today, Sam had just been exasperated. She had assumed Annie was going through one of the phases she hit every time one of her experiments reached a critical stage. She always disappeared at those times, but she usually came back a few days later, riding a high of scientific accomplishment the way a manic-depressive rode a high of dopamine. Only this time it had been weeks, Annie still hadn't crawled out from her lab, and she looked a long way from giddy with intellectual triumph. She looked almost haunted.

Annie's interest in science had always bordered on the obsessive, so it wasn't the disappearance or the single-mindedness that worried Sam. Her friend had been that way ever since grade school, which was about how long Sam had been nagging Annie to take a break now and then. Usually even when she was in the midst of one of her experimental breakthroughs and Sam came to drag her back to the world of the living, Annie would kick and scream but then spend hours describing her work to Sam in loving detail. This time, Annie hadn't said a word. If it weren't for the fact that she hadn't left the lab in two weeks, Sam would have shrugged off her worry and gotten on with her life. But Annie remained silent and didn't even mention the words "data" or "P value." It was creepy.

Not that it did Annie any good to try to explain her work. The length of time Sam had been trying to drag her friend out of her lab coat was also how long it had been since the two of them had shared a classroom. While Sam had struggled to master the intricacies of long division, Annie had been skipping grades like boxes on a hopscotch board. At fifteen, she had landed herself in the biochemistry department at Columbia University. She'd gotten her PhD at twenty-one. Her first PhD. She had two now: one in biochemistry and the other in molecular biology. Sam was lucky her bachelor's from CUNY hadn't been snatched out of her hand, rolled into a tube, and used by her professors to whack her a few times over her nose. An intellectual she wasn't.

Which, Sam figured ruefully, she should have thought of before she tried to lecture Annie on vitamin deficiencies. And Sam still didn't have an answer to the question she had come here to ask. Time for a change of tactics.

Where humor hadn't worked, maybe pity would. Or guilt.

"Annie, come on. Your mother is worried about you. And if that weren't bad enough, she's given up trying to reach you and turned on me instead. If I don't bring her proof of your continued health and well-being, I think she's going to challenge me." Sam watched her friend's face for any sign of weakening. "And you know what? I think she could take me."

"Don't be ridiculous. My mother is almost thirty years older than you, and she hasn't issued a dominance challenge in decades." Annie popped the fourth and last tube free and withdrew the needle, pressing a gauze pad against the puncture mark. Her movements remained as brisk and competent as always, but the shadows in the back of her eyes didn't escape the notice of someone who knew her better than a sibling.

"She hasn't had to. There isn't a Lupine in Manhattan who would be willing to accept one. We know when to show our bellies, sweetheart."

Annie's pen didn't even pause as she labeled the tubes. "I've never seen you show your belly to anyone, Samantha. Not even Graham."

Samantha felt her eyebrows shoot up. "You think I'd defy the Alpha of the Silverback Clan? Do I look suicidal to you? I can assure you the only reason our pack leader hasn't seen my belly is because he's never asked to. But I still do my crunches every day, just in case."

"Right."

Annie turned away so abruptly, she banged her hip into the counter and sent the vials of blood skittering toward the floor.

Sam's hand shot out and caught them before they had time to fall more than two or three inches.

"All right, that does it," she growled, slapping the vials back onto the counter with restrained ferocity. Guilt could go screw itself. She switched to threats. "You seriously need to tell me what's going on with you, Annie, before I tell your mother to come down here and find out for herself."

With both her palms, noticeably shaking, pressed to

the cool countertop, Annie bent forward and shook her head. "I can't."

"Why the hell not?" Sam figured she probably looked as confused as she sounded. She could feel herself scowling. "I'm your best friend. You told me when you had your first change, your first period, and your first orgasm. What could you possibly have to say that would freak me out?"

Annie shook her head, her dark hair falling forward to conceal her face. "I'm not worried about you freaking. I'm worried about you telling the Alpha."

Sam's stomach took a sudden trip on an amusement park ride, climbing into her throat before dropping so fast, gravity seemed to keep it airborne for a long, queasy moment. Damn it, this was going to be worse than she'd feared. Her instincts barked at her not to ask any more questions, but the words were out before she could stop them. "What do you mean?"

"Exactly what you think I mean, Sam."

Oh, shit. Her instincts shifted from trying to shut Annie up to trying to get her out the nearest door, window, or unreinforced concrete wall. Something very not good was going on here. So not good it bordered on bad.

For a second, she couldn't seem to remember how to speak, as if the primitive side of her brain had taken over and left her inarticulate and powerless. She watched while Annie calmly gathered up the blood vials and stowed them carefully in the small refrigerator on top of the counter. Her motions looked jerky and uncoordinated for the first time Sam could remember. Annie wasn't clumsy. She was smart, not always careful, and often oblivious, but she'd never been clumsy.

"Holy hell, An, what have you gotten yourself into?" she whispered.

Annie shook her head emphatically and slammed the refrigerator door. "Forget about it. I'm not dragging you any further into this than you already are. Right now, if the Alpha asks you, you've got no idea what's going on. You won't have to lie. Let's keep it that way."

"Are you serious?" Sam tossed the gauze into the trash and yanked down her sleeve. "Okay, (a) if Graham Winters asks me questions, you're right that I won't have to lie because I won't even need to open my mouth for him to realize something is wrong. And (b) how am I already involved in whatever it is I know nothing about?"

"I said forget it," Annie repeated, and headed for the door that Sam knew led down a short, cramped hall to her small, cramped office.

Sam stalked after her. "No, I'm not going to forget it. If I'm caught up in this, I deserve to know. And if it affects the pack as a whole, so does the Alpha."

Annie sank down into her battered leather desk chair and buried her head in her arms. "It's nothing, Sam."

Her voice was muffled, but Sam could hear the hiss of the water in the wall pipes if she concentrated, so it wasn't like she'd missed anything important.

"Bullshit. *Nothing* doesn't leave you smelling like a turkey on the third Wednesday in November."

"I shouldn't have said that before. You're not

involved. You have nothing to worry about. Now will you shut up and please go away?"

"Sure, that sounds exactly like what I'm going to do." Sam pushed the office door shut and leaned against the panel, crossing her arms over her chest. "You have to tell me what's going on, An."

The other woman looked up, her light brown eyes glinting behind her wire-framed glasses. Her spine lengthened, and her shoulders rounded as if to puff herself up and make her size as daunting as possible. Her lips pulled back from her teeth in what would have been a snarl if she'd been in her other skin. "Oh, I do, do I?"

Sam rolled her eyes. "Don't even go there, An. I love you like a sister, but I outweigh you by twenty pounds, and I can and will kick your ass if you make me."

Annie visibly deflated. "I know," she said, rubbing her forehead as if she could rub away whatever was bothering her. "I know, Sam, but trust me, it's better if I leave you out of this."

"*Kick* your *ass*, Annie."

It was interesting, actually. Sam could almost see the scales in Annie's head bobbing up and down as she weighed her stories and tried to decide what to share.

"It's just . . . work," she finally managed, adjusting her glasses in the nervous habit Sam knew meant she was lying like a cheap toupee. "Some research I've been doing on . . . us."

"Us?"

Annie's chin jerked up and down. "Yes. On Lupines."

Sam's stomach took another nosedive. "You mean on me."

"You've been an important source of research material."

"Shit." Sam blew out a breath and crossed the two steps to the chair in front of Annie's desk. She sank down and braced her forearms on her knees. "What exactly are you researching, Annie?"

"I'm decoding the genome."

"And how far have you gotten?"

"I've decoded the genome."

Sam blinked. Somehow the answer didn't surprise her. "But that should be a good thing, right? I mean, decoding a genome is the first step in finding new medicines and treatments for diseases and stuff, right?"

"Sure. It's huge. With this kind of information, we could find a cure for AIDS or smallpox or anthrax."

Her head was already bobbing up and down before the words actually hit. Sam froze. Those were three diseases to which Lupines were not particularly susceptible. By "not particularly," of course, she meant "not at all." A werewolf could eat a small village full of AIDS victims and not end up with so much as a case of the sniffles. Something in werewolves' genes just kept the human virus from getting a toehold in their immune systems.

"You don't look particularly excited about that," she said.

"Oh, it's a huge step. It could mean we'd finally understand what it is that makes us Lupine. We could find out what triggers our changes, what's responsible for our speed, even what it is about shifting that helps us heal what would otherwise be life-threatening wounds."

"But?"

Annie laughed, not sounding amused. "Secrets don't keep in science, and now that our biggest secret is out, it won't be long before the rest of them leak as well. We'll be the most popular kids in school."

The light dawned, and Sam swore. "And everyone will want to be just like us."

"Exactly."

"You'll have to stop, An. You have to put this stuff away. If human scientists got their hands on what you're telling me you're working on, we'd be the next great species of lab rat."

"You don't think I know that? I'm a certified genius, Sam. The thought had occurred to me."

"Come on. I'll help." Sam stood. "We'll grab everything together and get rid of it. I can take it back to the club with me and have them throw it in the furnace if I have to. Show me what to start with."

Annie shook her head, looking as if she wanted to cry. "I can't."

"Why the hell not? You know how dangerous this is, Annie. What's the matter with you?"

"Many, many things." She gave that laugh again, humorless and more sarcastic than anything else Sam had ever heard come out of Annie's mouth. "But at the moment, the problem isn't me. I think . . ." She paused. "I think someone started spying on me."

Sam blinked. "What?"

"It's mostly little things," Annie said, "but lately I've been feeling like I'm being followed. The person doesn't always smell the same, but I swear it's happening. I can feel my hackles rising whenever they get close, and a couple of times I've set things down, like on a table at a coffee shop or next to me on the subway, and half the time they go missing. Gordon thinks I'm being ridiculous, of course."

Sam said something her aunt would have shaken her by the scruff for if she'd heard. Gordon Entwhistle was a human who worked with Annie, when he wasn't busy trying to get himself some publicity or take the credit for someone else's hard work, and Sam had hated him on sight. Unfortunately, Annie hadn't been as discerning.

It probably hadn't helped that since she rarely left the lab, Annie didn't have a whole lot of experience with men, or a whole lot of opportunities to meet them. When a reasonably attractive—if you discounted the coating of slime—and reasonably intelligent—if you equated ruthless self-preservation and a wily, cutthroat sense of ego with intelligence—man waltzed into her territory and played the smitten flatterer, Annie had reacted like any woman in her situation would have: she'd developed a crush.

Sam set her teeth. "What does Gordon have to do with it?"

"He's been very interested in my work," Annie said, her shoulders hitching defensively. "Very supportive. He's helped out a lot, Sam. Two hands make the tests go a lot faster, after all."

"I'm sure."

She was. And she was also sure that two names on a paper published in *Science* would make Entwhistle's career plans go a lot faster, too.

"Don't look at me like that." Annie frowned. "He *has* helped. It's just . . . lately . . ."

"Well, maybe I'm being paranoid, but it feels like he's paying more attention than he used to. Not to me, but to the work."

"And?"

"It started around the same time I started to get the feeling of being followed. That just strikes me as a really big coincidence. I'm not sure I can trust him anymore."

Sam refrained from telling Annie she never should have. "You can't think he's the one following you? You spend most of your time in the same lab with him anyway, and it's not like you wouldn't notice if he kept showing up where you were outside of here."

"I know," Annie said. "But maybe he's involved in it somehow. Sam, I know this all sounds crazy, but I'm starting to get really scared. This work is significant. There could be a lot of people interested in it, if they knew about it, for all the wrong reasons."

Sam shook her head. "That's it, An. I don't care what your plans were; you *have* to tell the Alpha. And if you don't, I will."

"I can't. Not yet." She held up her hand when Sam opened her mouth to protest. "I've got time, at least a few more days, before things get to the point where we need to be worried. I'm keeping the key to my notes separate from the main data, and the results from my latest panels won't be in until the middle of next week. Until those are here, the data is too incomplete to be useful to anyone. I promise."

"Annie—"

"No, Sam, I mean it. I promise that if the danger was imminent, I'd go to Graham myself, but it isn't. And until I run tests on the samples I just took, I can't confirm half of what I've already done. It'll be okay."

For a long minute, Sam stared across the desk at her friend, reading her face, her eyes, and her body for the truth. It was her scent that finally tipped Sam's decision. She could smell nerves, yes, but not fear, and no traces of panic. Not yet.

Sam stood and nodded once. "I'll give you a week, Annie, but that's it. After that, I need to fill Graham in on what's going on. It's going to be bad enough going back to work with him this afternoon, let alone getting through the week."

Sam meant it, too, because Graham Winters wasn't just Sam's Alpha; he was her boss also. Sam worked with him at his office in Vircolac, the city's premier private club for the Other community. She served as personal assistant, assistant general manager, book-keeper, and go-to girl. She didn't make a habit of keeping secrets from the Alpha.

Annie nodded and stood herself, jaw firming. "Thank you, Sam. I owe you one."

Sam snorted. "You owe me about seven thousand, three hundred, and forty-two, but who's counting?" Shaking her head, she turned and opened the office door. "One week, Annie. The clock is ticking."

As Sam made her way back out of the lab and into the Manhattan afternoon, she sent up a silent prayer that the alarm wouldn't go off before they were ready for it.

CHAPTER 2

The Vircolac Club had been founded when Others first began to congregate in the New World in large enough numbers to require a private and safe place to gather. For most of the time since then, it had been run quite skillfully by the Winters family, and in addition to being the Silverback Clan's Alpha, Graham Winters also happened to be the club's current owner. As his personal assistant, Sam helped him with both club and pack business and had enough to do to merit a stack of message slips on her desk when she returned from lunch.

"Hey, Sam." Daisy Cliff, one of the club hostesses, had been monitoring the phones while Samantha was out, and she gave a cheerful wave when Samantha stepped back into her office in the town house's old front parlor. "It was pretty quiet today, but that could be because the Man is next door shoving a lunch fit for the Hundred and First Airborne down his wife's throat."

Samantha rolled her eyes. "He'll tell Missy that while she's nursing she's still eating for two, but Missy will tell him that he can shove his multivitamins where the sun don't shine, so it all evens out."

Daisy laughed, a light, trilling sound that proclaimed her part-Siren heritage more clearly than her penchant for really brief bikinis. "True, but things must be going relatively peacefully, because I haven't felt any tremors in the foundation."

"Thanks for holding down the fort for me, Dais, but you should get back before Richards decides I need another lecture about taking his staff away from their appointed positions."

Richards, the club's butler, liked to think of himself as a stern taskmaster, but Samantha and Daisy both knew he would have spared the hostess for the rest of the day if Samantha had needed the help.

"No problem. It's been quiet everywhere, including the dining room. Holler if you need anything else!"

Samantha nodded and waved Daisy out the door, but her attention was already focused on her message slips. She sorted them into two piles, the ones she could handle and the ones that needed to be passed on to Graham. Hers always turned out to be a lot bigger. Tons of people thought they needed to talk to her boss, but Samantha made a vigilant gatekeeper.

Focusing on work helped her push her visit with Annie out of her mind, and within a few minutes she had managed to relax. She'd given Annie a week, and she'd do her best not to worry about it before then. She had the majority of her callers dealt with by the time she scented the Alpha's return. She looked up just before he opened the office door.

"Hey, boss." She grinned as the polished wooden panels swung toward her. "How's it hangin'?"

Graham didn't even blink at her informal greeting. Their relationship operated on a level few others in the pack could have boasted of. Samantha was closer to the Alpha than anyone other than his mate, his cubs, and his Beta, so they tended to dispense with the formalities of rank.

"I swear that female is going to turn my hair gray before I'm forty-five," he growled, but the tone held no real menace. It never did when he spoke of his mate, no matter how much she might currently be driving him crazy.

"It'll look good on you," Samantha offered, still grinning. "Very distinguished."

Graham just sighed like a man much put upon and hitched his hip on the edge of her desk. "It's all right. I'm getting used to it. Besides"—his expression took on a distinctly mischievous cast—"I can always get her back and round out the family in a few months. Four is a nice, even number of pups, don't you think?"

"Oh, sure. And I'm sure if you gave it one more try, you could manage to have a daughter just like Missy. That would be so sweet!" She fluttered her eyelashes innocently.

Graham turned a little pale. "And deal with boys sniffing around a daughter of mine? Just whose side are you on, anyway?"

"I refuse to answer that question on the grounds that it may incriminate me."

"That's fine, because I know a way you can make it up to me."

Sam let her eyes narrow. "And what would that be?"

"I'm going to need you to do me a favor."

She shrugged and dropped her teasing glare. "Sure, no problem. I'll put it on your tab. What's going on?"

"The pack is going to start setting an example of interspecies cooperation."

Sam quirked an eyebrow. "You mean we don't already?"

The question was only half-humorous. The Silverback Clan had a long history of interspecies cooperation, dating back to the time before their Alpha had actually mated with another species. The fact that Graham's family had operated Vircolac for centuries and always opened its doors as neutral ground for all Others played a part in that, as did the pack's long association with the Council of Others. In fact, compared to a lot of the Others out there, the Silverback Clan looked a lot like a supernatural version of the United Nations. Only functional and quite a bit more effective.

"This time we're doing it specifically with the humans, and with the government in particular," Graham said. "I discussed it with Rafe and the rest of the Council last night. I think the consensus labeled it as a 'gesture of good faith.'"

"Which really means that Rafe wanted it, and the rest of the Council decided they'd rather watch the pack do the real work of it than dirty their own hands taking it on."

"Exactly."

Rafael De Santos, Felix werejaguar and head of the Council of Others, tended to get what he wanted from the Council, which was why he made one of the best leaders the Others had ever had. Managing that group was no mean feat when you considered that the rest of the membership consisted of the most powerful vampires, shape-shifters, changelings, and magic users in Manhattan. Still, one of the reasons that things tended to happen according to Rafe's plans was Graham. Having the Alpha of the Silverback Clan as a close friend and a staunch ally had often proved useful to Rafe. It looked like it was about to do so again.

Sam just shook her head. "Okay, so what are we on the hook for this time? More surveillance duty? Security for a contingent of humans from Trinidad and Tobago who want to consult with the Council on treaty negotiations with their local population of were–Gila monsters? I can round up volunteers. I'll ask for the ones who like palm trees and sunbathing. You know, to put the visitors at ease." Her words were joking, but she had already reached for the phone. Her job around here was to make things happen, and Sam was good at her job.

"Actually," Graham pursed his lips and developed a sudden fascination for his fingernails, "it's that word 'volunteer' that I wanted to talk to you about. You in particular."

Sam's head started shaking before he even finished speaking. "Oh no. You know what happened the last time you sent me on some other kind of assignment. It took me months before I could find where you'd filed the bar receipts."

"I handled the office just fine."

"You put them under 'M,' Graham, and when I asked why, you called them medical expenses."

The Alpha shrugged. "Don't worry. This time, you won't be going anywhere. This is a desk job."

Sam eyed him with growing suspicion. He wore his most charming smile, the one that said he was about to convince you to invest your last dollar in a housing development in the middle of the Okefenokee Swamp. Missy called it his Conner smile. Conner was the name of their second son.

Sam could already feel her feet getting wet. "Why doesn't that reassure me?"

Graham clucked his tongue. "Because you have a disturbingly suspicious nature, Samantha. I'm sure your family raised you to be more openhearted than this."

Considering the fact that the family who'd raised her had also raised him—in the pack, everybody helped raise everyone else's pups—that wasn't much of a stretch.

"And do you know why I'm suspicious?" she asked. "Because whenever you get that look—the one you're wearing right now—it bodes ill for me. So stop stalling and lay it on me. I'm a big girl. I can take it."

"We need to clear off some desk space in here," Graham said. "We're going to be having a visitor for a little while."

"Oh, my goddess! We're being *audited*?"

Graham shuddered. "Bite your tongue. No, nothing like that. I've agreed to let a select branch of the U.S. military have the opportunity to recruit pack members. Strictly as volunteers, of course. An army officer is going to be setting up a minioffice space with us for a few weeks."

Sam's glimmer of suspicion exploded in a siren-blaring and red flag—waving supernova of alarm. "Who?"

"Noah Baker."

Yeah, that's what she'd been afraid he would say.

On the surface, there was nothing wrong with Noah Baker. For a human, in fact, he'd made quite a few friends in the Other community since his sister had gotten mixed up with, and subsequently married to, a sun demon. Everybody seemed to like the man, from his demonic new brother-in-law, Rule, to Graham, to Rafe De Santos himself. Even Rafe's wife, Tess, liked Noah, and she wasn't one to suffer fools lightly, or even at all. But then, Noah Baker had proved to be no one's fool. A major in the army's highly selective and newly developed supernatural squadron, he had grit, training, and a cool head under pressure. Not to mention a talent for making large objects make even larger booms.

The only person Sam knew who *didn't* see the human as an all-around swell guy was Sam herself.

Something about Noah just made Sam's hackles rise every time he got within twenty feet of her, and it didn't seem to matter what form she was in at the time. Human, wolf, or were, Sam's teeth went on edge when Noah walked into a room and her hormones went haywire. She'd gotten to be friends with his sister, Abby, but with Noah, the best Sam could manage felt more like a tense cease-fire. And now Graham expected her to share office space with Noah?

Too much a Lupine to directly challenge her Alpha's word, Sam took a more subtle approach. "So he's going to be recruiting for his own unit? This 'spook squad' he's on?"

Graham nodded. "His own unit and a couple of new ones. Apparently, the Pentagon has been pretty happy with the way the squad has handled a couple of recent incidents leading up to and resulting from the Unveiling." The revelation of the Others' existence had set a few backs up around the world. Riots, demonstrations, and protests had been the least of the trouble. "I think their successes have inspired the army to expand, put together a few new teams."

"Do you really think many members of the pack will be interested? Playing well with humans is a new skill for a lot of us."

"To tell you the truth, I think it's a great opportunity. As loyal as our members are to the pack, it's got to chafe a lot of them to know they're not going to get ahead without challenging someone in a dominant position for a better place in line. That's why we get into trouble from time to time with things like the Curtis incident." Graham made euphemistic reference to the time his cousin Curtis had tried to rip his throat out and steal his mate, but Sam got his point. "This should give some of our gammas a good chance to get out from under my paw, so to speak."

"I'm sure no one has a problem with your paw, boss." But even as Sam said it, she uttered a mental curse. Graham made sense. Spending a lifetime in the middle of the pack didn't suit everyone. Graham's former Beta made a good example. Logan Hunter had chafed under the traditional pack system of hierarchy, and the only solution for him had been to leave

Manhattan and take over as Alpha of the White Paw Clan in Connecticut.

Graham making sense, though, failed to make Sam feel any better. All she could think of was the impossibility of getting any work done while a pair of very human and disturbingly intense hazel eyes looked on.

The Alpha flashed her a grin. "You may be nearly as biased as Missy."

Sam forced a smile of her own. "Not quite." She drew in a deep breath. "Well, you're the boss. When can we expect the troops to land?"

"How about now?"

Noah caught the flash of surprise and annoyance on Samantha's face and stifled a grin. He knew he made the Lupine tense just by walking into the room, but then, she did the same to him. Unlike him, though, he suspected Sam had no idea why they disturbed each other so badly. She probably wrote it off as lousy chemistry.

Oh, it was chemistry, all right, but Noah couldn't describe it as lousy. Not by a long shot.

Samantha Carstairs made Noah Baker feel about as predatory as her closest friends and relatives actually were. He might not get furry on full moons, but looking at the luscious female Lupine made him want to howl at one. It had been that way from the first time he'd set eyes on her, while he still thought she was a kidnapper holding his little sister captive. He'd taken one look at Samantha and felt his entire body go on alert. A few parts had even gone on *high* alert.

She had the body of an athlete, not as sinewy as a runner or as fine as a gymnast but covered in sleek, firm muscle and decorated with curves just generous enough to make a sane man look twice. Noah had looked more than that, taking stock from the top of her mane of wavy, richly brown hair to the tips of her feminine feet. Of course, by the end of their first meeting those feet had turned into paws and tried to pin him to the ground in the middle of the small park down the block, but even that hadn't put him off. He'd dated women with bigger vices than occasionally shifting into timber wolves.

After a second of silence, Samantha started to squirm and Noah deliberately shifted his gaze to the other werewolf in the room. Stepping inside, Noah set a cardboard file box down on the chair beside the office door. "Thanks for agreeing to put me up, Graham. I appreciate it."

The Silverback Alpha shook his hand, relieving the last of Noah's worries that the Lupine might still hold a grudge over the way his sister had briefly set the pack's Luna in harm's way a few months back when she'd been pursued by demons. Apparently, Graham didn't like having demons surrounding his wife.

"It's no problem," Graham said. "In fact, I was just telling Sam I think it might be good for some of our young males. Give them a place to channel their aggression other than in a dominance challenge."

Noah smiled. "I'll do my best."

He looked around the spacious room, taking note of the territory Sam had already marked. The huge cherry desk stationed in front of the door to Graham's private inner office had the look of a sentry's gatehouse, and Noah had no trouble picturing her fending off intruders and interlopers. Her area only took up one end of the grand old sitting room, though. There would be plenty of space for him. And he'd be near enough to give the electricity between them time to spar.

This grin he didn't bother to suppress. "Where would you like me to set up?"

Graham shrugged. "That's up to Sam. She's the one who keeps everything in its place around here."

It didn't take a mind reader to see that Sam wanted to put Noah outside with the trash. Or maybe to banish him to another continent. But that wasn't her decision.

Sam forced a pleasant expression onto her face. "I'll have one of the staff bring in a desk and some chairs. If we set them up near the fireplace on the far side of the room, it should give you some privacy for your sales pitch."

And get Noah as far from her as possible without banishing him from the room. Still. He'd save his fighting for other battles. "That works for me. Why don't you just tell me who on the staff I need to talk to, and I'll take care of my own supplies? I'm sure you have plenty of work to do without worrying about me."

"Great." Graham clapped Noah on the back. "I'll leave you to it, then. If you think of anything you need, just let Sam know. I'm putting her entirely at your disposal."

Noah saw Sam's eyes widen and her lips part to protest, but Graham had already retreated to his inner sanctum and closed the door behind him. Patiently Noah waited for Sam to turn her wary gaze back to him before he let the satisfaction bloom across his features.

"That," he said, his voice low and purring, "suits me perfectly. I can hardly wait to get started."

By four o'clock, Sam found herself wishing for a gun, a Valium, or a spot in the witness protection program. Noah Baker had obviously made it his life's work to drive her demented. She had to admit, he seemed to have a talent for it.

After fifteen minutes of discussion that had felt more like fifteen years—during which Sam asked questions about what furniture and supplies he would need for his area and he watched her with those penetrating hazel eyes that tracked every flicker of her breath—Sam had sent him off to see Richards about plundering from the other rooms of the club. The butler would be able to handle Noah while Sam took measurements to determine exactly how many bottles of Scotch would fit in the bottom drawer of her desk.

Laying her head down on a stack of paperwork, she gave a heartfelt groan. "This is never going to work."

"Don't be a pessimist," announced a familiar voice. "If I survived years of living in the same house with him, you can make it a couple of months in a shared office."

Sam groaned again, but she didn't need to lift her head to know that Noah's sister had let herself into the office. "I really don't need any more surprise visitors today, Abby, especially not ones with smart mouths."

"Better a smart mouth than a dumb one." Sam heard light footsteps and a slight rustling as Abby Baker settled herself in one of the chairs on the far side of the desk. "Come on, Sam. Aren't you being just a little bit melodramatic? I admit that my brother can be a pain in the *tuchis,* but he's not *that* bad. You managed to get along with him at my engagement party."

"I was dressed up," Sam grumbled, "and those little meatballs looked like they'd stain."

"With all the Lupines in the room, I doubt any of them would have landed."

Reluctantly Sam raised her head and propped her chin on her hand. "I'm sure that would have amused your family, to see all the werewolves leaping for flying meatballs. I can see your brother's face now."

Abby's friendly odd-colored eyes watched her sympathetically. "Yeah, I know he drives you crazy. That's why I came to lend you moral support. Rule just told me what was going on."

"Are you sure you didn't want to make sure I wasn't snacking on his femur?"

"Of course not. I'm over that old fear. You werewolves are just great big lap puppies." Abby's tone was airy, but her eyes twinkled.

Sam snorted. "Right. You should so work in our press office." Resisting the urge to whine like a two-year-old, she settled for making a disgruntled face. "I want you to know that it's because I consider you a good friend that I'm going to try to get along with him."

"And I appreciate that, even though I still don't get what it is with you two that constantly has you snarling at each other."

That was a question Sam chose not to consider too closely. "Just lucky, I guess."

Abby laughed. "I guess. But, hey, the other reason I came over was to ask if you had plans after work? Missy said the boys are playing poker tonight and they invited Noah to sit in. So Tess suggested drinks and DVDs at her place. Are you interested?"

A moment of introspection revealed Sam's choices: she could call Annie and fail miserably to coax her out of her lab, she could hang out with the lively group of friends no doubt included in Abby's invitation, or she could go back to her own apartment and spend the rest of the night brooding about a certain annoying new office mate. Gee, which of those sounded most appealing?

"Very interested," she answered, and glanced at her watch. "It's twenty till five. I've got a few things to finish up, but I should be able to get out of here on time tonight. I'll meet you guys at Tess and Rafe's?"

"Sounds good. I'm going to run out and pick up a couple of bottles of wine and some whole milk."

"Milk?" Sam blinked.

Abby grinned. "Missy still can't drink because she's breast-feeding, but she needs both the hydration and the calories, so you can tell your boss we're taking care of her. I'll see you later."

Sam waved Abby out the door and then looked down at her desk. If she was lucky—or if she shoved a chair under the doorknob—she just might be able to clear most of the pressing paperwork out of her in-box and slip out of the club without seeing Noah again. Then she'd have the whole weekend to brace herself for their next encounter.

Grimacing, she shook her computer mouse and brought her accounting software back up. She hoped Abby bought a *lot* of wine.

A n attack of doubt wasn't enough to keep a good soldier from doing his duty.

Noah was a very good soldier.

After spending a good amount of time instructing Vircolac's butler as to what he needed in his office area, Noah beat back the impulse to return there for the pleasure of tormenting Samantha for a few more minutes. Instead, he slipped out through the club's kitchens and walked the eight blocks to the second-closest pay phone. There he punched in the number trained into his memory.

"Yes."

The voice on the other end of the line didn't introduce itself, but then, neither did Noah. "They're setting me up today. By Monday, I should be able to get down to business."

"Good. Is everything going smoothly?"

"Yes, sir. The pack and the Alpha are being very cooperative." And he was learning to ignore the feeling he got from lying to all the people around him all the time.

"Make sure it stays that way. I shouldn't have to remind you, Major, that not only do we need results on this; we need them quickly."

Noah's mouth tightened, but the man on the other end of the line couldn't see that. "I'm aware of that, sir."

"Fine. I'll expect updates whenever it's feasible. I definitely want to hear something next week."

"Understood."

The click of the line disconnecting was the only reply Noah got.

Feeling grim, he replaced the receiver and turned toward the liquor store at the end of the block. Returning to the club with a couple of six-packs for tonight's poker game would explain his absence if anyone had missed him or, even less likely, had seen him slipping out. But Noah knew no one had.

He was very good at his job.

CHAPTER 3

It hadn't taken Noah very long after he'd learned of the existence of the Others to realize that, aside from the obvious, the differences between the species were actually remarkably few. Some things just never changed. Poker nights were among them.

The room on the second floor of Vircolac might be a little more elegant than the ones Noah was used to playing in—hell, half the time he ended up playing in a tent or a shack or inside a Bradley fighting vehicle—and the service was a hell of a lot better than he was used to. He could get accustomed to having a waitstaff bringing him a fresh, cold beer every time his bottle even threatened emptiness. But once he got past the surface polish, everything else looked and sounded pretty familiar, from the haze of cigar smoke to the flutter of shuffling cards. Poker was poker, and men were men.

Even, apparently, when they were also wolves. Or jaguars. Or demons.

"Five." Noah tossed his chips into the center of the table and listened to them click. He recognized that sound as well.

"See you."

"I'm in."

"Same."

Rafael De Santos clasped the stub of a very expensive, and mildly illegal, Cuban cigar between his first two fingers and leaned back in his chair. "See and raise. Another five."

Noah grinned. The werejaguar and head of the Council of Others said that so intently, as if the amounts they were betting wouldn't have gotten them laughed away from any serious table in Vegas. Noah liked Rafe. He had from the beginning. There was something steady and purposeful about the other man, for all his air of lazy elegance and weary sophistication. At first glance, a person could make the mistake of writing him off as too much of a pretty boy to worry about.

Noah wasn't that stupid.

He was, however, playing a very edgy hand. In more ways than one.

He threw in his chips and met the raise. "Let's see what you've got, Mr. Kitty."

"Three of a kind." Rafe arched an elegant brow. "You?"

Grunting good-naturedly, Noah tossed his cards onto the table. "Boot marks on my ass, apparently."

"That should teach you." Rafe grinned and leaned forward to rake in his chips.

Graham sighed and squeezed his hand into a fist, cracking open a handful of peanuts. "I don't know why we even bother playing with this bastard," he grumbled, and crunched. "His luck is better than Quinn's."

Noah had never met Sullivan Quinn but had heard of him. The Irish werewolf had come to New York at the beginning of the movement toward the Unveiling and ended up marrying Cassidy Poe, the granddaughter of one of the most influential members of the Council of Others. He and his wife split their time between Manhattan and Dublin these days. So far, their time in New York hadn't overlapped Noah's.

"Don't let the Irishman hear you say that," Tobias Walker snickered over his beer bottle. "He's a touchy son of a bitch."

"Why do you think I waited for a night he wasn't playing?"

Everyone laughed, and Noah tipped his chair back to indulge in a long, lazy stretch. His muscles felt unusually tight, whether from sitting at the poker table or from the tension of being constantly on duty, he wasn't sure. He didn't suppose it really mattered. He'd get out of the chair in a few hours. As for going off duty . . . that might take a bit longer.

Rule gathered the cards for his deal and shuffled the stack in his powerful hands. "Incidentally, Noah, your sister asked me to send you her love. She would also like to know if there is anything she can do to help you settle into your new office."

Noah chuckled. "I'm fine, but you can thank her for me."

The demon's mouth curled in a small, very satisfied smile. "It would be my pleasure."

The legs of Noah's chair landed back on the floor with a *thunk*, his mouth turning down in a scowl. "Hey, we talked about this. You promised no looks like that.

That's my baby sister you're thinking about . . . thinking about."

"Of course." Rule smoothed his expression back into its normally austere lines. "I apologize."

The other men at the table snickered.

"You realize he hasn't stopped thinking any of it, right?" Graham asked, grinning.

Noah snagged a fresh beer off the tray the waiter presented to him and glared. "Shut up, Fido."

"Whatever you say, pal, but I want you to know my sympathy for you is genuine. It drives me crazy enough, and all I've got is a few dozen female cousins." Graham shook his head. "I should send my parents a thank-you card."

"At the very least." Rafe picked up his new hand and began to rearrange the cards. "You do have everything you will need, don't you, Noah? Tess and I would be glad to assist if you think we could be helpful."

He shook his head. "I'm good. Graham's got all the information I need. I'm grateful the pack has been so accommodating."

Graham waved away Noah's thanks. "No problem. Like I told you before, I'm happy to help."

Noah forced a smile and looked down at his cards. Damn it, he'd prefer if they gave him a hard time. It would make his job easier in the end. Until then, he could at least change the subject. "You have. Sam's been great, too."

"She's great professionally. Possibly genetically, too. I gotta say, it can get annoying at times," Graham grumbled, but he was smiling while he said it. "But since without her babysitting skills Missy probably would have tried to divorce me ten times over by now, I try to bear up under the strain."

"You seem to be doing fairly well with that." Noah tossed back two cards, took two new ones. "Abby tells me she's been working for you for at least five years."

Tobias snickered. "You might say that."

Noah raised an eyebrow.

"Let's just say I've been paying her for about five years now. You could make a case for the fact that she's been working for me a lot longer than that." Graham took a drink from his bottle and saw Noah's expression. "She's one of those cousins I mentioned earlier. I may have sent her on an errand or two when she was younger."

"You could put it that way," Tobias laughed. "You could also say she was his minion. Or his retriever."

"You sure as hell wouldn't say that in front of her."

Tobias made a face. "Do I look that stupid?"

Graham turned back to Noah. "She was a helpful girl. You had a little sister. You know how girls are always trailing after you, pestering you. She liked it when I gave her jobs to do. It kept her happy."

"And off your back," Tobias pointed out.

"That, too."

The rest of the men at the table snickered.

"Oh, like none of you have tried anything similar." Graham scowled good-naturedly at the group. "Remember, I know your mates. I know what you've done trying to keep them occupied."

Noah watched the men in question grin and shift in their seats. None of them looked particularly disturbed by that statement. In fact, most of them looked pretty damned content with the world.

"Speaking of them," he said, "I'm surprised none of them has stuck a head in here tonight. They seem to be a pretty curious bunch."

"Oh, they are. But Tess invited them all to our home this evening," Rafe said. "She said that if we were going to indulge in our masculine pastimes, the ladies would need to arrange something to keep themselves occupied."

The clink of chips on the table heralded a moment of silence. A long moment. The men looked at one another.

Carefully Tobias laid his cards face down on the table and cleared his throat. "So, Rafe, did Tess happen to tell you what they had planned?"

Rafe shook his head slowly. "No, she did not. When I asked, she simply told me not to worry."

"That sounds . . . ," Rule frowned, ". . . worrying."

I'm in for fifty."

"I'll raise."

"I'll see that."

"Yeah? Well, in that case, I'm all in."

Sam rolled her eyes. "I thought it was the boys' night to gamble."

Tess De Santos raised her eyebrows and smiled over the rim of her wineglass, looking almost as feline as her werejaguar husband. "So? I'm feeling sporting."

"Me, too." Fiona Walker popped a grape into her mouth and looked cheeky, which pretty much counted as her normal expression.

"But do you have to sport with my love life?" Sam grumbled, refilling her glass with Shiraz.

"Trust me, Sam, where I come from, it's practically a rite of passage." Missy Winters smiled to soften her words, but Sam noticed she made no effort to take them back.

While the Silverback Luna was generally one of the softest-hearted people Sam had ever met, Missy had also met the Alpha through a series of nightmare dates her closest friends had arranged for one another. Those friends, frankly, terrified Sam, so she should probably watch what she said before Missy decided to throw her on their untender mercies.

"We all have your best interests at heart," Tess said. "I mean, how long has it been since you and Pete broke up?"

"What does that have to do with anything?"

Fiona grinned. "You mean aside from providing the info we need to handicap this little wager of ours? Come on, Samantha. We're girls. We gossip."

"But do you have to gossip about how long it's going to be before I get laid again?" Sam gulped more wine.

"Of course we do," Fiona said, her grin widening. "After all, the rest of us all have mates, so we know exactly when we're getting laid next. You're the only one with an element of chance for us to gamble on."

"Shouldn't you be in Faerie kissing royal ass right now?" Sam grumbled.

"Darling, I *am* royal ass." Which was technically true, although most of the time the Fae princess went out of her way to avoid the title and lived life like nothing more exciting than Tobias' wife. Sam noticed that Fiona wasn't afraid to use it when it suited her purposes. "But that's hardly the point. We weren't discussing my ass, spectacular though it may be; we were discussing yours. More specifically, we were basing a friendly wager on the fact that several of our mutual acquaintances would like to get a piece of it just as soon as you stop sulking about Peter."

"Sulking? I'm not *sulking*. I dumped him. Months ago. And for good reason. He was a wimp," Sam protested. Then she paused, her ears metaphorically perking. "Really? Several?"

Tess wriggled her eyebrows. "As in more than a few."

"Greater than a handful," Missy agreed with a grin.

Sam pursed her lips. "Like who? I want names."

"Nope." Fiona shook her head. "That would be telling."

"You *should* tell me. I'm the one you're all betting will be seduced before the next full moon. I think I deserve to know who you expect to do the seducing." Her indignation had no discernible effect on her friends.

"And spoil all our fun?" Tess asked. "Not a chance, fur face."

Sam shot a glance toward Abby, the only one present who might be persuaded to spill her guts if Sam played on her sympathies. But judging by her expression, Abby had no more idea of the names than Sam did.

"Were they this interested in your love life?" Sam asked her.

"Of course," Abby responded promptly. "Don't you remember? You were there. Among the interested."

So much for sympathy. Sam scowled. "Traitor. I should have gone and hung out with Annie at her lab."

"Why? One party pooper in a room is more than enough." Tess balanced the base of her wineglass on her knee. "And since Dr. Cryer told me she couldn't make it tonight because she'd be working, I'm pretty sure she wouldn't have had time for you any more than she had time for the rest of us."

"So why didn't Annie come tonight?" Abby asked.

Samantha had been waiting for this question. She'd rehearsed her response. Since she'd given it plenty of times over the past few months, she didn't think anyone would question it. Actually, it made a good distraction from anyone snooping too closely into why Annie really hadn't come. Sam pasted on a scowl. "Three guesses."

Tess raised an eyebrow. "Because she's a huge geek who couldn't be dragged out of that lab of hers if you tied her to the back of the bull herd in Pamplona?"

"That's reason number one. I'll let you have the others guess reason number two."

"Ugh." Missy wrinkled her nose over her milk glass. "Don't tell me she's still crushing all over that creep Gordon?"

Samantha nodded and sipped her wine. "Unfortunately."

"And it hasn't penetrated her admittedly narrow field of vision that there's a reason no one she knows likes him?" Tess asked.

"As far as I can tell, no one on the planet likes him," Abby said.

"This may be true."

"Forget liking him; I don't trust him," Samantha grumbled, trying to sound disgruntled. It wasn't hard. That much of her story was absolutely true, and it was nothing she hadn't said before. "He doesn't smell right. I don't know why Annie hasn't picked up on that."

"Because love is blind. And tasteless. And apparently odorless as well," Tess said.

"Still, it's not right. And it's beginning to tick me off."

Fiona sighed. "Well, she is a big girl, so I suppose we don't get to pick her friends or her boyfriends. Though I have to say, if we were in Faerie, *I* would get to."

Tess snorted. "It's good to be the princess."

"Damn skippy!"

"I don't want to pick her friends or her boyfriends," Samantha said, affecting an air of righteous worry. "I just want her to be better at picking them herself."

"Considering that she never leaves the lab, I suppose it makes sense that she'd fall for him," Missy said. "I mean, she never goes out. The only men she ever sees are oblivious old scientists with as much sex appeal as the average eggplant. So when Gordon came along—under fifty, in decent shape, and reasonably attractive . . . if you ignore the slime quotient—and started paying attention to her . . ." She shook her head. "It almost seems inevitable."

"That doesn't make it any better."

"No, but if you look at it from another point of view, at least she's acknowledging that another sex exists and is in possession of some interesting bits worth a closer examination," Tess said, her gaze fixing pointedly on Samantha.

Who shuddered quite authentically. "Please, do not make me picture Gordon Entwhistle's 'bits.' I could conceivably never sleep again."

Tess unfolded her legs from beneath her and leaned forward to set her empty wineglass on the coffee table. "You know what I mean. I think it's time we took a closer look at the lack of a social life of someone already in this room."

Samantha suppressed the urge to shout, "Look! The sky is falling!" and make her escape while the others were distracted. As much as she wanted to move the subject off Annie, she did not make an acceptable substitute.

Come to think of it, she wasn't sure her friends could be distracted. "Hey, just because I'm the only one in the room who hasn't been taken in by some smooth-talking thing in pants and started adding to the looming global population crisis is no reason for you guys to get bent out of shape."

"We're in perfect shape. We just think you should join us."

Samantha looked askance at Missy. "You do realize that made you sound like some kind of cult leader, right? Were you about to offer me some Kool-Aid?"

"Not at all." Tess picked up an open bottle of Syrah and topped off Samantha's glass. "Wine is ever so much more useful. Have some more, Sam. It will take your mind off other things."

"Off-guard, you mean," she muttered into her glass, but she sipped anyway.

"Semantics. We're all friends here. What could you possibly have to worry about?"

The trouble with friends, Samantha reflected, was that they caused the only kind of worry worth stressing about. Especially friends like these.

CHAPTER 4

The night air was as crisp and clear as it ever got in Manhattan by the time Sam left Tess and Rafe's a little before 1:00 A.M.

Sam breathed it in, automatically sorting the scents of car exhaust, humanity, asphalt, and Others. She caught a whiff of coffee, too, from the little shop down the street, and a hint of water. They'd have rain before the weekend was out.

Glancing up at the sky, Sam's eyes strayed automatically to the half-moon floating high in the darkness, visible the way the stars never were in the city. In a couple of weeks, the moon's call would prove irresistible, but for now she walked in its silver light through the De Santoses' swanky Upper West Side neighborhood toward the subway and her own more modest apartment in Gramercy. She looked forward to the moments of peace.

She'd enjoyed spending the evening with her friends, but she had to admit her mind hadn't been entirely on the merriment. She'd been too busy brooding about Annie.

What the hell had the girl been thinking? She'd genetically engineered them a whole barrelful of trouble, and somehow she'd managed to put Samantha right in the center of it.

Not that Sam believed even a bit of it was deliberate; Annie didn't operate that way. The idea of malicious intent made Sam frown and blink behind the lenses of her glasses, as if someone had suggested that the Earth's crust actually consisted of rock candy. Annie had just been doing what Annie always did, seeing a scientific question that no one else could answer for her and finding a way to answer it herself.

When the woman got her teeth into a problem like that, she was like a dog with an especially juicy bone— no pun intended—and she worried the thing down to a nub until she found what she was looking for. You got used to it after a while, and it started to seem almost natural. The sun rises in the east, the moon pulls the tides, and Annie Cryer figures stuff out. The only problem with that was the fact that a bunch of other people would really, *really* want her to share her latest discovery.

Sam shoved her hands deeper into the pockets of the jacket she really didn't need and kicked at a stray pebble. Whether or not Annie had intended to make a mess didn't affect the fact that someone would have to clean it all up. Every instinct in Sam's body screamed at her that it should be the Alpha, but she'd promised Annie a week and she wouldn't go back on her word. Graham would have to stay in the dark until next Friday. With any luck, by then Sam would have thought up a plausible story to disguise the fact that she'd been lying to him for a week. Because lying to one's Alpha tended to greatly reduce the average life span of a Lupine.

Gagk. Maybe she could just call in sick next week. Say she'd caught a cold, or the flu, or the Ebola virus. Anything. Of course, that would stand a better chance of working if Lupines were actually susceptible to human diseases. She sighed, beginning to understand why some pack members preferred to work in non-pack-related businesses.

But on the other hand, if she survived until her promise expired, she'd be providing Annie with a whole other medical marvel worth studying . . . And Noah Baker would be right on the other side of the office watching the whole excruciating thing.

Groaning, Sam stalked down to the nearly empty subway platform and leaned against a pillar to wait for her train. Talk about that old "insult to injury" thing. She'd have a rough enough time keeping her cool around the Alpha, but fate had to toss GI Joe into the mix, too? Exactly which god's shit list had she worked her way onto?

Noah Baker drove Sam absolutely out of her mind; he had from the first minute she'd seen him, right before she'd tackled him in the middle of the neighborhood park down the street from the club. At the time, she'd thought he was kidnapping Abby, not realizing he was Abby's brother, there to help her escape from the pack's custody, so Sam had taken him down in an effort to protect the girl she'd been assigned to guard. If she'd known how rolling around in the grass with that particular human would affect her, she might have pretended to be blind, deaf, and dumb when Abby had

made her break for it. It would have saved Sam a world
of trouble and made a positive impact on her sanity.
Not to mention the soothing effect on her libido, because Noah Baker made her want to sit up and beg.

She couldn't explain it. In fact, when she tried, it
short-circuited something in her brain that she figured
she should probably keep in working order. But no
matter what she tried to tell herself when she had full
possession of her faculties, the minute he got within
twenty feet of her she ended up in thrall to her own raging hormones. It was embarrassing, damn it. She was a
grown woman and a Silverback; she shouldn't get
weak in the knees at the scent of a human, no matter
how rich and musky his spicy scent was. It shouldn't
matter to her that his body was more toned than some
of her fellow pack members, including a few on Tobias's elite security staff. And she damned sure
shouldn't be able to remember what that body had felt
like when it had pressed against her almost six months
ago now. Maybe this was the evidence that her claim of
never having been sick in her life didn't hold water after all, because just thinking about the feel of Noah
raised her temperature to positively feverish levels.

The train ride back to 23rd Street took fifteen minutes, which wasn't nearly enough time for her to wrest
her thoughts away from Noah. Once she dropped her
guard enough to let her mind go there, it practically
took an act of God to yank it away again. Even telling
herself scornfully that she ought to know better than to
develop a crush on a human didn't make any difference. She was a sick, sick puppy.

It might be different if Noah had ever done anything

to indicate he had any real interest in her. Oh, he flirted, sure, but in the same recklessly casual way he seemed to flirt with all women, with the possible exceptions of his sister and the wives of those men he knew could eat him raw and smile while they picked their teeth. Sam had no reason to take him seriously, aside from her own schoolgirlish stomach-fluttering reaction to his presence. For all she knew, he viewed her the same way he viewed Gina, the breakfast shift waitress Sam had seen bring him coffee during some of his visits to the club. He gave Gina that slow, crooked smile, too. It didn't mean anything.

If it had, he would have asked Sam out months ago, not treated her just like any other casual female acquaintance. The jerk.

Rolling her eyes at herself, Sam walked the last two blocks to her apartment and debated jogging her way through the neighborhood in a bid to dump some of this restless energy. Between worrying about Annie and lusting after Noah, Sam felt charged up and a long way from ready for bed, but as safe a neighborhood as hers might be, this was still Manhattan. Even though Sam felt confident in her ability to kick the ass of anyone stupid enough to bother her, she preferred not to have to do such things in public. She got along well with her neighbors; she didn't need to go scaring them. Some knew she was Lupine, some didn't, but knowing something and seeing a live-and-in-Technicolor demonstration were two different things.

Stifling a growl, she dug in her pocket for her house key. She should just go inside and go to bed. Clearly both problems currently driving her demented would still be there in the morning, and she'd need her energy to deal with the kids on her weekly visit to her aunt and uncle's house. Even though her own pups had long since grown up and left the den, Aunt Ruby's house always strained at the seams with all the youngsters running around. She was the official Silverback nanny, and the entire pack knew that if their young needed minding, Ruby Howell could do the job with skill and good humor. Heck, she'd survived raising Sam after her mother took off; what more proof did anyone need?

So, Sam would go get herself some sleep, get through her visit with Aunt Ruby—whose sharp eyes were certain to see something was bothering her—and then use the rest of her Noah- and temptation-free day to tackle the one problem she just might have a little influence over. She'd make one more attempt to talk some sense into Annie. And she'd keep her fingers crossed while she did it.

It couldn't hurt, right?

By the time Noah returned to his room at Vircolac, the sky outside his window had lightened to a wintry gray streaked with vibrant flashes of pink and orange. It was sunrise, and he was just now getting to shuck his clothes and become reacquainted with Graham Winters's extraordinarily comfortable mattresses. And Noah had been worried this assignment wouldn't keep him as occupied as Noah had grown used to. Christ, he was an idiot sometimes.

He slipped between the cool cotton sheets with a

muffled groan and indulged in one long stretch before stacking his hands on the pillow behind his head and blinking up at the fancy plaster ceiling of the bedroom his host had assigned him.

"You'll stay at the club," Graham had told him a week ago when he'd been trying to give the Lupine the address of the hotel the army had booked for him. "That will give you a lot more access to the pack members you're trying to recruit, and I don't think I'm tooting my own horn when I say you'll be a lot more comfortable at my place than you would in that one. Besides, if you're in a hotel, Abby will worry and then she'll tell Missy she's upset, which will upset my wife and generally put me in a very bad mood. So think of it as a kind of community service act."

The only trouble with that, Noah reflected with a grimace, was the fact that his current assignment required him to lie to that community with every damned breath he took, and he didn't like it one bit. The constant knowledge that he was deceiving the people he now thought of as friends gnawed at his gut like an ulcer.

This was why he hadn't gone into military intelligence, he acknowledged. He hated lying to people who mattered. It pissed him off, especially given how he felt about being lied to, and he didn't like to think of himself as a hypocrite. He'd much rather be blowing stuff up than dancing around with the undercover bullshit. Bombs he got. They made perfect sense, an elegant sequence of physical and chemical reactions with predictable results and measurable impact. Lies were trickier; you never knew who might get caught in it when they blew or who might wind up in the path of their shrapnel. Lies were messy, and Noah considered himself an orderly man. He didn't like them at all.

And neither would the Others, if they ever found him out. He couldn't picture any of them dealing well with the sense of betrayal his little stack of lies would undoubtedly cause, and while he knew perfectly well they posed no physical danger to him—they weren't the type to repay his actions with violence—he stood in very large danger of causing irreparable harm to some relationships that meant a hell of a lot to him. His sister, for one, would not be pleased. It had taken her a while to assimilate to the world she'd become part of when she'd fallen in love with and married a demon, but she was part of it now, and Noah knew the Others who surrounded her had come to be both friends and family to her. And as timid as his baby sister might look at first glance, Noah knew for damned sure she wouldn't hesitate to take a swing at him if she found out what he was doing.

Hell, he reflected, Abby's reaction was likely to be the one he had to worry about least. As mad and hurt as she might be, she was still his sister, and she would still love him in the end, no matter how long it took to forgive him. It was the other Others who were likely not to forgive so quickly. Others like Samantha Carstairs.

Noah swore into the lifting darkness. Just the thought of her name caused a tug somewhere in his gut, not to mention the reaction it caused a few inches to the south. He couldn't explain what it was about the woman that got to him, but whatever bug it was had burrowed its way under his skin the first time he'd set eyes on her. By now, it had exploded into a full-blown infestation. He wanted her like a drug, a craving that nothing else seemed to take the edge off of. Half the time all he had to do was look at her and he'd be sporting a hard-on to scare a life-long hooker.

He'd never understood it. It couldn't just be Sam's looks. They were fine enough, all sleek curves and warm, animated features, but not the kind to stop a man in the street and make him forget which way he'd been going. But that was exactly how Noah felt when he looked at her, as if everything in his mind had been evicted by the burning, pounding need to *have* her.

What made it even worse was that Noah knew she had a similar reaction to him. He couldn't vouch for whether or not it was as intense, as consuming, as the one he had to her, but he knew he affected her. It showed in the way her muscles tensed whenever he got close, the way she looked at him, the charge of hot electricity in the air of any room that confined the two of them together. He knew she was just as aware of him as he was of her. It made him think that if circumstances had been any different, their situation couldn't have lasted too much longer before both of them wound up naked. And probably sweaty. But what would happen if she found out the truth?

She'd try to rip his balls off.

Noah acknowledged it with a wry twist of his mouth. He'd known Sam long enough to see the temper that burned beneath her civilized exterior. It wasn't something she'd lose control of often—in fact, Noah wouldn't be surprised to learn she'd never truly allowed it out of her grip—but he knew it was there, and knew the force of it unleashed would be something to reckon with. The way he saw it, if he was going to get Sam all worked up, he didn't want it to be with rage. Which meant she couldn't be allowed to know why he was really here.

Which meant he'd have to keep up his lies.

Cursing, Noah flipped onto his stomach and pounded his pillow into a tight ball. The only thing this situation had going for it was the fact that he didn't have to pretend to be someone else. He might have to lie about his intentions, but at least he still got to act like Noah, so she couldn't claim she didn't know the real him. She knew him well enough. If fate smiled on him and he got through this assignment clean, maybe she'd never have to find out what had happened. If she didn't know, she couldn't hate him and she wouldn't have any reason for kicking him out of her life when he tried to make himself a permanent place in it.

It was the first time in his life that Noah had ever used the word "permanent" in relation to a woman, but as he let his eyes drift closed he knew in his gut that it would also be the last.

CHAPTER 5

Any Other who'd grown up before the Unveiling, which was pretty much all of them currently out of diapers, got used to lies. Not destructive ones, not the kind that tore people apart, but the little ones that kept them together. White lies.

Or in this case, Sam thought, dove gray ones.

Annie's lab had a minimal security system, electronic locks on all the working-area doors, and guards who patrolled the high-security labs during the hours when the lab was officially open, but today was Saturday and no one was supposed to be in the lab. Sam knew Annie would be, though, which was why she'd come out here. Maybe in an empty lab in the more relaxed atmosphere of the weekend, she'd be able to talk some sense into her friend, get her to stop hiding things from the Alpha and do what their laws required her to do, which was keep Graham in the loop and let him decide how to move forward. It might be a pipe dream, but at the moment it was what Sam had.

Determination and a couple of those white lies got her through the building without attracting much attention. Not that she saw many people on a Saturday, but the janitor who had looked at her curiously and the one lab tech she'd run into had been easy enough to get past with the dropping of a few well-chosen names and the mention of a pressing deadline. The names she knew from stories Annie had told her, and the deadline was a pretty sure bet. According to Annie, the intersection of science and academia practically ran on deadlines.

Sam made her way up to the fifth floor easily. She'd taken the stairs rather than the elevator, partly because she still had a few traces of last night's excess energy to burn off, but mostly because she knew the security cameras didn't film the stairwells as they did the elevators. She wasn't sure why she felt the need to be so cautious, but when her instincts told her to do something, she didn't spend a lot of time second-guessing them. They were usually right.

Pushing her way into the fifth-floor corridor, Sam took a quick but thorough look around and made her way across the building to Annie's lab. Even with light puddling in from the windowed labs on one side of the hall, the light levels were low. The university must not feel the need to run up their electric bills when no one was supposed to be around to notice. The dark didn't bother Sam. She could see in pitch-blackness, let alone this, but the dimness did trigger something Lupine inside her that said low light was when unexpected things happened. It kept her slightly more aware than usual of her surroundings. At the moment, they felt peaceful.

That didn't mean the hair on the back of her neck

wasn't ruffled, just that it hadn't yet stood on end and started to vibrate, but Sam would take what she could get.

Turning the corner, she spotted the entrance to Annie's lab, as well as the fall of artificial light that spilled out through the reinforced window set high up in the door panel. Just as Sam had suspected, Annie was still here, still working. Glancing at her watch, Sam shook her head and just hoped her friend had at least had the sense to lie down during a few of the twenty-seven hours since she'd last seen Annie.

The indicator light on the electronic lock glowed a steady red, so Sam lifted a hand and knocked on the heavy wood. From inside the lab she heard something that sounded like a muttered curse, then a rustling and the tap of footsteps. Neither the curse nor the steps sounded like Annie's. Frowning, Sam knocked again. Harder.

A second later the door swung open and she had to swallow a curse of her own. Instead of Annie's petite form, Sam found herself looking at a masculine, handsome, and thoroughly slimy figure in a white lab coat and sharply creased khakis.

"Gordon," she managed, trying not to sound quite as disgusted as she felt. "I was looking for Annie."

Gordon Entwhistle, PhD, looked less than thrilled to find Sam standing on the other side of the door. She knew very well that he liked her just about as much as she liked him, and she liked him as much as she liked root canals and flea infestations. Theirs could be called a loathe-hate relationship.

"I'm afraid you've missed her. She's stepped out for

a little while." Gordon didn't sound afraid at all. He sounded hostile. Sam occasionally wondered if he ever sounded any other way. Around her, he never had.

"Oh, that's odd, because she told me to meet her here at three," Sam lied, making a show of glancing over his shoulder at the clock on the wall. "It's just that now, isn't it?"

He shrugged, his jacket lapels parting to reveal one of the expensively tailored shirts he always wore. This one was pink. The word "popinjay" popped into Sam's head. Old-fashioned and pretentious. Just like Gordon.

"She must have forgotten to tell you we would be working all afternoon. You know how she can be when she's occupied with something significant. She forgets the little details."

Meaning science was important, but her friend wasn't. Had the man actually spent the last six months working with Annie and still not learned a damned thing about her?

Sam suppressed the urge to scoff.

"Believe me, I know Annie." Sam's words carried an edge she wondered if he would even notice. "I'm sure she just forgot to tell you I'd be stopping by. We'll probably just run out for a cup of coffee. I'm sure you can spare her for half an hour."

Gordon's mouth tightened. "That's where she's gone, actually. She ran down the street to fetch us coffee, since the food services in the building aren't available on the weekends. But—"

"Perfect," Sam said with a cheer as false as her smile, the one that showed a lot of her teeth. "I'll just wait here for her, then. I promise to be as quiet as a mouse."

"Ms. Carstairs, there are regulations against visitors entering the laboratory. I'm afraid I can't allow you to—"

"Sam?"

Turning, Sam saw Annie hurrying up the hallway carrying a cardboard drink tray in which nestled three gently steaming paper coffee cups. At least one of those, Sam knew, held tea. Annie couldn't stand the taste of coffee.

"Hey, An. I was just telling Gordon that you were expecting me," Sam said, trying to sound casual and cheery and no doubt failing miserably. This was not her kind of lie. "Did you get me extra cream?"

"I always do," Annie said, and freed one of the coffee cups to hand to her. "Gordon, you're blocking the doorway. Sam and I can't get in unless you back up."

Silently and obviously unhappily, Gordon stepped back to allow the women into the lab. When he shut the door behind them, it latched with a decidedly frustrated click.

Sam sipped her coffee, rich with extra cream, and silently gave thanks that Annie had played along. She knew very well that they hadn't made any arrangements for Sam to visit today, and Annie could easily have given her away. The fact that Annie had brought Sam a coffee when she'd gone out for herself and Gordon was entirely chance. She'd probably suspected Sam would stop by after their conversation yesterday, but the timing had been pure dumb luck and a by-product of how well Annie knew her friend. Judging by the scent of tension on Annie's skin, though, Sam got the impression she might just be glad for the interruption.

"I'm sorry I took so long," Annie said. It took a Lupine sense of hearing to detect the nerves in her voice. "The line at the coffee shop was insane. I guess that's what happens when the weather turns colder."

Gordon pried the lid off his cup and looked down at the dark brew with a scowl. "How many sugars did you tell them, Annie?"

He always said her name as if speaking it left a sour taste in his mouth. He probably wished he could call her something more dignified, like Ann or Anna, but Annie wasn't a nickname. It was the name Vivian and Joel Cryer had given to their daughter, and everyone else who knew Annie knew it suited her all the better for its informality.

"Three, Gordon. Just like always. Is it too sweet?"

"No, it's like tar," he snapped. "It tastes like they didn't put any in here."

"I'm sorry about that. I'm certain I told them the right thing." She blinked behind her glasses quite innocently. "Well, maybe it can be salvaged. After they got it wrong the last time, I brought a canister of sugar from home. It's in my lower desk drawer, if you'd care to help yourself to some."

The man's scowl deepened and he opened his mouth, no doubt to utter even more complaints, but Sam raised an eyebrow in his direction, and his jaw snapped shut. Without a word, he turned on his heel and stalked through the door into Annie's office, taking his coffee with him.

The minute the door swung shut, Annie set down her cup, grabbed Sam's shoulder, and began to hustle her to the door.

"What's going on, Annie?" Sam hissed.

"Hush. He'll be back in less than ten seconds." Annie's voice was low, as if she didn't want to be overheard. She had one arm wrapped around her friend's waist and her head bent toward her, a pose of affectionate closeness. Annie's other hand slipped into the pocket of her lab coat and returned with a sheet of white paper, neatly folded. With their bodies between her hand and her office, no one could see her movements. "Take this and go home. We can't talk about this now, especially not with him here. Besides, I still have six more days. You promised."

Confused but feeling seriously unhappy with the situation, Sam slipped the paper into her jacket pocket and took a deep breath. She smelled that same tension, coupled with nerves and a tiny whiff of fear. Her stomach clenched.

"I know what I promised," she said, speaking quietly and pulling away to look squarely into Annie's face, "and you know I'll keep my word, but there's some fine print in this contract, Annie, and you know very well what it is. If you or the pack is in any immediate danger, all bets are off. I'll go straight to the Alpha, and damn the consequences for both of us."

Annie held her gaze for a long second, then nodded. "I know, and that's fair." Her mouth twisted into a little smile. "You always were the responsible one, Samantha. It's part of what makes you Sam."

Leaning forward, Annie wrapped her arms around Sam and gave her a hug. Startled, Sam returned it and felt a small hand slip something else into her pocket. She fought to keep her expression from giving anything away even as the knob on Annie's office door began to turn.

"Thanks for the coffee," Sam said in her normal voice, watching out of the corner of her eye as Gordon stepped back into the room. "We'll meet up again when you're less busy. Maybe at the end of the week."

The warning in Sam's voice was subtle, but she knew Annie understood. They were both under a deadline.

"That sounds good. Now I've got to get back to work, so get out of here."

A playful shove accompanied the word, voiced in an equally lighthearted tone, and this time Sam received a hidden message of her own. Annie wanted Sam gone. Really gone. So much for her plan to lurk out in the hallway and listen to the conversation inside the lab. If Annie felt compelled to tell her not to do it, she had a good reason. Damn it.

"See you later, Annie. If you can yank yourself free, give me a call this week."

Annie nodded and smiled, but she was already turning back to Gordon. Sam wondered if the man even noticed the reluctance in his co-worker's body language. Probably not. Most humans were clueless about that kind of thing, and from what Sam could tell, Gordon Entwhistle was more clueless than most.

As she made her way back toward the stairwell, she reflected that in this case his cluelessness might be a good thing, especially if it extended to whatever Annie had slipped into Sam's pocket. Whatever it was, it wasn't what she had gone to the lab hoping to take away with her, but at least it would give her something to focus on until Annie came clean to the Alpha.

Something that didn't come in a set of military fatigues.

This time, Noah wasn't sneaking out to a pay phone. Saturday meant the first of his weekly check-ins with his handler for this mission, and that meant in-person contact.

The diner sat at the edge of Vircolac's neighborhood, squatting between the historic district and the more relaxed though still outrageously expensive areas of the Upper East Side. It looked beat up and comfortable and enormously out of place—just the sort of thing for a soldier feeling like a fish out of water. Noah could only assume that's why the handler had chosen it.

As arranged, Noah plunked himself down at the counter with his newspaper at ten minutes after 0900 and hoped the coffee he immediately ordered would do something to make up for his lack of sleep. He'd only gotten about three hours of it. He'd worked on less before, but he hadn't liked it and he didn't like it now.

He waited ten minutes, which was just long enough for him to finish his first cup of coffee and order a second, along with a plateful of French toast, ham, and eggs. He could already smell the ham frying.

At 0925, the stool next to him swiveled away. When it turned back, it held a muscular figure with a bald head, a close-cropped goatee, and skin the color of Noah's coffee. He had to work not to show his surprise.

The newcomer set his cell phone down on the counter between the two of them and ordered coffee and the breakfast special—a stack of pancakes the size of his head with a gargantuan omelet on the side—then he flipped open the pages of a current issue of *Sports Illustrated*.

Noah lifted his paper to make room as the waitress brought his plate. He thanked her and reached immediately for the pepper. "Couldn't find the swimsuit issue?" he muttered.

"That's out in February. This is October. Peasant." The man's voice was deep, gravelly, and almost as familiar as Noah's own. Which was hardly surprising, considering Derrick Carter had been serving on the spook squad with him for almost four years.

"You should talk." Noah forked up a bite of breakfast and shot Carter a sidelong glance. "When did they start letting you off your leash in public?"

"I'm reformed. Besides, they're so worried about you staying housebroken, they figured they had to cut me some slack. It's now my job to follow you around with a roll of newspaper. I figured the magazine would work just as well when I smacked you across the nose with it."

Noah hid his grin by stuffing it full of ham. He hadn't expected Carter to be his live contact. Somehow, he'd gotten it into his head that it would be a superior officer, and Carter was right on Noah's level. He wasn't going to argue, though; he liked Carter. And even better than that, Noah trusted him.

"You'd have to catch me first," Noah said, finishing his second cup of coffee and gesturing for a refill. "So what's the news from home?"

Carter accepted his own plates of food—two of them, both in danger of spilling over—and shook his head. "No news is good news, my man, at least on my side of the equation. If I were you, though, I'd try a different tactic on yours."

They each applied themselves to their breakfasts. When Noah's plate was nearly empty, he shoved it away.

"It's been one day," he pointed out. "How much news are they expecting?"

" 'Bout as much as always."

"Which means more than I have."

"You know the drill, Boom. They want papers, if you can get 'em. Photos if you can't. And they don't seem inclined to be patient."

Noah ignored the nickname his unit used just to torture him, though Boom was better than the full version. What grown man wanted to be called Boom-Boom, even if it did refer to his ability to make things explode? It made him sound like a Vegas showgirl.

"In-persons still weekly?" He reached for his wallet and drew out a couple of bills, dropping them on the counter.

"Rain, shine, or coffee shortage."

"Then tell them they'll have news next week. Till then, if they need me, they know how to get me."

Neither man looked at the other as Noah stood and grabbed his paper and the cell phone Carter had planted for him.

"Ten-four, my man. Cell's as secure as we can make it." Carter sipped his coffee. "Watch your back."

"Trust me, Hoss," Noah muttered, heading for the door. "I got that covered."

CHAPTER 6

Sam walked through the front door of Vircolac on Monday morning with a serious case of the grumps. That's what came of spending most of her weekend poring over pages' worth of Annie's handwriting, only to decide by one o'clock this morning that they might as well be written in Sanskrit for all the sense they made to Sam.

Waving to Richards, she let herself into her office and dumped her bag on her desk, but she didn't flick on her computer as usual. Instead, she grabbed her keys and unlocked the door to Graham's inner office. Flipping on the lights, she crossed to the cabinet built into the far wall and opened it to reveal a small safe. Entering the combination, she opened it and pressed the mechanism inside that opened a panel in the opposite wall housing the Alpha's real safe. Quickly she stuffed the paper and the pocket notebook Annie had handed her Saturday into the bottom drawer and locked everything back up. Since she hadn't been able to make anything out of the notes, she figured the best thing she could do with them was keep them safe. And what safer hiding place could she find than a secret safe guarded by a werewolf and his entire top-notch security team?

Retracing her steps, she returned to her desk and powered up her PC, storing her bag in her bottom drawer while the operating system loaded. The message light on her phone blinked frantically, and a stack of pink message slips sat in the middle of her blotter, evidence of an average weekend at the club. Other than her trip to the safe, everything appeared to be on a normal Monday schedule. It was just Sam who felt like the world had gone off-kilter.

She had the phone to her ear and a pen in her hand when the office door opened. As she looked up, an automatic smile for her boss curved her lips but froze when her gaze landed on the figure in the doorway. His crisp olive dress uniform made his skin look golden and emphasized the breadth of his shoulders and the firm cut of his jaw. Sam felt her mouth go dry, then begin to water as if Pavlov had just rung his bell.

"Good morning," he rumbled.

Had his voice always sounded like that? All rough and gravelly and warm? Had it always made her thighs clench together?

She blinked up at him stupidly.

His grin widened. "I brought some breakfast." He waved a box of doughnuts under her nose. "And I asked the kitchen to send over a pot of coffee. I'd have brought that with me, too, but I wasn't sure how you take it."

"Light," she muttered, still dazed and wondering if she could make herself look like a bigger idiot. Maybe if she really put her back into it . . .

"Good. I told him to put cream and sugar on the tray." Setting the doughnut box on the edge of her desk, he hitched his hip on the wood beside it and folded his arms over his chest. One eyebrow arched curiously. "Do you find the disconnected-line tone oddly soothing?"

Jerking back to reality, Sam discovered herself holding the phone receiver to her ear while it blared the strident beeps that indicated she'd finished her call to the voice-mail system and forgotten to hang up.

Oh yeah. She obviously had unplumbed depths of idiocy still to strive for.

Flushing, she hung up and struggled for some scraps of dignity. "Good morning. I'm sure Richards took care of stocking your desk over the weekend, but if you discover there's anything you still need, feel free to let him know." Okay, that just sounded rude. "Or me." She forced a smile. "I'd be happy to help."

His lips twitched. "Oh, I'm sure you would. You made that clear on Friday."

She felt her cheeks growing even redder, but she couldn't think of a reasonable answer, so she clenched her teeth against the urge to babble.

He stood for a second, just grinning at her, then reached down and pushed the doughnuts closer to her. "Not hungry?"

She wasn't, but since she hadn't eaten breakfast, she didn't really have much of an excuse not to be, and she sure as hell wasn't going to tell him she couldn't eat while his presence had her stomach doing the rumba through her abdominal cavity. There was such a thing as oversharing.

"I'm not much of a breakfast eater," she said, hoping

she wouldn't choke on the lie. Normally, she started her day with a nice hunk of meat and maybe a piece of toast, for the fiber. The fact that she hadn't done so today would catch up with her sooner or later. She tried to be polite and give herself an out at the same time. "Thanks for bringing them, though. I'm sure Graham will enjoy them. He's got a heck of a sweet tooth. And I'll have one later, once I'm more awake."

"If you're not into breakfast, you must be a big fan of dinner."

She nodded before she stopped to think.

"Great," Noah said, looking the slightest bit smug. "Then you can have it with me. How's tomorrow night sound?"

How did it *sound*? Like she was supposed to be able to hear anything over the buzzing in her ears. "Um, what?"

"Have dinner with me tomorrow night," Noah repeated patiently. "I even promise to spring for something better than doughnuts."

His crooked smile turned her knees to jelly filling, so at the moment she had doughnuts on the brain. She was also really glad she was sitting down.

"I can't."

Noah raised an eyebrow. "Why not? If you don't like breakfast, you have to eat sometime and a woman can't live by lunch alone. Why not dinner?"

Frantically Sam searched her mind for an excuse. There had to be one in there somewhere. One that didn't involve the phrase "because I'm afraid I'd attack you over the table and get us both arrested for public indecency."

"I—uh." She swallowed. "Tomorrow's Tuesday."

"Yeah, that's what usually happens after Monday. So what?"

"So, I can't go out to dinner. I'll have to work in the morning."

"I wasn't planning to take you to Greece, Samantha. We can sit down to dinner before ten. I can even have you home before ten, if you want."

She ignored the amusement in his voice and shook her head. "I don't go out on weeknights."

He sighed. "Okay, then how about Friday night? You don't work on Saturdays, do you?"

"No, but I have plans early on Saturday."

Noah gave her a level look. "If you're trying to brush me off, you're going to have to be blunter than that. I'm a soldier. We don't take hints; we take orders."

A little surprised to actually hear him giving her an out, Sam opened her mouth to tell him she wasn't interested in going out with him and found the words catching in her throat. Because she *did* want to go out with him. She also wanted to stay in with him. Hell, she just plain wanted him, and there really was no good reason why she couldn't go on a date with him, was there?

She thought about it for a second. True, he wasn't Lupine, but that didn't matter as much these days as it had in the past, especially not since the Alpha had taken a human to mate. There weren't any laws against dating outside the pack, and it wasn't like Sam was contemplating marrying Noah anyway. It was just dinner.

And, if she was really lucky, maybe some hot, sweaty sex.

Pursing her lips, she felt some of her tension drain away to be replaced by a quick buzz of awareness of the attraction between them. Her lips curved into a smile.

"I'm not brushing you off," she said, finally sounding more like herself. "I really do have plans on Saturday morning. It's one of my cousins' birthdays, and I promised my aunt I'd help rodeo the kids during the party. But I'm free Saturday night."

She didn't even have a chance to hold her breath; his smile turned warm and sexy again and took it away before she could even inhale.

"Good. How about I pick you up at your apartment at seven?"

She nodded. She opened her mouth to say more, but the office door swung open and Graham walked in, sniffing avidly.

"I smell doughnuts," he said, eyes sparkling with avarice. "Gimme."

Snorting, Noah pushed away from her desk and nodded to the still-closed box. "Right there, but I brought them for everyone. You'll have to share."

Graham scowled over the Boston cream that already filled his mouth. "Share?" he mumbled.

"Share," Noah confirmed, reaching around him to snag a jelly-filled. "Sam hasn't had any breakfast. She needs them more than we do."

Chewing and swallowing, Graham turned his frown on her. "Why didn't you eat? You're not getting sick, are you?"

"Would you relax? I'm fine." Sam grabbed a chocolate glazed and leaned back in her chair, trying to appear casual to Graham and to put some head-clearing distance between herself and Noah. "I just overslept. I didn't have time for anything before I left home. Unless you wanted to answer your own phone until ten."

Graham's horror at that thought showed clearly on his face.

"I didn't think so." Smirking, she set her doughnut down on a napkin and turned to her computer screen. "Now if you boys will excuse me, someone around here has to keep things running. I have work to do."

Graham snagged a second doughnut from the box and beckoned to Noah. "We've been dismissed, soldier. Come on into my office for a few minutes and I can give you some names you might want to put on the top of your interview list. I've been thinking about this all weekend. How do you think the army would feel about taking on a couple of . . . creative thinkers?"

The two men disappeared into Graham's sanctuary, but not before Noah left her with another one of those sexy smiles and an even more devastating wink. It took Sam three full minutes before she remembered her computer log-in.

It was going to be a very long week.

To her surprise, Sam actually managed to get a good amount of work done that morning. Graham and Noah stayed closeted in the inner office for nearly an hour, which gave her hormones time to chill out and stop driving her quite so out of her everloving mind. By the time Noah emerged to take his place at the desk across the room, she was elbows deep in the month's expense reports and barely had time to smile at him between keystrokes.

He didn't bother to interrupt her, just took a seat and got down to business. At 11:00 A.M., the first of his candidates walked in, and from that point on neither one of them had the time or the energy to so much as throw the other smoldering glances. They were too busy doing their jobs.

He did five interviews that day, and Sam knew each and every one of his candidates. All were Silverback, and though most of them were a good five or even—gagk—ten years younger than her, pack was pack. One of them was a cousin, and Sam had babysat for two of the others. All of them said hello to her on their way to their appointments, and she had to stifle the urge to ask them what they thought they were doing. She hadn't yet decided whether or not she approved of the idea of Lupine soldiers serving in a human military establishment. The idea gave her an instinctive pause or two. After all, there were certain members of the government who still hadn't embraced the idea that Lupines were people, not animals to be used as lab rats or weapons. She could only hope Noah's superiors counted among the enlightened.

Plus, all these guys were adults. They had the right to make up their own minds, and if some or all of them wanted to join the military, it wasn't any of Sam's business.

Besides, she had bigger things to worry about. As she left for lunch, she cast a glance at Graham's office and thought about the paper and notebook she'd locked in his safe. Those were her business. She just hoped she proved to have a head for it.

Working undercover and probing the interests and skills of the Lupines he interviewed turned out to be less of a challenge for Noah than working in the same room with Samantha Carstairs. The woman played hell with his libido, not to mention his concentration. Hearing her low voice when she answered the phone, seeing the sway of her hips every time she walked into Graham's office, even smelling the sweet, spicy scent of her whenever the air stirred in Noah's direction had altered the fit of his uniform trousers in ways he felt certain the army had never intended.

He was also pretty sure the army had never intended for him to be thinking about whether or not he'd be able to taste that scent on her skin while he was asking potential recruits about their interest in exploring advanced degrees in science on the government's dime.

Oh, well. That's why it paid to be adaptable.

By the time he ushered the last of his interviews out the office door just after six, his battle with frustration had spread to two fronts. The first sat across the room at her desk, calmly clicking away on her keyboard, but the second had developed over the course of the last seven hours. None of his carefully chosen subjects had responded to any of his carefully worded questions. He'd spent all day doing a job he was beginning to hate, and he didn't even have anything to show for it.

Unless you counted the zipper marks on an extremely sensitive part of his anatomy.

Concealing his frustration behind a blank expression, he finished making notes in the folder in front of him, then flipped it shut and rose from his chair to indulge in a long stretch. He hadn't spent this long at a desk since high school. It reminded him exactly how much he preferred the action of field duty.

He saw Sam's head turn quickly away from him and felt his mouth curve in satisfaction. She must have been watching him stretch, but she didn't want him to know she'd been watching. That was a good sign, and it reminded him that his day hadn't been a total loss. She'd agreed to a date. He stifled the impatient growl of hunger that reminded him it was still five days away. He could wait that long. Just.

Strolling casually across the room, he shot a quick glance toward Graham's closed door and saw that no light seeped from underneath. He must have left for the day while Noah was conducting his last interview. That meant he and Sam were the only ones left in the office. His hunger changed from a growl to a purr as he leaned one hip against the edge of her desk.

"So I don't suppose I can convince you to take a walk on the wild side and move our dinner to tonight, can I?"

Samantha fiddled with her mouse and shook her head, but she kept her eyes on her open e-mail program, not on him. "Sorry. It will have to be Saturday. It turns out there's some stuff I need to do tonight anyway."

"I didn't realize Graham was such a slave driver."

"He's not." Evidently, she had run out of e-mails to

distract herself with, because she finally turned to face Noah. "It's personal stuff, around my apartment. Nothing major, but I'd like to get it done and over with." Her fingers fiddled with a pen, rolling it back and forth across her blotter, but her expression was blandly curious as she changed the subject. "How did your interviews go? Did anyone volunteer to be an army of one?"

"Not yet, but I think things went pretty well." He accepted her change of subject, along with his unwelcome waiting period. "I answered a heck of a lot of questions, though. You Silverbacks aren't the most trusting bunch I've ever run across."

"Can you blame us? Even you wouldn't be all that excited to find yourself looking into a silver bullet, would you?"

Noah frowned. "Does that really happen?"

He knew there was a lot of prejudice in the world against the Others. He wasn't naïve enough to believe otherwise, but he found himself less than enamored of the idea of any yahoo bigot threatening Samantha. The thought made his fists clench.

Sam shook her head. "Not much. Before the Unveiling, the few humans who caught us in the act tended to be less than friendly, but these days most of them are too afraid of a lawsuit if they go vigilante." Her mouth curved in a wry smile. "One of the many advantages of public recognition, I guess."

"I guess." Noah let his fists relax and tried for a casual smile. "But I promise I'm not working with the black hats. I think enlisting could be an important opportunity for some of your pack mates. And in the current economy, you can't fault it as a career move."

"That's what Graham said. Not the career move part, but the opportunity part. I'm not so sure I agree. Although I suppose it's good that at least we're not at war at the moment."

"It is a good opportunity," he insisted, his tone serious. He meant it, too. He might not have learned very much about biological research from the Lupines he'd interviewed today, but he had learned that he'd be happy to have one or two of them under his command. "They'd get training, education, and a rewarding career. They'd have a greater purpose and the opportunity for advancement that's only limited by their own ambition. They could become leaders. The army would let them use the skills they were born with in a positive, controlled way. We wouldn't be looking to put a muzzle on their instincts; we would be fostering them."

"Using them, you mean. For your own ends."

"That's one way of looking at it. The other is to consider the alternative."

Sam frowned. "What alternative?"

"Staying in the pack and living their whole lives knowing they'd always be followers."

"Well, that's a little harsh." Sam glared up at him, but Noah could see his bluntness had struck home. She knew he was right, but he was sure she didn't intend to let him get away with insulting her people. "You make it sound like we're all Graham and Missy's lackeys. That's not how it works. We're not masters and slaves; we're family."

Noah nodded. "I can see that. Getting to know you and Graham and Missy and Tobias and the others had made that pretty evident. It's a nice thing to see. But the service can become a family, too. If there's anyone in this world I trust as much as Abby, it's my unit. We're brothers." His grin flashed then, white and wicked. "And the best part is, when we're on duty, Dad is never around."

She watched him for a minute, then nodded. "It's not my decision anyway. If they have to be eighteen to join up, then they're old enough to make their own decisions. I have to say I was a little surprised to see who you interviewed, though."

"Why's that?" He fought not to tense, to sound unconcerned, only vaguely curious.

"Somehow I was picturing you rounding up all the big bruisers and rushing them off to boot camp. I didn't think you'd have much use for guys like Adam Forrester and Tim Youngblood. They're geeks."

He chuckled. "You thought I was looking for jarheads? Those are marines. We like soldiers who already have a thing or two between their ears. You'd be surprised at how technical and scientific the armed forces are becoming. We like geeks almost as much as the tech industry."

"I guess so. If those two enlist, you'll be getting two of the biggest. From what I hear, school can't keep up with Tim. They had to ship him to science classes at NYU. And Aunt Ruby tells me that if he weren't so bone-deep honest, the things Adam can do with a computer would have gotten him arrested years ago."

Sam smiled, and he felt himself relax a fraction. Not completely, because he hadn't expected her to catch on to the pattern of his interviews so quickly, but enough. He'd have to be careful around Sam. More so than he had expected.

"I've got to get moving," she said, pulling a tiny leather backpack out of one of her desk drawers and leaning down to shut off her PC. "I've got stuff to take care of at home."

Noah stood with her and began fastening the buttons on his uniform jacket. "I'll walk you home."

She shot him a disbelieving look that melted into one of frank amusement. "I live in Gramercy, Noah. I wasn't planning on walking. I'll catch the subway."

"Then I'll ride with you."

"Don't be a jerk. I'm a grown woman. I can take care of myself. In fact, I'm Lupine; I could take care of you, too."

He shot her a sideways glance full of heat. "As I recall, the last time we tussled, it ended in a draw. It will be interesting to see who wins the rematch."

Sam froze for a second, then shrugged into her backpack with what looked to him to be very deliberate nonchalance. "As *I* recall, the last time we 'tussled' ended in a demon attack."

"I can guarantee that we won't start the rematch unless we're very much alone."

He'd pitched his voice deliberately low, letting the huskiness of his desire creep into it and rumble between them. He saw no point in concealing from her the fact that he wanted her. Hell, he didn't think he could do it if he tried. What he hadn't counted on was her reaction. He watched the ripple race up her spine with fascination and found himself wondering what it would feel like if she gave one of those full-body shivers while he was inside her.

Sam drew herself up, deliberately drawing on a

mask of cool challenge. But when she met his eyes, hers had gone just the slightest bit hazy. She wanted him, too.

"I haven't agreed to a rematch," she said, stepping out from behind the protection of her desk and walking deliberately around him, far enough away to maintain some distance but not so far as to give him the impression he scared her.

He knew he didn't scare her, just like he knew he threw her off-balance. Both truths pleased him.

She headed for the door, her chin up, her expression a study in confident unconcern. Noah couldn't resist. As she walked past, he caught her arm and turned her, bringing her close enough that he could feel the heat radiating off her body. He wondered how much of it was because of her Lupine metabolism that kept her body temperature hovering just over a hundred degrees and how much of it was a reaction to his nearness.

Maybe it was time to find out.

Deliberately he straightened from his half-seated position on the desk and aligned their bodies so he could feel her heat along every inch of him. He had to grit his teeth against the sensation in order to maintain his control.

"If you won't let me take you home," he rumbled, releasing her arm to stroke his hand up over her shoulder until he cupped the back of her neck, "then I'll have to say good night right here."

Squeezing gently, he shifted closer and slowly, intently, lowered his mouth to hers.

He gave her plenty of time to pull away, but she didn't. Instead, she stood very, very still, not resisting but not melting against him in the way he craved. He kept the kiss light, brushing her mouth with soft, teasing little contacts, enjoying the plush, velvety giving of her lips beneath his. She was the softest thing he'd ever touched, and he wanted to touch a lot more of her.

He let the hand cupping her neck firm by degrees until the pressure brought her closer to him and he felt the hot shudder of her breath against his lips. The tip of her tongue followed, tracing the seam of his slightly parted lips, gathering his flavor like nectar to a hummingbird. She teased for a long, tense moment, then retreated, and he followed as helplessly as a sailor steering for the Sirens' rocks.

Her lips parted, luring him deeper, urging him on, and he battled the urge to rush, instead progressing with almost excruciating slowness, savoring every minuscule change in texture and flavor. The surface of her lips felt like velvet and tasted like spun sugar, but beneath, the tender inside of her mouth felt like hot, damp silk and clung just as enticingly to his probing tongue. She tasted of honey and almonds, like an exotic Middle Eastern treat, and the soft skin beneath his hand felt as hot as a sandy desert. He could have devoured her then and there and felt nothing but the satisfaction of a craving fulfilled.

But this wasn't the place.

Slowly, reluctantly, he drew back, easing from the kiss by the same mind-numbing degrees that he'd entered it. With a fierce sense of satisfaction, he felt her lips cling sweetly to his for a moment before he raised his head.

He looked down at her, taking in the fog in her

golden eyes, the heavy lids, the slick sheen of her mouth, and wanted to give a primitive grunt of satisfaction. He settled for a lazy smile.

"Take care of yourself, Samantha," he purred, letting his hand caress her nape as it withdrew and feeling her tremble with another of those full-body shivers. "I'll see you in the morning."

She nodded, blinked, then stepped back, putting a buffer of space between them. He saw that her fingers had clenched around the thin straps of her backpack until the knuckles looked white against the dark leather. His smile widened.

Stepping forward, he put his hands on her shoulders and gently turned her to face the door. It required a tiny nudge to start her moving. She didn't say a word, just stumbled out into the hallway, pulling the door closed behind her, more out of habit, Noah guessed, than intent.

For the next five minutes, he stood staring at the blank wooden door panels and grinning like a prize fool. Saturday couldn't come fast enough.

CHAPTER 7

Samantha felt Saturday looming before her like a bottomless pit and cursed the day Noah Baker had been born. Or at least the day he'd hit puberty and condemned a generation of helpless women to lust and confusion. It was Wednesday night, she still hadn't made any appreciable headway on the situation with Annie, and every bloody time Sam sat still long enough for her mind to wander, it wandered right back to Monday's mind-altering kiss.

She swore to the moon, Noah Baker's lips were like LSD. She'd almost been able to feel the circuitry in her brain rewiring itself. How else could she explain the fact that one kiss from him had done more to upset her equilibrium than the sum total of all her past romantic relationships combined? It was ridiculous.

Scowling, Sam dropped her dinner dishes in her kitchen sink and poured herself another half glass of wine. Her thinking had been cloudy for the past three days, so she didn't need to add a haze of alcohol to the equation; but at the same time, tension had her wound so tight that if she didn't find a way to release it, she'd wind up snapping under the sheer pressure.

Her libido whispered that it knew of a fabulous way to release her tension. . . .

"Like I haven't thought of that," Sam growled to herself, taking her wineglass and settling herself at the pine desk in the corner of the living room.

She'd thought of little else since Monday. All she had to do was pause for breath and she could feel the warm weight of Noah's hand cupping the nape of her neck, taste the rich spice of his mouth, feel the hard length of him pressed up against her body. Goddess, another two and a half days of this and he'd be taking her for dinner in the cafeteria at Bellevue.

Powering up her laptop, Sam tried for the millionth time to figure out what it was about Noah that put every one of her nerve endings on high alert. Sure, he was a raging babe, but she'd seen plenty of gorgeous men before. She'd even dated a few of them, and she was related to a hell of a lot more, but no one had ever affected her the way Noah did. Even the first time they'd met, when she'd attacked him because she'd thought he was kidnapping Abby, Sam had felt the flare of heat between them. At the time, she'd written it off as a side effect of the adrenaline caused by the fight, but it hadn't gone away. In fact, it had gotten stronger every time they'd met for the entire last six months. Ruefully she acknowledged they were both lucky nothing had taken to bursting into flames anytime they got within ten feet of each other.

Nothing, that is, other than her sex drive.

Sam would have loved to blame that on the moon, on hormones, on her heat cycle, but none of them seemed to have much effect on it. She wanted Noah all the time, not just when she was in season and not just when the moon was full. It was like an addiction she couldn't shake. Seeing him every day at the office this week had only added fuel to the flames. By the time he picked her up on Saturday, he'd be lucky she didn't throw him down on the stoop and rape him.

The thought of the expressions on her aunt's and uncle's faces if she did that gave her pause. She'd realized yesterday that if Noah wanted to go out at seven, he'd have to pick her up at Aunt Ruby and Uncle Henry's place in Brooklyn. There was no way Sam would have time to finish up with the kids, get home, and get ready in time. Which meant that when Noah came to get her, he'd have to meet her family.

When she'd told that to Noah yesterday before leaving work, he'd taken it in stride, shrugging his broad shoulders and asking her to write down the address for him. She didn't think it had dawned on him just what meeting her family would entail. This wasn't just a polite nod to a couple of aging parents as he escorted her out the door. She was Lupine, for heaven's sake, and Saturday was little Evie's sixth birthday. The entire family would be at the house to celebrate. Noah would be looking at a solid wall of adult Lupines, probably fifteen to twenty of them, all of whom felt they had a right to know Sam's business, especially if Sam's business involved dating a human.

It wasn't so much that they would object to her date with Noah on principle, just that they would have a good deal of concern about the possibility of her getting hurt. If Sam chose to date someone in the pack, there were rules everyone expected would be followed, and certain repercussions would be meted out if anyone broke them. Humans didn't know the rules and couldn't be expected to follow them; therefore, they presented a special kind of concern for certain members of her family. Including Aunt Ruby and Uncle Henry.

They had been the ones to raise Sam. Her father had never been in the picture, a rogue with a chip on his shoulder who had claimed her mother and just as quickly discarded her again, only to end up on the losing end of a dominance challenge before he was even aware he'd sired a pup. And Sam's mother, young, selfish, and unable to cope with the responsibility of raising a child, had dropped her off on Ruby and Henry's doorstep before taking off for parts unknown. Sam had always figured she'd gotten the better bargain. Her aunt and uncle had loved Sam as much as their own children and had raised her as one of them. No one had ever spoken of her mother, Ruby's wild younger sister, and that had suited Sam just fine. Cindy Meadows hadn't wanted her daughter, and Sam hadn't needed her mother. Sam had grown up fine and healthy and well-adjusted, thanks to Ruby and Henry, and as an adult she rarely spared a thought to the woman who had whelped her. The Howells were all the family she needed.

Unfortunately, they'd always been a little overprotective of Sam, maybe to make up for the abandonment she'd experienced in infancy, and that protective instinct would carry over into their meeting with Noah this weekend.

Guiltily Sam wondered if maybe she should warn him.

She pondered the issue while she brought up her Web browser and pulled out the notebook she'd been using to keep track of the information she'd been able to dig up on Annie's experiments, molecular biology, and cross-species DNA manipulation. At the moment, the pages remained distressingly empty. Sam had found very little, and most of what she had dug up she didn't really understand. Sam considered herself an intelligent woman, but the vocabulary these Web sites used made her feel like a four-year-old at an astrophysics convention.

For all intents and purposes, she reflected ruefully, she supposed that's exactly what she was.

Typing a new search term into the browser window, she hit the go button just as the phone rang. She reached absently for the receiver and murmured a distracted hello.

"Hey, gorgeous," a familiar voice greeted her. "What are you wearing?"

Sam laughed and leaned back in her chair. "That depends. Is this going to be a dirty phone call?"

"Would you let me get away with that?" Noah asked.

"Mm, probably not. I've never been a big fan of remote-control sex."

"Me either. I'm a hands-on kind of guy."

She snorted through a chuckle. "I never would have guessed."

"So, what are you doing right now?"

"Just some research," Sam dismissed. "I'm trying to answer some questions for a friend of mine. You?"

"Paperwork." A note of disgust crept into Noah's voice, making Sam grin. She could easily guess how he felt about that aspect of his job.

"Ah. So, what did you need me for?"

There was a short pause on the other line, then a husky laugh. "Now that's a loaded question if I ever heard one, sweetheart. How much time have you got?"

"Like I said, I'm not into dirty phone calls. I meant, why did you call?"

"Because I wanted to talk to you."

"About what? It couldn't wait until morning?"

It must have been Noah's turn to snort. He did it with authority. "Samantha, this is what people do when they have a personal interest in each other. They talk to each other. Since you refused—again—to go out with me before Saturday, I figured a phone conversation was the next best thing. Sooooo . . . how are you doing?"

"Noah, you just saw me three hours ago. I'm doing the same now as I was then."

"Samantha," he growled, amusement and frustration warring in his voice, "either we can have a nice, casual, getting-to-know-you conversation, or I can go back to asking you what you're wearing and what color panties you have on. What do you want it to be?"

"I'm good, thanks," she said, pursing her lips and staring at the list of Web sites her search engine had pulled up. "And you?"

"Impatient. Saturday is too far away."

"I'm pretty sure it's arriving at the usual time." That didn't mean her stomach didn't do an excited little flip at the thought of his eagerness to see her. It made her feel less vulnerable to know she wasn't alone in that. "Don't you have enough to keep you occupied in the meantime?"

"Sure, but that doesn't mean I can concentrate on it. For some reason, my mind would much rather concentrate on you."

"Your mind?"

"No phone sex, remember? My mind. Among other things."

His voice had deepened on that last bit, but Sam decided to leave it there. Before she forgot that she should. "Okay, so am I supposed to tell you about my day? Oh, wait. You were there watching the whole thing."

He sighed. "Has anyone ever told you that you're a hard woman to get to know?"

"Absolutely not. I'm an open book."

"Written in invisible ink."

His grumping sounded more good-natured than irritated, so Sam just sipped her wine and waited, her gaze idly scrolling down the list of search results on her monitor.

"All right," he said. "Why don't you tell me about this birthday party you're having on Saturday?"

She felt her eyes widen with surprise. "You want to hear the details of me spending an entire day riding herd on a couple dozen six-year-olds? I'm not sure your stomach is strong enough for that."

"Sweetheart, I've been in combat. After an hour or two in a war zone, I don't think a birthday party is going to faze me."

Sam laughed out loud. "You haven't spent much time around six-year-olds, have you?"

"No, but that's Abby's fault. She's been slacking on providing me with nieces and nephews."

"Somehow, I don't think that will be a problem for much longer." She thought about the electricity that sparked between Abby and Rule and grinned. "So after Junior's sixth birthday party, give me a call and we can have this conversation all over again."

There was a short pause before Noah rumbled, "I'll put it in my calendar."

His voice sounded close to a purr, and Sam felt her stomach do something acrobatic. To distract herself, she focused briefly on her computer and hit the button for the next page of search results. "Six-year-olds can be surprisingly . . . creative."

"I know I was. My parents still haven't forgotten about the time my best friend and I devised a creative and clever plan to keep in touch through the summer while he went on vacation with his parents fifty miles away."

"What was the plan?"

"Smoke signals."

Sam choked on a mouthful of wine. "What did you set on fire?"

"My schoolbooks. But when that didn't make a big enough blaze, I threw on my parents' toboggan."

"And they let you live? What did your friend use?"

"Oh, Joey had ambition," Noah informed her, and she could hear his grin. "He went for the boat shed at his parents' cabin on the lake. That one took two fire trucks. My mom just used the kitchen fire extinguisher."

"And where is Joey now?" she laughed. "Prison, perhaps?"

"Not Joey Jenssen. Like I said, he had ambition. He's a high-ranking employee of the USDA, as a matter of fact. In the Forest Service. Fire and Aviation Management."

"Good goddess, there goes Montana."

"So far, so good."

"What happened to the two of you? Did your parents decide Joey was a bad influence?"

"Nope. They were too busy worrying I'd be a bad influence on him. When Mom got pregnant with Abby, I think she went to church every day for the whole nine months, just to pray for a civilized child. It worked, too. Abby saved all her troublemaking for after she was all grown up."

Sam laughed. "She was that good all along, huh? Even as a kid?"

"Oh, she was worse as a kid. I don't think she managed to get grounded once in her life. 'Goody Two-shoes' doesn't even begin to describe my sister's childhood."

"While you, I'm guessing, only got more creative as you got older."

"I tried," he said modestly. "Do you want to hear about the time I made a citizen's arrest of my fourth-grade teacher?"

Sam grinned, enjoying their banter. And the butterflies in her stomach that seemed to appear every time she spoke to him. She'd been attracted to other men, obviously; she was almost thirty and a healthy young Lupine in her fertile years. She'd even had crushes before, but this was different. It felt better, stronger, more intense. This felt like the kind of thing that she'd seen develop all around her—between Graham and Missy, Tess and Rafe, Abby and Rule—and never thought she'd have herself. This felt like . . . home.

Before Sam knew it, she looked down at the time in the lower corner of her computer screen and saw that more than an hour had passed in flirtation and conversation. She blinked and realized she'd been staring at the same search results for almost forty minutes, which made for a less than effective bit of legwork.

Hastily she hit the button for the next page. She was supposed to be working tonight, digging up information on Annie's research and on whoever might be trying to get their hands on it, not passing notes with the cute boy in study hall. Where the heck were her priorities?

"In my pants."

Sam jolted in her chair. "What?"

"That's where Abby had hidden the hamster Mom said she wasn't allowed to have. In the pocket of the pants I kept in my bedroom closet," Noah explained, sounding almost as if he admired his sister's creativity. "Let me tell you, there's nothing quite as peculiar as putting on an old suit and feeling it move around you. I almost fainted, like a gothic heroine."

Laughing weakly, Sam determined to focus at least half her attention on the task at hand. She could flirt with Noah on Saturday night. For now, she had work to do.

". . . worst trouble you ever got into?"

How should she know, considering the answer might change within the next week?

"I was a perfect angel." She settled for obvious sarcasm.

Noah laughed. "Now why do I have a hard time picturing that?"

"I have no idea. It's the truth. I—" Sam's gaze scanned down the roll of search results and locked on number 47. She felt her heartbeat stumble, and the flip her stomach gave this time did not count as anything close to fun. "I have to go."

"What? Why?" Noah sounded confused.

Realizing how abrupt she had sounded, she tried to force a teasing note back into her voice. "I just looked at the clock, Noah. It's almost midnight, and we both have to work in the morning. We can talk more then. Bye."

She hung up without letting him get another word in, her hands almost trembling. She didn't think she should plan on a second career on Broadway. She couldn't act worth a shit.

Helplessly she felt her gaze drawn back to the words on her computer screen. She really, really hoped they didn't mean what she thought they meant.

The search engine had turned up an academic reference, a citation in some scientific journal from three or four years ago. The title read: "The Theory Behind the Manipulation of the Structure and Function of the STN4 Gene's Effect on Muscle Strength: Can Science Create the Supersoldier?" The author was listed as the National Task Force on Strategy and Medical Research.

Cursing with words she hadn't even realized she knew, Sam picked up her phone again and dialed Annie at the lab; she didn't even bother trying her apartment first.

Three rings, then Annie's voice mail clicked on. "Hi, you've reached Annie's machine. Leave me a message, and I'll call you back. Bye."

Sam swore again and was about to hang up when the recording continued.

"Oh, if this is Sam, do me a favor and check your e-mail. Thanks."

She had her mailbox pulled up before the beep could sound. Lowering the receiver, she hit the send/ receive button and waited impatiently for her new messages to download. Three were spam; one was a coupon to her favorite catalog; the fifth was from Annie.

Sam double-clicked.

hey, sam,
you must have tried me at home, which is a good thing. don't call the lab right now, 'cause i can't talk here anyway. i know i agreed to one week, but i need just a couple more days. i swear we'll talk on monday, with the alpha, too. I've booked some time on thursday and friday at a lab run by a friend of mine at MIT, so I'll be gone til the weekend. i'm not taking my cell. you can yell at me on sunday. love you, a.

Sam finished the note and said something she wasn't even sure she understood. It ended with the relatively benign "that little *twit*!"

No wonder Annie hadn't answered her phone. She knew perfectly well that Sam would have stopped her if she'd known about this plan ahead of time. Not only was it breaking the agreement they'd made to tell the

Alpha everything on Friday, but it also left Sam in a position where she couldn't even tell Graham herself. She didn't understand Annie's research; if she tried to explain what was going on, she'd sound like an idiot and she'd never be able to convey the seriousness of the situation. She might be able to make Graham understand she was worried, but unless he got the *why* of it, he'd just pat her on the head and tell her to let him know when something happened. The explanation would have to wait until Annie returned.

Samantha swore again and slammed her fist down on her desk, not even wincing when the wood cracked under the stress. Annie Cryer had played her. Like a five-cent jukebox.

Noah hung up the phone and scowled at it hard enough to melt the plastic. What the hell had happened? One minute he'd been talking to the woman he hoped to see naked in the very near future—and getting a pretty good button-loosening vibe going—and the next she was brushing him off like dandruff. What the fuck?

He searched his brain for something he might have said to set her off but came up blank. Sure, she'd sounded a little distracted there at the end, but he'd figured she was getting tired, and he could live with tired. He could live with ending the call, but it pissed him off to know she'd used "tired" as an excuse just to get him off the phone. He knew she had another reason for hanging up on him, and damned if he'd let her get away without telling him.

On the plus side, she couldn't hide from him. Avoiding someone who worked in the same office—in the same room—as you did required a kind of talent he felt pretty confident Sam didn't possess. Werewolves might have some pretty impressive skills, but the list didn't include invisibility. He'd see her downstairs tomorrow and impress upon her his dislike for being brushed off. He just hoped he'd calmed down some by then, or the impressing might wind up taking the form of a few stiff smacks to her backside.

When his phone rang, he reached out to snatch it up again, only to find dead air. There was no call on the other line, just a dial tone.

Cursing, Noah replaced the receiver and sprinted to the closet. Pulling his firm-bottomed duffle down from the top shelf, he pried up one corner of the floor of the bag and extracted a small black box. Two seconds later, he was tugging the line out of the base of the phone and reconnecting it with the box between the phone and the wall jack. When the phone rang again, he just stared at it. After the second ring, it went dead for another ten seconds.

The third time it rang, he picked up the receiver. "This is one."

"I've been waiting for an update."

"I got the cell. The contact said it was secure. I'll call when I have news."

"It is. So is this. I had hoped you'd have news now."

"I'm collecting information. I've had to space out the interviews with the contacts I'm most interested in to keep the Others from noticing the pattern. They're not stupid."

"That's all well and good, but we need results. We can't wait on this forever. Things move fast in this field."

"I move fast, too," Noah gritted out, "but I don't rush. I can either do this right, or I can do it quick. Quick *and* right would require an entirely different kind of operation."

"Should I be reevaluating your role in this assignment, Major?"

Reevaluate your fat ass, Noah thought, his jaw clenching. "No, sir. I'm just letting you know how I see things."

"I may reevaluate anyway, unless you can show me some progress."

Noah hesitated, but he didn't want the general to start seriously considering Plan B. Noah didn't know what it was, but he would guess it involved a heavy hand and some consequences for the Others that he'd rather avoid.

"I have a name. A woman," he continued before the voice could ask who it was. "The brightest of the kids I've been talking to look at her as some kind of genius. Albert Einstein and Marie Curie and Gregor Mendel all rolled into one. She'd got at least two PhDs, one of which is in molecular biology."

There was a pause on the other end of the line. "Have you checked her out?"

"Not yet. I just got the name today, and she's apparently not a social butterfly. I've been trying to figure out a way to meet her, but I don't think it will be an easy thing to orchestrate."

"If you can't make it happen, find another way to

get the information," the voice ordered brusquely. "You've got until Monday. After that, I'm going to have to reevaluate the strategy."

The line clicked dead in Noah's ear.

"Bastard."

Unhooking the encryption box, Noah stowed it back in its hiding place and settled himself in to brood. He hadn't lied to the man. Noah's first good lead of this whole nightmare pointed at a female Silverback by the name of Annie Louise Cryer. She made every one of the science geeks he'd been interviewing sigh with envy, and she apparently took her work so seriously that she never left her lab or attended any but the absolutely mandatory pack functions. Few of the kids who knew about her knew her very well. They treated her more like a legend than a pack mate, and not a single one had been able to tell him where he could arrange to bump into her. Somehow, he didn't think wandering nonchalantly into a reportedly secure lab at the university where she worked was going to cut it. She might be able to guess he had ulterior motives.

He ran a hand roughly over his close-cropped hair. Damn it, between the conversation with Sam and the conversation about his assignment, he felt ready to chew nails. The thing he wanted to do—namely, Sam—refused to get done, and the thing he wanted no part of, this goddamned lie he was telling to people he'd started to consider friends, seemed to be pulling him in faster than quicksand.

His gut had told him not to take the assignment, and he should have listened to it. He had plenty of leave saved up; he should have taken it and stayed the hell out of this mess. He had never felt comfortable with the idea of using lies to get information out of the Others. They'd been remarkably cooperative all through this Unveiling thing, always wanting to find ways to work with the human establishment for the benefit of both sides. So why did the Pentagon feel it had to get its information on their scientific research through covert operations? None of the answers Noah could think of made him the least bit happy. The main one was that whatever the military wanted to do with that research was something the Others wouldn't agree to, and that made his back itch, right in the center where he couldn't reach to scratch it. It was a sign for Noah that somehow he'd ended up standing downwind just as the shit was about to hit the fan.

The other reason was that the information the Pentagon needed was something it didn't want anyone else to know it had. That idea didn't make him any happier. People didn't usually hide things unless they expected to eventually use them to get the upper hand on someone else.

On top of that were the lies. Every damned minute they got harder to keep up. He liked the Others he knew, and more than that, he respected them. He hadn't had quite as many prejudices to overcome against the Others, not after serving with some of them for years before the Unveiling that announced their presence to the world. He'd liked the folks his sister had introduced him to right away, and the Alpha of the Silverback Clan was no exception.

Neither was his personal assistant, who happened to be the other reason that Noah's deception had begun to make him so goddamned uncomfortable. The attraction between him and Sam had flared from the beginning, but over the last week he'd started to think it might be something more than just chemistry. It might be something worth pursuing, worth keeping hold of for more than a few weeks. Might be the beginning of a relationship.

Frustrated, he took to pacing the confines of his suite at the club. One of the good things about staying in a club for true night owls was not having to worry about disturbing anyone in the wee hours. Below him, he knew the club would be hopping. No one would notice his restless footsteps.

How the hell could anyone ever build a relationship surrounded by so many lies? It wouldn't be founded on those lies, since the attraction between them was very real and he'd never told her anything about his past or his family or his character that wasn't true. But the lies were still there, eating away at the framework he was laying like acid etching steel.

For all his combat experience and advanced tactical training, he couldn't for the life of him see a way out of the trench he'd already dug. In fact, the only thing he could see was a way to dig it deeper. As much as he hated what he was doing, he hated the idea of anyone else doing it even more. At least Noah respected the Others, and he would go out of his way to make sure that he accomplished his mission with the highest possible level of respect for them and their culture. Whoever else the general sent might not be so considerate, or even considerate at all, which meant that Noah had to make sure he got the job done.

With a sick sort of fury, he realized that the best way to get the information he needed on Annie Cryer would be to see what Sam could tell him. As a friend to the Luna and assistant to the pack Alpha, she had to know most of the pack, at least by reputation. She would have to know something about Cryer. So Noah just had to think of a way to get Sam to share it with him without raising her suspicion. He had to pump her for information when what he really wanted was to pin her against a wall and demand that she tell him what the hell was bothering her so he could fix it and get on with his real goal of pinning her to a mattress. Which he was pretty sure she wouldn't want him to do if his strategy of using her to complete his secret assignment succeeded and she found out about it.

Noah already had too many secrets to keep, but now he added one more to the list. And hoped that the dangerous game he played wouldn't cost him anything harder to replace than his job.

Like his heart.

CHAPTER 8

Noah discovered on Thursday that for a were-wolf, Samantha Carstairs could prove as slippery as a greased piglet.

He made a point of heading downstairs to her office early, since he'd noticed that she rarely arrived less than fifteen minutes ahead of schedule herself, but this morning her desk sat empty. Even after Graham arrived on the dot of nine, it stayed that way. Finally, at nine thirty she raced in like a whirlwind and dropped her backpack in the middle of her desk. Noah rose from the seat he'd taken while he waited, intending to go over to her and ease at least part of his frustration by forcing her to tell him what was bothering her. But Sam didn't even spare him a glance, just grabbed a pad and pen and hurried into Graham's office, closing the door behind her. Cursing to himself, he sat down to wait. And wait.

And wait.

In the end, Sam spent all morning closeted away with the Alpha. Noah pretended to work and to carry out his business, but even during his one interview of the morning he kept one eye on the clock and felt his frustration grow with every single tick.

She would pay for this one.

When twelve thirty rolled around and she still hadn't returned to her desk, he tried an experiment. Snagging his uniform jacket, he shrugged into it, calmly fastened the buttons, and exited the office as if he had no more devious a goal in mind than lunch. As soon as he pulled the hallway door shut behind him, he turned and pressed his ear to the wood. Just as he'd expected, it took less than five minutes before he heard the interior office door open and Sam's voice thanking Graham for helping her get caught up. She sounded nervous and guilty when she added that if he needed her, she'd be having lunch at her desk today and in the afternoon would be in Richards's office going over the semi-annual employee reviews. She expected to be tied up until quitting time, when Noah supposed she planned to sneak out before he laid eyes on her again.

Not on his watch.

Moving quickly, he spun the door open and shot toward her desk. Considering he was human and Sam Lupine, he couldn't move fast enough to make a grab for her, but the office setup worked in his favor. Instead of trying to reach her, which she would assume he'd do as soon as she saw him, he countered speed with strategy, entering the room and immediately cutting off her primary means of escape. Her desk occupied the corner to the right of the door and formed a sort of alcove with a large wardrobe used for supplies butting up against one end of the L-shaped desk. At the other, shorter end of the L, there was a three-foot gap between the end of the desk and the wall of Graham's office that was the only way behind or out from behind the large piece of furniture. Noah placed himself in the middle of that opening and waited.

Cornered behind her desk, Sam met his intense gaze with a glare and folded her arms across her chest. He felt a surge of triumph, not because he'd blocked the path between her and the rest of the room, but because if she had really wanted to get away from him, there were at least a couple dozen ways she could have done it. One of those ways would have been to go right through him. He had no illusions about the fact that even though he was strong and fit, stood at least six inches taller than her, and outweighed her by more than fifty pounds, she still could have kicked his ass. She would always be stronger and faster and fitter; it was a genetic fact. But the fact that she chose not to use her superior physical abilities to get away from him told him she might be half as caught up in him as he was in her.

"What do you want, Noah? I have work to do."

"You just told Graham you were going to lunch."

"I just told Graham I was *having* lunch. At my desk. While I work. Alone."

Noah shook his head. "Very bad for the digestion. Come eat with me. We should talk."

"No."

"No to eating? Or no to talking?"

"Take your pick."

"You can't avoid me forever," he told her, taking a

careful step closer. "Sooner or later, you're going to run out of work or excuses or other places you have to be, and then you'll have to talk to me whether you like it or not. Why not now? Over lunch."

She scowled at him. "Because I don't want to. So go mind your own business."

"I'd rather mind you." He took a second step, still cautious. "I want to know why you brushed me off so fast last night. You seemed to be enjoying our conversation, and I think it was pretty clear that I was. Right up until that last minute. What happened?"

"I don't want to talk about it."

"I do."

"Well, that's just tough. This is not the right time or the right place." Her voice held exasperation and a hint of nerves. "It can wait."

"I can't." Another step. He could see tension lurking around her eyes, and he didn't like it. "I think now is exactly the right time. As for the place . . ." He shrugged. "I offered to take you someplace else. You refused."

"Because it's not appropriate," she snapped, and her eyes glinted. "This is where I work and this is when I work. I'm not going to fight with you here. Especially not just because you got a bruised ego just because I didn't beg you to stay on the phone with me until all hours of the morning. You'll get over it."

Noah eased forward until he stood so close, she had to lift her chin to keep eye contact.

"You think that's why we need to talk?" He let himself give a small smile and shook his head. "You've got it all wrong, sweetheart. I don't want to talk about me. I want to know what's bothering you."

S am looked up at Noah and frowned. She wasn't exactly thinking clearly at the moment, not with her mind racing in twelve different directions over Annie and him and the pack and a cartel of mad military scientists. And not with him wearing that uniform that made his shoulders look a mile wide, or with him standing so close she felt bathed in his scent. He didn't wear cologne, thank the moon, but if she could have bottled the smell of him, she could have made a fortune. He smelled of musk and man and warm skin, all underlain with the clean, subtle spice of his soap. She could have licked him, just to savor that scent. Clearly he already threw her off-balance, and now even his words had stopped making sense.

"What?" She shook her head to try to clear it.

He gave a long-suffering sigh, grabbed her backpack with one hand, and used the other to grip one of hers. "Come on." He towed her behind him. "We can talk and eat at the same time. If you can't take too much time from work, we'll just go across the hall to the club dining room."

That got Sam's attention. She dug her heels into the rug and shook her head. "No. We can't talk in there."

He paused, looked down at her for a second, then changed course for the front door. "Fine. The deli down the street is excellent. We'll go there."

Sam tried to muster up a protest, but nothing came

out. Instead, ten minutes later she found herself sitting at one of the deli's five tiny tables and bumping knees with Noah. She unwrapped the white paper from her sandwich with great concentration and wondered why she hadn't just refused to go with him. It wasn't like he could have forced her, so why was she here?

Because, she acknowledged, for the first time in her life, something bothered her that she couldn't share with her pack.

Lupines were sharers, by nature and nurture, and Silverbacks shared more than most. For millennia, it had helped ensure the pack's survival, and Sam couldn't be sure it wasn't still helping. There really was strength in numbers, and when one pack member had a problem, he turned to the pack for a solution. Pack meant protection, security, family, and safety, and Sam was starting to feel like this situation with Annie had taken all those things away from her. If she couldn't turn to her pack, whom could she turn to?

Her subconscious, apparently, had nominated Noah.

He'd taken one bite of his sandwich, chewed, and swallowed before his patience quite obviously ran out. "So what could you possibly have been doing while we talked last night that set this off?" he demanded, his gaze as blunt as his question. "Because you're not going to try to tell me it was something I said."

Her head shook before she could stop it, destroying her chance for an easy excuse. "No," she admitted. "It wasn't you."

"Then what was it?"

She fiddled with her roast beef. Part of her wanted to crawl into his lap and ask him to fix everything, to tell him the whole messy story, even though she knew perfectly well there wasn't anything he could do. The rest of her had almost thirty years of training in pack protocol and kept reminding her that the pack took care of pack problems. Of course, the Alpha seemed happy for Noah to involve himself in the pack, and if Graham trusted him, the pack trusted him.

She felt a strange pounding in her head and realized she must be developing her first real-life headache.

She would have preferred to skip the experience.

"Samantha," Noah prompted, his foot nudging hers under the table. "Tell me."

"It's a long story."

"I have faith in you. Condense."

She quarter-smiled. It was too small to qualify as half. "It's complicated, too, and you've probably never even heard of most of the players." She saw him about to protest and lifted a hand to stop him. "Which *means* that you'll have to stop me for questions if you get lost."

She saw him relax fractionally, and this time her almost smile at least felt genuine. She still didn't feel a hundred percent comfortable about sharing any of this with him, but she felt compelled to do so. Who else could she share it with? Outside the pack and the friends close enough to be privy to all the pack's business, Noah was the only one she could think of whom she could trust. Plus, she liked that he wanted to know. She liked that he was interested in what bothered her, as well as what turned her on.

"I guess it all boils down to the fact that I'm worried," she said, pushing away her half-eaten sandwich and leaning her forearms on the table. "About my best friend. I think she might be in trouble."

"I'm guessing that's not a euphemism for 'pregnant.'"

That startled a laugh out of her. "Hardly. She doesn't even date. If she were pregnant, we could start a new religion."

Noah reached out and took her hand in his, rubbing a thumb across her knuckles. Sam tried to concentrate on something other than how incredibly good it felt.

"Tell me."

"She's been acting a little weird for weeks." She stared down at their hands, her smaller and paler one cuddled in his large, callused grip. "Canceling plans and working day and night, but that didn't really bother me. She loves her job, so when she's caught up in something, she'll do that, just disappear and focus all her energy on it until she's satisfied. She does it once or twice a year. I'm used to her ignoring phone calls."

"But?"

"But this time she's disappeared."

"Your friend is Lupine?" Noah asked, and she nodded. "Are you afraid something has happened to her? Have you tried calling her family to see if any of them have heard from her?"

She shook her head and used her free hand to brush her hair away from her face. "No, I know where she is. She sent me an e-mail."

Noah stared at her for a minute, his brows drawing together in confusion. "I don't get it. If you know where she is, how are you worried that she's disappeared?"

"I'm not explaining this well." Sam blew out a

breath. Her scattered explanation illustrated how disorganized her thinking had become. Too many worries, not enough solutions. "I'm not worried that something *has* happened to her. I'm worried that something is *going* to happen to her."

It was the moment of truth, and Sam didn't even hesitate, just told Noah the truth and knew instantly that she would feel better for having said it. "Annie is a scientist, and I'm afraid that the research she's working on now could get her into a lot of trouble. Not even the Alpha knows what she's doing, but from what I can understand of what she's told me—and that's not a lot—everyone on earth is going to want to get their hands on her data. She may have found a way to isolate the genetic sequences that made Lupines strong and fast and make their senses so acute, and that would mean there might be a way to give those traits to other people. Like humans."

CHAPTER 9

Noah felt his pulse stutter and hoped like hell Sam was too preoccupied to notice. He had to fight to keep his breath even and his muscles from tensing in shock. Annie Cryer was Sam's best friend?

Human or not, he felt like letting out a howl just then. Could any other part of this miserable assignment possibly go wrong? Maybe he could get shot in the balls by a cherub with bad aim, or something. That would perk him right up.

Mentally gritting his teeth, he blew out a breath and shook his head. "I'm afraid you lost me, sweetheart."

"Don't worry; I've lost me, too."

"Is something like what you're saying even possible?"

"If Annie says it is, then I believe her. Don't ask me to explain how, because I don't have the slightest clue," she said, "but there must be a way. I mean, I read in the paper a few months ago that scientists in England or someplace had found a way to splice some human genes into a mouse. When you think about how genetically different a human and a mouse are, doing the same thing with a human and a Lupine would have to be easy."

"Okay, I'll take your word for it. But what makes you think this has anything to do with Annie disappearing?"

She frowned and nibbled on her lower lip while Noah tried not to stare. "We're both operating purely on speculation, but she thinks someone has been watching her. And one of her colleagues is . . . less than trustworthy. He's all about the glory of the latest discovery. She's afraid, and I have to agree with her, that if someone wanted to know every last detail about her work, it wouldn't be hard for them to get it out of Gordon."

Noah listened carefully to the story, because this was information he needed, but it wasn't easy to take it all in while wrestling with the urge to roar and trying to maintain an expression of mild concern. He deserved a frickin' star for this. To hell with a bird.

Sam told him about the fears the Others had, especially the Lupines, about being used as lab rats or guinea pigs, or, even worse, being drafted to fight wars their species had no part in. She described Annie's behavior at the lab on Friday and Saturday, Entwhistle's attitude, and the way Annie seemed to think he'd become extra curious lately. Then Sam mentioned the paper she'd found with the military-sounding committee listed as the author and her suspicions about what the government might want to do with Annie's data.

"I tried to get her to go to Graham," Sam explained, "but she made me promise to give her a week. She said she was near a breakthrough that could change the whole situation, so like an idiot, I agreed. Her week is up tomorrow, and now she's disappeared. And I can't go to the Alpha without her. How the hell would I explain any of this? I don't even understand any of it myself!"

Noah nodded in sympathy, his mind racing. If not even Graham knew about the things Sam was telling him, she and Annie had done an unbelievable job keeping their secret. No wonder he hadn't been able to find out much from the pack members he had interviewed. The real source had been sitting right in front of him all along. Slowly working her way into his heart.

He stifled the urge to punch the wall. What the hell was he supposed to do now? Choose between them? His job and the woman who made him consider for the first time what it would be like to make a family of his own? Whose sick idea of a joke was this?

Sam squeezed his hand. "Noah? Are you okay? You look . . . upset."

"I'm fine." Carefully he schooled his features into relaxation. He could not afford to screw this up now. It sucked so bad already that he sure as hell didn't need to make it worse. "I'm just suffering one of the downsides of being a man."

"Which is?" She sounded wary.

He laughed. "Nothing embarrassing, I promise. I'm upset because one of the things men have in common is that we want to fix things. I want to fix your problem for you, but damned if I can think of a way to do it. It's . . . lowering."

And it was. What was even more lowering was the knowledge that fixing the problem he'd come here to handle would mean making her situation even worse.

Again she squeezed his hand. "Don't worry. I didn't tell you all this so that you could fix it for me. Though if you come up with any ideas, let me know." She smiled at him wryly.

Could he possibly feel like a bigger piece of shit?

"I will." He searched her face. "What are you planning to do?"

"There's not all that much I can do, really. Not until Annie comes back, which she said should be on Sunday. I've been poking around a little to see if I could dig anything useful up on the kind of experiment Annie's doing. Maybe if I found what other groups were doing, I could find out who might want to get their hands on her data most urgently. That's how I found that article. But other than that, I feel like I've hit a brick wall." She pulled a face, one that made Noah want to kiss her and smooth it away. "Annie's the planner. She's the brains of the duo. I've always been more of the dumb muscle."

At that, he did kiss her, leaned over the table and brushed his mouth over hers. "Samantha Carstairs, I think 'dumb' is the second-to-last word in the world I would use to describe you."

"What's the last word?"

He grinned at her. "'Ugly.'"

She burst out laughing, which had been his goal. "Thanks. That puts things into perspective, now doesn't it?"

"I hope so." He made a show of glancing at his watch. "Wrap that sandwich back up. We need to get back to work. I have an interview in another fifteen minutes."

"I'm not hungry. I'll just throw it away."

"No, you won't." He snatched it out of her hand before she could take it to the trash can and rewrapped the white deli paper around it. "We're taking it with us. You didn't eat enough for a church mouse, let alone a grown woman. You can snack on it at your desk."

Holding the sandwich in one hand, he recaptured hers in the other and led her back out to the sunlit sidewalk.

They walked a few paces hand in hand before he looked down at her and found her watching him with a slight smile on her face. When their eyes met, she leaned into him, bumping her shoulder against his.

"Thanks for forcing me to have lunch with you, Noah," she said. "And for making me talk. Somehow just getting the whole story out makes me feel a little better. Of course, I still wish I knew what to do about all of it, but I'm glad it got it out. So, thanks for listening."

Noah smiled down at her while shame crept down his spine like a scorpion, looking for the best spot to sting.

"Anytime, sweetheart," he murmured. "Anytime."

It amazed Sam how much work she accomplished that afternoon, not to mention that she was able to finish the rest of her sandwich while she did it. Her appetite had come back, and she felt like at least part of the weight she'd been carrying around since last weekend had lifted from her shoulders. Everything wasn't fixed—not by a long shot—but talking to Noah about it had at least made her feel more capable of dealing with whatever happened. Somehow, he had that effect on her; he just made her feel better all around. It was a little scary.

For all that her friends liked to tease her, Sam *had* had a few dates over the years, even a couple of serious relationships. Once, right after she'd finished college, she had been sure she was in love. She'd been gearing up for the whole thing—mating, marriage, pups, the whole shebang. It hadn't been until she'd ended the relationship after finding that her lover's definition of "mate" differed drastically from hers—she had believed it meant happily ever after, and he'd thought it meant happily ever after a different piece of tail—that she'd started to think that the emotion she had felt had more to do with expecting love than actually finding it.

Lupines tended to mate young. Despite their life spans being roughly equal to or greater than those of humans, a higher proportion of them died from violence—challenges, wars, attacks, and feuds—than humans, so there was a dip in Lupine mortality between the ages of twenty and forty. It meant they lost the largest percentage of their population during prime breeding years, so they tended to make up for the losses by mating and having pups young. By the time she got out of college, Sam had been twenty-two and ready to settle down. Or so she had thought.

When she looked back now, she was glad for how things had worked out, but it had skewed her perspective on relationships in ways she was just beginning to notice. It had made her think relationships were things best approached intellectually, based on common backgrounds and common goals. She'd thought of lust as absolutely the worst first step in finding a mate, until she'd met and lusted after Noah, only to find out he offered her a lot more than a tremble in her tummy. He made her laugh, he made her think, he made her crazy, and he even made her feel safe. He lightened her heart, damn him. How was she supposed to protect herself against that?

Why should she have to?

Sam's fingers froze over her keyboard as the question flashed in her mind. Why should she have to? Why wouldn't it be okay for her to develop a relationship with Noah? A real relationship, the kind with strings and no expiration date? What was stopping her?

She tried to think logically. She didn't know of any laws against it. The Lupines had gotten rid of the ban against interbreeding centuries ago, and the humans hadn't had time to enact one since the Unveiling. Hopefully, by the time they thought of it, Rafe and the Council of Others would have gathered up enough political influence to keep that from happening. The pack would accept it; they could hardly refuse to, not with the Alpha mated to a human female. Everyone could see they'd produced three healthy pups, with another on the way. Sam didn't even think her family would object. They'd been among Graham's earliest supporters when he'd announced his mating, not just because he was a relative—a third cousin on her mother's side—but also because they were fair people who made judgments based on character, not species. So why should Sam try to keep from letting anything develop between her and Noah?

True, she didn't know if he felt the same way about

her. He flirted with her outrageously, and he didn't hide the fact that he found her attractive. He obviously wanted her; she had no doubts about that. She didn't know if it meant any more to him than sexual attraction, but who could ever tell that? If she'd met him in a bar or at a Howl or on the subway and started dating him, she still wouldn't have known if he wanted a relationship with her or just a way to pass the time. Should she let a fear of being dumped one day keep her from trying? It would be a sad day when Samantha Olivia Carstairs let fear keep her from anything.

Feeling a smile spread across her face, Sam glanced down the room to where Noah sat talking to Bobby Metcalf. Noah's attention was focused on the young Lupine as they spoke quietly but earnestly. Her smile widened. Noah had told her when they got back from lunch that he had an off-site interview later this afternoon that would take him out of the office starting at four. He didn't expect to return until after seven, he said, so he would see her in the morning.

Samantha turned back to her computer, humming softly. Somehow she thought she'd see him—a lot more of him—much sooner than that.

CHAPTER 10

To hell with Lupines, generals, military intelligence, molecular biology, and his whole current situation, Noah thought as he stripped off his uniform later that evening.

He'd made it home just after seven o'clock, right on schedule, but he hadn't been in Brooklyn interviewing another potential Lupine recruit. He'd been at the public library digging up everything he could find on Annie Cryer and Gordon Entwhistle and the task force who had written that damned paper. Then Noah had made a couple of quick phone calls on a variety of public pay phones to ask some highly placed sources to dig even deeper. And finally, he'd wasted nearly twenty minutes going through the slow, painstaking process of getting a message to the general to let him know he had information to pass on. All of it left him feeling dirtier than a five-dollar whore.

A quick shower didn't do much to change that, but then, Noah hadn't expected it to. He toweled himself briskly dry, then pulled on a battered pair of blue jeans and grabbed a beer from the small fridge in his suite on the club's third floor. As long as he was screwing Graham Winters and the entire Other community, he might as well drink the man's beer and watch pay-per-view sports on the massive flat-panel television in his room.

He twisted the cap off his bottle and stretched out on the bed with a grunt, thumbing on the remote. He'd seen Graham downstairs when he'd come in, an encounter that had failed to sweeten his mood. Graham had been as friendly and welcoming as ever. He had, in fact, invited Noah to have dinner with him and Missy and the kids at their home next door, but Noah had refused. He'd pleaded fatigue, paperwork, a headache, and possibly bubonic plague. He couldn't remember. All he'd been able to think of was the sick, twisting, sinking feeling in his gut that had settled there that afternoon and gotten steadily worse as his day progressed. At this rate, he figured by morning his abdomen would have turned inside out through his belly button and his problems would be over. He'd be dead. No more secrecy or deception required.

It sounded like heaven.

Brooding, not even half his attention on the game in front of him, he nursed his beer and tried to think of any possible way in which he could make his current assignment not suck. After ten minutes in which he could have sworn he heard the sound of crickets chirping inside his skull, he gave up and decided there was only one thing he could do tonight.

Get stark, raving, stone-cold, red-hot, ass-over-teakettle drunk.

Gulping down the rest of his beer, he got up and

wandered back over to the fridge and opened the cabinet beside it. Score. Minibar.

Although it wasn't like any other minibar Noah had ever seen. Instead of those tiny airplane bottles of assorted liquor, Noah found generous bottles—about 375 milliliters each—of name-brand vodka, tequila, gin, light rum, dark rum, Scotch, and bourbon. He also spotted a bottle of very nice cabernet sauvignon and remembered seeing a similarly pleasing pinot grigio in the fridge when he'd grabbed his beer. This place was better than a frat house.

Bypassing the mirrored silver tray bearing four crystal shot glasses as well as the matching rocks glasses on the shelf above, Noah grabbed the Scotch and headed back for the bed.

Time to get to work.

He uncorked the bottle, savoring the hollow little pop it made, and took a second to inhale the rich, tangy scent of good liquor before raising it to his mouth and taking a healthy swig. He gave himself half an hour, tops, before he was flat on his back singing the song his unit sniper had taught him about a lovely young girl from East Indonesia.

Bringing the bottle back for a second dose, he froze at the sound of a gentle knock on his bedroom door.

He glared at the white-painted panels and debated ignoring the person on the other side. Eventually they'd have to give up and go away. It was probably Graham, come to persuade Noah into food or a card game or some other friendly activity guaranteed to send his already low opinion of himself straight into the gutter. Well, he didn't need anyone to remind him what a heel he was. He could take care of that just fine on his own, thanks.

The knock came again, more insistent this time. Holy hell. These people were determined to see him straight to damnation on the first bus south. Graham knew Noah was in here. If he didn't answer the door, he'd look like as big a jerk as he really was. He had to at least open the door and come up with some excuse for being an unsocial git. Likely it would be a lame excuse, but he still had to give it a try.

Taking another slug to fortify himself, he set the bottle on the bedside table and forced himself across the short distance from bed to door. Yanking it open like a bandage off a wound, he prepared to fake civility. He blinked for a minute at the empty space directly in front of him before his gaze dropped six inches and collided with Samantha's.

The breath sighed out of him like he'd just taken a power left to the solar plexus. What was she doing here?

While he stared down at her stupidly, she hitched the straps of her little black backpack higher on her shoulders and offered him a smile.

"Hi," she said, and her husky, familiar voice went to his head in ways the fifteen-year-old Scotch had never even attempted. "Do you mind if I come in?"

Automatically he stepped aside to make way for her, and she strolled across the threshold before his brain started working well enough to tell him what a stupid idea it was. He took his time closing the door, trying to buy enough time to reclaim his power of speech, before he realized that shutting himself in a room alone with

Sam and a bed did not qualify as the brightest moment of his life. When he turned back to her, he found those bright golden eyes watching him intently.

"It occurred to me that I didn't thank you for listening to me spaz this morning," she said, her lips curving into a small, self-deprecating smile.

Ah, shit. She had to remind him of the moment when this whole situation had gone straight down the crapper, didn't she? Was there no sense of justice in the world?

He crossed to the television and lowered the volume. No way was he heading toward the bed where he'd left the remote. "You came all the way back here for that?"

He winced at the way that sounded even as the words were leaving his lips. But Sam didn't seem to take his rudeness to heart. "I wanted to. It's not like this is such a trek from my apartment. It's a fifteen-minute subway ride."

"You could have waited until tomorrow."

With perfect nonchalance, she took a seat on the end of his bed and crossed her legs. "I didn't want to wait."

It had to be the Scotch making those words sound like an invitation, he thought, shaking his head as if that would clear it. The effort failed spectacularly. Her graceful movements as she crossed her legs drew his eyes like a laser guidance system. He noticed immediately that the stockings she'd worn during the day had disappeared, leaving him an unencumbered view of her naked and lithely muscled legs.

Sweet Jesus.

Forcing his gaze higher, he realized her stockings

weren't the only change she'd made since leaving the office. He recognized the skirt with the few wide pleats that she'd worn all day. It had looked completely professional in the office when it had been paired with a matching gray flannel suit jacket, but the jacket had disappeared and been replaced by a snug white tank top and a soft-looking pink cardigan with a disconcerting number of unfastened buttons. The two halves clung together by virtue of just two buttons, one between and one immediately below her breasts. Everywhere else, the sweater gaped open, revealing the clingy fabric of the tank top below and making him picture the scene minus that particular garment. The mostly unbuttoned cardigan would frame her breasts while exposing the soft, smooth skin of her chest and belly. . . .

He stifled a groan and wished he could stifle his other instinctive reaction so easily. Somehow just changing her damned shirt had transformed her skirt from an attractive piece of business attire to something out of his darkest naughty schoolgirl fantasies. Was she trying to kill him?

Her smile curved a fraction wider, and Noah realized he'd been standing there staring at her like a drooling idiot for God knew how long. Struggling for an air of calm, he leaned one shoulder against the wardrobe that housed the television and shoved his itching palms into his pockets.

"So, I thought you were the kind of responsible citizen who didn't go out on school nights," he challenged, giving the whole "best defense" thing a shot. "Isn't that why you refused to go out with me until Saturday? I would have thought this was past your bedtime."

The hot, bright glitter in her eyes couldn't possibly have prepared him. One minute, Sam was sitting on the end of his bed watching him with an intent golden gaze and looking like something out of an erotic film; the next, she was pressed full-length against him with her husky whisper echoing in his brain.

"You're right," she purred. "In fact, I should be in bed right now."

Then her mouth closed in on his and his world exploded.

She tasted of heat and woman and wild, unfathomable need. His hands came up and clenched around her upper arms as if he couldn't decide whether to haul her closer or push her away. Pushing her away was never an option. If he could have gotten inside her skin, he would have done it. Instead, he'd just have to get inside of her.

His surprise lasted less than a second. That was how long it took before he dove headlong into the kiss and made his own needs clear.

He had so very, very many.

She might have led the way into the kiss, but within seconds of following her lead, Noah had outpaced her. Her parted lips taunted and tempted, her tongue playing with his until he realized he had no patience for games. No matter how beguiling. Tugging her against him, he plunged into her mouth, avid and rapacious.

Her welcoming moan, the eager pressure of her lips, the clenching of her fingers on the tops of his shoulders convinced him that his greed hadn't bothered her. In fact, she met him want for want. He barely had to tighten his grip on her arms for her to plaster every one of her sweet curves against him. He nipped at her lips, and she opened for him wider. He shifted his hips to nestle the ridge of his erection against her soft mound, and her legs parted, body melting to welcome him even nearer.

She was the most sensually responsive woman he'd ever touched, and thirty seconds after he got his hands on her, he knew that if he didn't get inside her soon, he would die.

Releasing his grip on her arms taxed his willpower, but she made up for his fortitude by wrapping them around his neck and using the new leverage to haul herself up against him. His palms skittered down the long line of her back, over that infuriating, teasing excuse for a sweater. They squeezed the curve of her hips, savored the instinctive giving, before sliding around to cup her lush backside. She wriggled against his touch, a cat begging to be stroked. Instead, his hands tightened, and he lifted her off the floor.

Her legs parted instinctively, then eagerly, curling around his hips, her ankles locking together at the small of his back. Her pelvis tilted, dragging Noah's reality with it. The action brought the sweet warmth of her center into perfect alignment and nestled it tight against the length of his cock. If it hadn't been for his worn-out jeans and her tiny panties, he would already have been inside her.

His frustration poured into her mouth on a low, rumbling groan. She answered by shimmying her hips and nearly making him come in his pants. As it was, he gave himself another ninety seconds. Tops.

Huge strides took them to the bed in the shortest

time possible. He tumbled her down on the downy coverlet, more savage than suave, but when he dragged his mouth from hers he detected no outrage in her small, wicked smile. Only pleasure. And anticipation.

He braced his weight on his arms and leaned over her, deliberately rocking his hips against her softness.

"I want you," he ground out, and he could barely recognize the voice as his own. It sounded tight and rough and brutally frank, but he saw excitement flare in her eyes. "I want to get inside you, so deep you forget which way is up. I want your ankles on my shoulders and your nipples in my mouth—"

She cut him up with a sharp nip to his chin. "Don't talk." She yanked her sweater and tank top off over her head and threw them aside. "Don't talk. Do."

The rosy satin of her bra shimmered up at him, but pretty at it was, he hated it with a passion all out of proportion to its sins. He wanted it gone. Reaching out, he flicked open the front clasp and revealed an infinitely more beautiful sight beneath. Her blush pink nipples had tightened into hard little nubs just begging to be sucked. He couldn't stand to disappoint them.

His mouth closed over the first, tongue lashing out to rasp across the sensitive flesh. The attack made her moan and shiver beneath him. When he clamped down and began to suck in strong, rhythmic pulls, she cried out and grabbed for his waistband.

"Off!" She fumbled with the metal button at his waist, her body arching under the onslaught of his attention. "Want you."

Her panting demands barely registered. He left her to deal with her problem, too entranced by the soft, warm weight of her breasts to let himself be distracted, no matter how worthy the cause. He rubbed his cheek over the soft undersides, feeling his evening stubble rasp over the velvety skin. Turning his head, he nuzzled her, savoring her warm, musky scent and the way her flesh gave so willingly to his slightest touch. He could play with her breasts for hours, but Sam had other ideas.

"I said *off*!"

She gave what he suspected was a very restrained tug under the circumstances, and his jeans never stood a chance. The rivet holding the metal button in place snapped, and the button flew across the room to ping against the outside wall. The zipper didn't even pretend to fight back, splitting apart to free his impatient arousal.

He looked down at his ruined clothes and felt his lips quirk. "Well, why didn't you say so?"

Her eyes narrowed and she wiped the smile off his face by the simple expedient of wrapping her hand around the base of his cock and dragging it toward the tip in a long, tight, exquisitely torturous milking motion.

His head fell back and his eyes squeezed shut as he groaned like a dying man. Every muscle in his body shook with the strain of his epic battle not to come. He nearly lost it when she reached her goal and rubbed her thumb over the head, massaging the small bead of moisture into the painfully sensitive skin. "Shit!"

Balancing himself on one hand, he darted the other beneath her skirt, fisted it in the fabric of her panties, and yanked. They disintegrated in his hands, eliciting a grunt of satisfaction. Shaking off the scraps, he grasped his cock and fitted himself to her entrance, swearing again at the slick, soft heat of her. He gave a brief thought of regret to her skirt and his jeans still between them, dampening the pleasure of skin against skin, but it was too late to pause. Gritting his teeth, he slid his hand around to her ass and held her in place while he thrust home, impaling her on his thick length.

She screamed, a short, sharp, breathless cry that he prayed wouldn't bring Tobias and a whole platoon of his security staff barging through the door, mostly because he couldn't have stopped if they had. At that point, he figured the Queen of England could have sat down next to them on the bed to give a televised address and he couldn't have stopped. It was way too good for that.

Sam had arched beneath him, lifting into his thrusts, and he could feel her muscles trembling against him. Hell, he could feel himself trembling. He felt like he'd just plugged his dick into a wall outlet; that's how intense the electricity between them felt. The sensation forced him to grit his teeth to keep from coming before he got all the way inside her.

Walls of slick velvet clung to his shaft, parting reluctantly, making him feel like some kind of marauding barbarian, which in turn only made him even harder. He was amazed his heart could still beat, considering the center of his circulatory system was currently positioned between his legs. Or, rather, between Sam's legs.

Blowing out a harsh breath, he slipped his hand out from between Sam and the mattress and slowly eased his weight down onto her torso. Already their skin had grown damp with sweat and they clung together like Velcro. He slipped both arms under her rib cage and curled them up, hooking them over her shoulders and trapping her in place. Jaw clenching, he looked down at her and slowly flexed his buttocks, easing his last inch into her and feeling himself nestling high against her heart.

If he had died right then, Noah knew he'd have gone straight to hell, because where he was at already qualified as heaven. The only hell would be separating himself from this woman, and he had no intention of letting that happen.

Slowly, achingly slowly, he began to move, easing himself away from her, only to slide home again, drawn by the magnetic pleasure of being inside her, of feeling her holding him, squeezing him, as if she, too, could not bear for their flesh to be separated.

Every stroke wrenched a groan from him and a thin, ragged cry from her. He felt his breath sawing in and out like a bellows, felt the heat radiating off her like a furnace, and reveled in the knowledge that he was the one who had stoked that fire. He began to move faster, caressing her with his length, caressing himself with the hot clasp of her silken walls. His fingers dug into her shoulders and he worried briefly that he might be bruising her, but if he was, she never noticed. Her own hands were clenched in the bedsheets, fisting them into ragged knots. He wondered briefly why she didn't touch him, but the eager way she matched him, thrust for thrust, drove every other thought from his mind.

All rational thought had left him. There was only

her body, tight and wet around him, soft and strong beneath him, filling his mind the way he filled her body.
Her scent wrapped them in a cloud of heady musk,
mingling with the heat of his skin and the rich, earthy
smell of sex. He sucked it in with every grasping breath,
unable to get enough oxygen, unable to get enough of
her. Unable to get enough.

Feeling desperate, he shifted. His hands left her
shoulders and grasped her thighs, pulling her legs wider.
He slid his arms under her knees, hooking his elbows
beneath her legs and pressing his arms forward until he
forced her legs high and wide. The position left her
open and vulnerable, sent him nudging even deeper,
and he felt the tension in her coil tighter.

She took every inch of him, drinking him in like
rainfall in the desert. He felt himself seeping into her,
becoming part of her in a way he hadn't known was
possible. He thrust harder, his shoulders hunching with
the effort. With another woman, he would have worried he was hurting her, but Sam was with him every
step of the way. Her ragged, breathless cries held nothing but pleasure, reverberated with it, formed an an-
gelic, ecstatic chorus in time with their movements.

Fear teased at the corner of his mind. He hadn't expected anything this intense. He hadn't expected the
Earth to shift on its axis beneath them. As much as he
had known that Samantha was different, that something
about her spoke to him in a way no other woman ever
had, he hadn't realized that by taking her, he would make
her his. Every hard stroke within her body deepened his
claim on her, but the truth of the matter was, he was the
one changed by it. He was marking her, absorbing her,

taking her, and pressing her into the fabric of his being so that being removed from her would be like losing a limb. He could survive the loss, but he would never be whole.

A high, thin cry broke from her lips and dragged Noah back to the magic of their mating. He stared down at her, watched as her eyes flew open and that intense golden gaze locked with his. Her mouth opened as she struggled to breathe, and the look on her face held both terror and awe as she arched her back and tumbled over the cliff into climax and dragged him, shuddering, with her.

It seemed to last forever. He poured himself endlessly into her, shaking so hard he worried he might snap with the strain. Through the whole thing, she pressed up against him, taking all of him, whimpering in helpless pleasure. Her body drank him in, made him a part of her, just as she had become a part of him.

As he slumped, shuddering, atop her, Noah buried his face in the curve of her neck and acknowledged that nothing would ever be the same again.

S he slept, the sleep of the righteously exhausted, if not the innocent. She drifted off with Noah sprawled on top of her, pressing her into the mattress like a dead weight that she would have died to keep with her. His weight didn't bother her; she was more than strong enough to support him, and she loved the closeness of feeling his heart beat against her skin, his breath sigh against her ear. She loved all of it, and yet somehow having this much of him only made her ache with the need for more.

Never satisfied, she acknowledged ruefully. Always wanting more and wanting it her own way. That was Sam—a dozen demands and a flowchart to keep them straight.

She imagined showing Noah a flowchart of what she wanted to do to him and chuckled as she drifted off. She'd like to see his expression.

As it was, she saw his face all the while she slept.

CHAPTER 11

Noah hadn't gone limp with exhaustion. It was panic, pure and simple. With maybe a little shell shock thrown in.

He lay atop Sam's delicious half-naked body with his face buried in her neck, because no power in heaven or on earth could have compelled him at that moment to meet her gaze. Hell, at that moment he felt so low he didn't know if he could even look that high.

He couldn't feel sorry for making love to her. God, he'd be living for the rest of his life on how it had felt the moment he'd first slid inside her. That wasn't the problem. The problem had to do with how he'd felt when he'd realized he never wanted to leave. Not just her body, but her presence. Their joining had forged a link between them, one he feared he could never break. And he couldn't imagine ever wanting to.

But what would she do when she realized that he'd been lying to her all this time? Not about them, obviously, not about his attraction to her, but about everything else. He'd told a lot of lies, and most of them put the pack she called her family in danger.

Christ. He'd be lucky if all she did was refuse to ever see him again. Even ripping his balls off seemed to fall on the mild end of the range of possibilities. She'd want to rip him open and eat his liver, and she was more than capable of doing so.

Her breathing had deepened into the steady rhythm of sleep. Carefully Noah disengaged their bodies and eased himself off her. She made a whimpering sound and shifted onto her side, curling away from him and snuggling her backside against his hip, but she didn't wake. He held his breath for a long moment anyway. Then he counted to a hundred for good measure before he began to extricate himself soundlessly from the bed.

He grabbed a fresh pair of jeans and fastened them in the dim light of the bedside lamp, watching Sam for signs of stirring.

She didn't move.

Face grim, he grabbed the cell phone Carter had dropped him and slipped noiselessly out of the room. He'd scouted the location of the exits when he'd first arrived, subtly of course, and now he headed for the one that got the least use. The stairs to the roof existed not for the convenience of the guests but for the owner and the chef, who grew herbs and some vegetables in the greenhouse up there. Noah figured Graham was tucked in bed with Missy right about now, and he doubted he'd run into anyone harvesting chervil at midnight.

That didn't stop him from reconnoitering the area as soon as he got there. Nothing stirred in the open space, and the only living things he found in the greenhouse had roots. He activated the cell and roughly pushed in a number.

"Alpha."

Noah winced. He had a whole new appreciation for the military's use of certain vocabulary these days. "I need a debrief."

"Have you secured the target?"

"That's not the issue."

"Then why are you calling?"

Why the hell was he calling? He damned sure didn't want to call his ability to complete the mission into question. All that would accomplish would be to get him replaced by someone who didn't give a shit whether the pack survived the experience or not.

"I have a name that may be involved, but I need more info. I want a file."

"What's the name?"

Noah hesitated. "Gordon Entwhistle." He spelled it. "Scientist at NYU. Works in a microbiology lab. He's become of interest."

"I thought last time you mentioned a woman."

"It's starting to look more complex than I initially thought."

"The deadline hasn't changed. If you've got sources, you need to interrogate them. We need this information."

Noah clenched his teeth. This was why he'd held back, why he still hadn't given them Annie's name. She wasn't a person to them; she was a source, something for them to tap into and discard. "Get me a file, and I'll get you some answers."

The pause on the other end of the line vibrated with displeasure. "Your contact will be at the rendezvous at twelve hundred. Your clock is ticking, Major."

Once again, the line went dead on a threat.

Noah didn't bother cursing. The sound would carry too far on the still night air, and it wouldn't make him feel any better anyway. He was starting to think only a miracle would do that.

Shoving the cell into a pocket, he stalked toward the edge of the roof and wished he had someone to throw off. With every hour that passed he felt more and more like he'd gotten trapped in some nightmare, and for the life of him he couldn't wake himself up. He tried to imagine a worst-case scenario option, but his mind wouldn't even go there; it skittered up to the part where Sam shut him out of her life. There was no point in thinking about that, because he wouldn't let it happen. Sam was his now, and damned if he'd let her go.

A small part of him appreciated the irony. He'd known a few Lupines before he'd gotten mixed up with the Silverback Clan, so he'd picked up a few key details about their culture. He knew that in general they tended to view sex in a very earthy way, as something natural and instinctive that felt damned good and shouldn't be allowed to get all complicated with a bunch of extraneous bullshit. But he also knew how strongly attached they were to the idea of mating, how they genuinely believed that each one of them had one destined mate, the person whom they could recognize in an instant and who would be the end of the road for them. Once a Lupine mated, he or she became completely devoted to that partner, so that words like "divorce," "infidelity," and "betrayal" didn't even enter into the vocabulary. Lupine males also tended to be primitively possessive, guarding their mates from cross-eyed glances, let alone the occasional come-on from other men. Lupines used words like "claim" and "mine," the kinds of words that made most women look around for the nearest blunt instrument, but for the first time in his life, Noah completely understood where they were coming from.

He acknowledged, not without some discomfort, that he felt precisely that way about Samantha. In his mind, he already called her his, and with his body he'd done his damnedest to imprint the message on her. He knew that after taking him inside, she would have taken on his scent. Any other Lupine in the area would have known it, too, and the idea gave him a deep and very basic sense of satisfaction. He wanted everyone else to know she belonged to him, especially other Lupines.

Stupid he wasn't, and he realized that in getting involved with him, Sam had taken a chance. She was risking disapproval from not just her family but also her entire community. She was cutting herself off from the road they expected her to take, probably even the road she'd assumed she would take herself. He would find a way to reassure her about that later, but in the meantime he wanted everyone else to know it was done, and no one would be turning back. He wouldn't allow it.

Christ, he sounded more like an animal than most Lupines. Either an animal or a two-year-old. *Mine, mine, MINE!*

The click of the rooftop door opening snagged his attention. Light streamed in from the staircase, casting a golden glow onto the tarred surface. Sam's head peeked out and her eyes searched the darkness.

"Noah?" she called softly. "Where are you?"

He shifted, knowing her sharp eyes would catch the motion. "Here."

Sure enough, she shut the door and headed unerringly toward him. "What are you doing up here?" she asked, stepping close and cuddling unhesitatingly against his bare chest.

He let his arms come around her to pull her even closer, and he lowered his head to rest his cheek on her tousled hair. "Couldn't sleep. I was feeling a little wound up."

He felt her smile shift against his skin. "Funny, I thought I'd wound you all the way down."

"Sweetheart, you've got a lot to learn," he chuckled, pushing his dark thoughts from his mind. He'd have enough time to worry about that stuff later. More than enough. "I've wanted you for six months. One quick tussle, no matter how amazing, is not enough to make that go away."

"Hmm. So are you telling me I've got my hands full with you?"

"No, but if you move them around to the front and down a couple of inches, I can guarantee you will."

Her laugh was deep and throaty and made his gut clench into a tight fist. God, she slayed him. Laid him out like a prize trout ready for the filleting knife.

"And here I thought you'd be cold, standing up here without a shirt on."

"Not with you in a half-mile radius." He ran his hands over her bare arms. She'd left her sweater downstairs, but she felt pleasantly warm, reminding him that she'd just climbed out of bed. He felt his body tighten at the thought. "I could melt a glacier."

"You've certainly melted me."

Instead of heading down, her arms slid up, circling his neck and bringing his head down to hers. Her face was turned up, her mouth parted in invitation, and he slid inside with a groan.

How the hell could she taste so sweet? So much like home?

He pressed her closer, his hands roaming over her sweet curves, memorizing the feel of her, slipping under the hem of that flirty, maddening little skirt and finding her warm and soft and very, very naked.

"Shit," he groaned, tearing his mouth from hers. "You're trying to kill me."

"Don't be silly." She wriggled her hips and pressed her delicious bottom into his hands. "Why would I kill you? I'm not nearly done with you yet."

And she never would be. He'd keep her with him if he had to fit her with a collar and leash. Or himself with a whip and chair. Whatever worked.

Growling, he lifted her high against him and headed for the stairs. Sam wrapped her legs around his hips and hung on for the ride.

"I guess this means you might have a piece or two of unfinished business yourself," she teased, grinning down at him.

"What I have," he bit out, "is a dick so hard it's preventing blood from circulating to any other part of my body. If you don't want to be responsible for my arms and legs going gangrenous and falling off, you'll have to help me think of a way to cure it." He had her down the stairs and was pushing open his bedroom door in less than thirty seconds. He considered telling her she was lucky he hadn't just leaned her up against a wall along the way.

"Oh, I can think of several. In fact, as far as I can tell, there's really only one question to be answered here."

"What's that?" He carried her inside and kicked the door shut behind them.

As he laid her on the bed and stretched out over her, she tightened her arms around him and lifted an eyebrow. "Can we take our clothes off this time?"

CHAPTER *12*

Considering how much trouble she had walking on Friday morning, you'd think Sam would have been grateful that Noah spent the day playing least-in-sight. She ached in places she hadn't known it was possible to ache in, and she had been wishing fervently for a bathtub full of Epsom salts since before she'd cracked open her eyes just after dawn. She couldn't say since she'd first woken up, because, quite frankly, Noah had woken her before dawn and made sure she didn't think about anything except him until the sky had bloomed all pink and orange outside.

So technically, her first thought had been about him and the amazing, breathtaking, heart-stopping feeling of having him slide into her like a piece that had always been missing. Her second thought had been about the Epsom salts, and her third had been about coffee. Lots and lots of coffee.

She'd finished most of the mini-pot in his room before he'd climbed out of the shower—one she'd refused to share on the grounds of the Epsom salt thing—and had been sitting on his bed wrapped in her own slightly damp towel when he'd told her he'd be spending most of today out of the office.

"I thought you did your off-site interviews yesterday?"

He tossed aside his towel and tugged on a pair of boxer briefs, then reached not for his uniform pants but for a pair of worn-looking fatigues. "It was. This isn't an interview. I have a meeting on base with my commanding officer."

That surprised her. He hadn't mentioned the meeting yesterday, not even to Graham, and she had thought his commanding officer was in North Carolina, at Fort Bragg, where Abby had mentioned he was based. "In Manhattan?"

"I wish. No, that's why I'll be gone all day." He shrugged into his shirt, bent his head to the buttons. "The CO is paying a visit to Fort Monmouth to the C4ISR team. So I have to head down to Jersey."

Sam watched his efficient movement and reminded herself that even if she wanted to jump him right now, she probably wasn't capable of following through. But damn, that thing about men in uniform was proving to be oh so true. Noah in a uniform, at least, definitely sent her pulse spiking.

She shook her head. "And in English that means . . ."

He gave her a rueful grin. "Fort Monmouth, New Jersey, is headquarters of team C4ISR, which is mil speak for command, control, communications, computers, intelligence, surveillance, and reconnaissance."

"Yikes. No wonder you guys use so many acronyms," she laughed, and stood, crossing to him to run a hand over his broad shoulders, smoothing the fabric over his skin. She had been looking forward to the torture of being in the same room with him today, watching him work and quietly lusting after him. The fact that he wouldn't be there to torture her disappointed her. "Sounds like an impressive group, though. I'm surprised you're not in a dress uniform."

"My CO likes to see us looking battle-ready, and since this is a damn sight more comfortable, I'm not about to argue and maybe shoot myself in the foot." He grabbed her hand and pressed a hard kiss to her mouth. She fought to keep from going under. Goddess, he got to her fast. "And keep your hands to yourself, lady. You had your chance, and you turned me down. We could have conserved gallons of water this morning and single-handedly saved the planet from ruin."

"Oh, I'm sure that was your motivation."

She stepped back anyway. She could see his mind was already on business, and she wondered that she should feel this odd sort of jealousy for his job. It made no sense. It wasn't like he was going to a strip club; he was going to an army base. And she wasn't his mate anyway. She didn't have a right to like or dislike where he went.

Ignoring the little jolt inside her at the use of the term "mate," she decided that was a world of trouble she didn't need any part of at the moment. She had to get to work soon herself. At least her commute would be easy this morning. Ruthlessly she shoved the thought of mating aside and reminded herself to breathe.

Draining her coffee, she set the mug next to the sink, while Noah replaced the items he'd left on the dresser last night into his pockets. She saw him glance her way.

"What?"

"What are you going to wear to work today?" he asked, eyeing her towel as if he expected her to march downstairs wearing nothing else and was less than enamored with the idea. "I should have gotten us up earlier and run you home so you could pick something up."

"All taken care of." Smothering a grin, she grabbed her backpack from the floor where she'd dropped it last night and pulled out a handful of slinky black fabric. He almost sounded like a Lupine with that remark. "Stretch poly-cotton blend. I packed it small, but I could have shoved it in the space of a toothbrush holder and this stuff wouldn't wrinkle." She grabbed a hairbrush from the depths and gestured behind her to where an actual toothbrush sat beside the sink. "I came prepared."

He lifted an eyebrow and stalked toward her. "Did you think I was that easy?"

His hands slid under the edges of her towel, and she shivered. "Not at all. But I knew that I *was* that easy."

He traced the curve where her waist met her hip, and her towel gave up the struggle. It parted and slithered to the floor. His gaze devoured her, and she found herself wondering if she might be capable of a whole lot more than she'd originally thought. His lips touched her shoulder and she sighed. Capable or no, she'd be more than happy to give it the old college try.

"Wow, you weren't kidding," he murmured as she shivered under his touch, her mind gone blank and cloudy with lust.

"About what?"

"You are easy."

Her eyes flew open to meet his laughing gaze, and she mocked a growl, popping him on the shoulder. "Creep. Get your lousy paws off me. I've got to get ready for work, and I know when I'm not wanted."

She stuck her tongue out at him and heard him laugh. Then his hands grabbed her hips and tugged her back against him.

"Then you know that not wanting is definitely not my problem." He pressed the evidence of that against her bottom. "But we both have to get to work, so you'll just have to wait a few hours to seduce me again, you shameless hussy."

"You loved it."

"Damn straight." She felt his lips press a kiss to the top of her head and his hand give her ass an affectionate pat. "I've got to get moving. There's no telling how long this will take today, but I'll give you a call when I'm on my way back to the city."

Sam nodded and reached up to kiss his cheek. "Okay. I'll see you when you get back."

He smiled and left.

It took her a minute to catch her breath, a minute of standing stock-still and stark naked in the middle of his temporary bedroom before her heart started beating again.

Oh, shit, she was in so, so, *so* much trouble.

Her legs shook, forcing her to sink down onto the edge of the extremely rumpled bed. Her eyes stared unseeing at the wardrobe while her mind raced to come to grips with the idea that the *m* word might not have been so far off base.

Okay, stop and look at this rationally, she told herself. You've thought you were in love before, remember? And it didn't work out. Don't go jumping into something on the basis of a chemical attraction and one night of mind-blowing sex. Things could change. This could wear off. It could go nowhere. In two weeks, you could be back to just annoying each other. This doesn't have to be forever.

When her heart lurched at the thought, she knew. It wasn't just forever; it was Fated.

Her head spun, and the room danced crazily in her field of vision. She lowered herself back onto the bed, staring up at the ceiling. Her breath had gone shallow and shaky, but that had nothing to do with the fact that she'd just run headfirst into the knowledge that somehow, completely unintentionally, Sam Carstairs had managed to find herself a mate.

Ack. It wasn't supposed to happen this way, she thought, while Fate chuckled in the background. Sam knew that one day she'd find her true mate, the one destined for her. She'd witnessed it happen several times over the last few years. It was an epidemic, but she hadn't expected to catch anything just now. Especially not a big, tough human who didn't even blink at what she was and who could hold his own against her in a stubborn contest. What had Fate been thinking?

Sam needed to talk to somebody, she admitted, someone who could understand what she was going through when she didn't quite know if she understood it herself. Her mind went immediately to Missy; then she frowned. Missy would get some of it, since she'd mated outside her race herself, but Missy was in the opposite situation. She was human, and her husband was Lupine. She would get the feeling of culture shock, but she couldn't possibly understand the weirdness of trying to feel feminine around a man you could rip in two if you really had to.

You didn't have any trouble feeling feminine last night, a smart-alecky part of her subconscious whispered.

She scowled, but it had a point. She hadn't had any doubts last night that Noah was a man and she was a woman and they fit together exactly the way nature had intended. She didn't remember even a moment of worry that he might find her strength unappealing. Given the fact that he'd spent most of the night demonstrating exactly how appealing he found every last inch of her, that shouldn't surprise her. What did surprise her was that she couldn't recall any moments where she'd worried about hurting him, either.

Sam hadn't dated many humans. First, there hadn't been that many that attracted her. Noah was unique that way. But also, in the back of her head there had always been the knowledge that it would be so easy to hurt one. She knew her own strength, had grown up knowing it, and there had always been plenty of pups around to remind her to be gentle. There were some pretty significant differences, though, between playing with pups and playing bed games with a man.

She'd always assumed that holding back at a time when all her instincts wanted to let go would be uncomfortable and awkward, but that hadn't been even close to the case last night. She hadn't held back anything. Sure, she'd been aware of what she was grabbing and how tight she held on, but not out of a sense of obligation. It was as if Noah's touch drained her strength and at the same time left her able to move mountains. She hadn't had to think about not hurting him; it had never been an issue. Her power had been tempered for her. Judging by the soreness in her thighs and deep inside her body, she figured he'd walked away with fewer bruises than she had.

Not that she would have traded a single one.

So much trouble.

Pushing herself off the bed, Sam began to dress automatically. She pulled on the sexy undies that Noah hadn't stayed around long enough to see and slipped on the soft knit skirt and top she'd waved at him earlier. Her bag of tricks also contained stockings, makeup, and a hairbrush, which she used by rote while her mind churned over and over the same information. By the time she walked downstairs and let herself into the office at fifteen minutes before nine, she figured her brain could officially be scooped out and spread on toast.

The door stuck when she tried to shut it behind her. She frowned and turned to see Missy calmly blocking the way.

"Handy of them to have installed a subway stop on the club's third floor," the Luna said, lips pursed against what Sam strongly suggested was a smile.

She felt herself blushing. "Uh—"

"And it looks like it's right next to Noah's room," Missy continued. She entered the office and shut the door behind her before slipping into the armchair in front of Sam's desk. "In fact, from what the maid who was cleaning the room next door to his tells me, it looks like it's right *in* Noah's room. Fancy that."

If anything, Sam's cheeks got even redder. "Luna," she began respectfully, "I—"

"Oh, hush." Missy grinned, folding her hands on her lap and looking smug. "I hate when you call me that. We're friends. I'm teasing you, not asking you to state your intentions to make an honest man of him."

That was when all the color drained out of Sam's face and she had to lower herself into her own chair like a ninety-year-old with bursitis. "Um, right."

Missy's eyes widened. "Were you *planning* to make an honest man of him?"

"I don't know what I'm doing."

She heard a pause and wondered if maybe Missy hadn't understood her through the hands she had buried her face in. That did tend to muffle things.

When the Luna finally spoke, it failed to reassure Sam. "That's the first sign."

"The first sign of what?" Sam raised her head enough for a glare.

"Falling in love."

"What is?"

"Confusion."

"Confusion is the first sign of falling in love? Then I must have been wild over my high school geometry teacher."

"Don't be a twit," Missy dismissed sweetly. "You know what I meant. And trust me when I tell you I'm speaking from experience here. This kind of confusion means big changes in your future, my dear."

Sam shook her head. "It does not. I'm just . . . re-adjusting to the whole relationship thing. It doesn't mean anything more than that."

"Mm. And I suppose that's why you smell like Noah even after what I assume was a reasonably thorough shower?"

Damn it, that was the worst thing about Graham getting his wife pregnant so often. While she was carrying a Lupine pup and for the first few months afterward, while the pup was still nursing and utterly dependent, she got to share in some of the benefits of being Lupine. Including the enhanced sensory perception.

"I don't know what you're talking about."

"Oh, Sam, honey, trust me when I tell you that you can't brazen this one out," Missy laughed. "The minute Graham walks within five feet of you, he's going to know exactly what happened. That's why I brought you this. I was talking to Richards when you came down the stairs and I smelled you from the dining room doorway."

Still frowning, Sam held out her hand to accept a small amber bottle. "What is this?"

"Well, perfume wouldn't do you any good. Graham would take one whiff and know you must be hiding something. So I brought one of Tess's scented-oil blends. Thank heavens she knows how to put together something that smells nice to both Lupines and non-Lupines. Put some on. Graham will smell something different, but hopefully it will mask the Noah smell enough that he'll put it down to Noah having spent the last week in this room."

Sam sighed and unscrewed the bottle cap. "I really still smell like him?"

"Honey, you reek." Missy smiled to soften the statement. "Not in a bad way, though. I like Noah. He smells pretty good, even to an old married woman like me."

"An old married woman like you should know better than to go around smelling other men."

The words flew out before Sam could stop them. Once they registered, she raised her eyes to Missy and sighed. "Oh, damn."

The Luna laughed. "Don't worry about it. It comes to us all, eventually. Remember the little incident I had with Lucy what's-her-name the first time you and Annie introduced me to her? All she had to do was say Graham's name and I was ready to scratch her eyes out. And I knew very well she'd actually slept with him at some point. I think you can rest assured that I've never known Noah quite that well."

Sam shook her head as she applied the oil and refastened the cap. "This is really not a good time for me to be finding a mate, Missy."

"And I will give you an 'amen' there, because you are preaching to the choir, sister." Missy's lips twitched with wry humor. "I think if you did a little survey around here, you'd find that not one of us was ready for that. Fate tends to make it happen anyway."

"Yeah, well, I think Fate needs to take a little vacation."

"Trust me, that particular bitch is never off duty." Missy looked around the room and raised an eyebrow. "So where is your hunka-hunka burnin' love today?"

Sam glared back. "Noah, which is the name he prefers to go by, had to go down to New Jersey for some work thing. He'll be back this evening."

"Well, when you see him, give him a big ol' kiss for me. I need to go give Junior his second breakfast before he decides to get nasty." She paused in the doorway and sent Sam a smirking grin. "I'll send Richards in with a pot of coffee for you. If you need some linament, you'll have to put that request in yourself."

Sam threw an eraser at her, but it bounced harmlessly off the back of the door.

So much for finding someone sympathetic to talk this through with. If all Sam's friends, most of whom were mated themselves by this point, were going to treat her crisis so casually, she'd be better off without them.

Sighing, she turned her chair to face her monitor and powered up her PC.

And hoped Richards would hurry with that coffee.

W hen Noah entered the diner at five minutes before twelve, he bypassed the counter and took the back corner booth. He slid into the seat with his back to the wall and fixed his eye on the door to wait.

He wasn't feeling patient.

Since leaving Sam naked and rumpled in his room, he'd spent the morning quietly fuming. He'd known from the beginning that this assignment was bad news, but he was just starting to understand how monumentally screwed up things had gotten. A few phone calls to numbers he wasn't supposed to know had put him in touch with people he wasn't supposed to talk to. One of them had let him know that one of the reasons the general was so determined to rush this mission and get his information had to do with the other noses currently sniffing around the same research Noah had been sent to uncover. Apparently, the North Koreans, Chinese, Iranians, and several well-known terrorist organizations all had a particular interest in this area. Rumors had even suggested that someone had put out a few feelers on the possibility of putting the research information out on the open market. Noah hoped like hell it hadn't been Annie, for her sake as well as Sam's. No way would he be able to protect her if that was true. Even if he wanted to. But the idea of anyone selling that kind of information to groups with a malevolent intent did not inspire his chivalrous nature.

Needless to say, by the time Carter slid into the booth opposite him, Noah's expression had scared the waitress so bad, she'd never come back to bring him the iced tea he'd ordered.

"Your face is gonna freeze like that," the soldier said, pulling off his sunglasses and hooking them in the collar of his T-shirt. "Of course, in your case, I don't guess it matters much. It's not like it could get much worse."

"I'm not in the mood, Hoss. You're supposed to be bringing me a present."

Carter ignored him and turned to catch the eye of their waitress. She still didn't look happy about serving their table, but when Carter flashed her his crooked, blindingly white smile, her eyes widened. She hurried over. Minus Noah's iced tea.

"Hey, sugar," Carter drawled. His sugary southern accent always seemed to come out around women, and they always sucked it up like hummingbirds. "Can we get us a couple of iced teas? And I'd surely love if you'd bring me the biggest burger your kitchen can manage."

"Absolutely." The waitress sounded breathless, a condition that hadn't afflicted her when she'd brought Noah his menu and run away with his drink order. She didn't even look up when she collected the menus and said, "And you?"

"Reuben." Noah tried to soften the bark in his voice to keep from scaring her before he got his food. She did manage to flash Carter a flirtatious smile, though, so he couldn't have traumatized her too badly. He waited until she'd made it back to the counter before he held out a hand. "Where's my file?"

"In the drawer marked 'Pains in the Ever-lovin' Ass,' unless I miss my guess." Carter ignored the hand and ladled sugar into his tea. "If you're asking about the file on the lab coat, we'll get to that. But I've got other info for you first."

"What?"

"Command is sending in a B-team. They're setting them up in a safe house about fifteen blocks up."

Noah's jaw set. "Annoying, but not surprising. What aren't you telling me about it?"

"I'm telling you what they told me."

The pronouns finally registered. "You're not leading the team?"

"I'm not even on the team. None of us are. This crew is imported. Sent up from New Jersey, of all places." He managed to make it sound like one of the lower pits of hell. "Never heard of a single one of them, but the general talks about 'em as if they were the next best thing to the Second Coming. Been through 'advanced paranormal training' or some shit like that."

And the badness just kept piling up. One of these minutes, Noah was going to find himself drowning in it. "Spook squad 2.0."

"Apparently."

They both sat back while the waitress delivered their food. As soon as she left, Noah leaned forward again. "You got an address on that house?"

"Sure. It's not even a secret. It's in the file. General wanted you to know about it, quote, 'in case of need.' If you want my opinion, he just wants you to know he's got someone looking over your shoulder."

"Yeah, I share that opinion." He watched Carter drown his fries in ketchup and frowned. "You got anything else on them?"

Carter grinned. "Naw, but I can tell you that in a remarkable example of coincidence, one of your own team members has a good friend in an apartment across the street from the house. Jammer's got himself a great view of their comings and goings. You know, just by coincidence."

The thought of their communications officer keeping watch on Noah's watchers was the first decent news he had heard in days. "And can I assume, since he's currently on leave, that Jammer's location is not something the general knows a lot about?"

"I think that would be a safe assumption. If one were going to make one."

"I owe you, Hoss."

"Oh, I put it on your tab, Boom. Don't you worry."

He picked up his burger and met Noah's gaze, his expression suddenly intent and serious. "How bad is it?"

"It's starting to look like a royal cluster fuck. In more ways than one."

"Need some lube?"

Noah shook his head. "For now I got it covered. But do you still have that pager I told you to get rid of?"

"Of course."

"Good. If things get rough, I might send for take-out."

Carter grinned again, this time straight on and savage. "Twenty-four hours, boss. We deliver."

"Good. It won't be through the cell. In my experience, 'secure' only means 'secure to outside tampering.'"

"Pay phone's better. Random ones, at least three to six blocks away."

"I'm the one who taught you that trick."

"Yeah, but I perfected it. In fact, I picked out three of them for you. Locations are on a note inside the file."

That got Noah's attention. "A, B, and C?" On his team, standard procedure included having a Plan B, just in case something went wrong. An "oh, shit!" option. Plan C was the final backup. The "aw, fuck!" last resort.

If Carter had already scouted out three phones, it meant none of his team felt real comfortable being out of communication during this operation. If they thought they had something he needed to know, they'd get a message to him telling him which phone to head to based on the level of urgency involved.

Carter nodded. "A, we need you; B, we saw smoke; C, grab your kitty cat and run, 'cause we got ourselves a five-alarm barn burner."

"Fine. Only use 'em if you need 'em." He looked down at the manila envelope in his friend's hand. "Am I going to like what's in that file?"

Carter handed it over with a shrug and reached for a soaking French fry. "I doubt it. Guy sounds like a real winner. He the one who developed whatever it is everybody's after?"

"I don't think so, but the one who did thinks he's been acting weird lately. He might be the loose lips that sink this rowboat."

"What about the girl?"

Noah's eyes narrowed. "What girl?"

Carter snorted. "The one who left the little souvenir on your neck."

Noah had noticed the bruise while he was shaving that morning, but he'd hoped his collar would cover most of it. Especially the impression of Sam's tiny, even teeth.

"No." His denial was automatic. Sam might have gotten dragged into all this through her association with Annie, but she wasn't involved. And even if she had been, he would have kept anyone else from finding out about that.

"Okay, if you say so. But if you want my opinion, women who get themselves caught up in the middle of military operations? Not generally the kind you take home to Mom."

He had to fight not to picture exactly that—bringing Sam into his parents' comfortable old farmhouse upstate and watching her charm his dad and help his mom with the dishes.

"No one's bringing anyone home," he said, forking up a mound of Swiss-covered corned beef. "And no one's caught up in anything. It's just a mission."

Carter just raised an eyebrow and chomped a fry. "Whatever you say, Boom."

CHAPTER 73

S amantha, you've been washing that pot for ten minutes now. I think it's clean."

Sam jumped and splashed herself with soapy dishwater. "Sorry, Aunt Ruby," she muttered. She quickly rinsed the pot in question and set it in the drainer to dry. "I was distracted."

"I never would have noticed."

The two women stood in the kitchen of Ruby and Henry Howell's house trying to make a dent in the mess generated by seventeen six-year-olds and their associated parents and guardians. The women had already run two loads through the dishwasher and had made a good start on number three, but the dishes just kept coming. Part of that could have to do with the fact that the food kept coming as well. No one had ever gone hungry at Aunt Ruby's house on a regular day. On celebration days, like Evie's sixth birthday, they didn't even go satisfied. As far as Ruby was concerned, it was stuffed or nothing.

Finishing her latest batch of pots, Sam pulled the plug and let the sink drain to be refilled with clean water before she started on the empty serving trays from the last round of provisions. Several of her cousins had just left for the backyard loaded down with newly filled ones, and it was better to keep up with these things as they happened rather than wait for everything to be over. If they tried that, they'd be scrubbing until Memorial Day.

"So what time is your boyfriend coming by to pick you up?" Ruby asked as she arranged slices of ham on a large platter. Her slim, capable hands held surprising strength, even into her sixties, and her posture was just as straight as always. She looked like she should be a farmer's wife somewhere in the middle of the country, not a real estate agent from Brooklyn. She had that kind of strong, capable, salt-of-the-earth look to her.

And one of the sharpest minds Sam had ever met, which was why Sam didn't let the casual tone of the question fool her. "I never said he was my boyfriend, Aunt Ruby. But he's coming at seven." She glanced at the clock. "Any minute, I suppose."

Ruby stopped her fussing and planted her hands on her hips. "You can tell me he's not your boyfriend until the cows come home, young lady, but you'd better not say any such thing in front of your uncle or your cousins. Not if you're going to come to a party smelling like that."

This time, Sam couldn't even attempt to brazen it out. "It's not what it seems like—"

"Samantha Olivia, I might be getting old, but I am not an old fool. And this nose still works just fine. If the man on your skin is not the man who's going to be knocking on this door in a couple of minutes, then you and I need to have a serious talk. That's not the way I raised you, and I certainly hope it's not the way you're intending to live your life."

"They're the same man, Aunt Ruby," she sighed, drying her hands on the dish towel. "It's just . . . more complicated than it seems."

Ruby laughed, her handsome features softening. "Darling, it always is. That's how you know it's worth it."

"What do you mean?"

"It doesn't mean anything if you don't have to work for it, Sam."

The back door of the kitchen opened and Sam's uncle Henry strode up from the backyard, her cousins John and Robbie on his heels.

"My Sammie has always been a hard worker," Henry bragged, wrapping one arm around her shoulders and hauling her against his side. "Ever since she was a little girl."

Sam smiled and returned her uncle's one-armed hug. "Thanks."

"Yeah, she worked my last nerve a time or two," John drawled, snagging a slice of Ruby's ham and getting his hand smacked in the bargain.

He leaned up against the door frame leading into the hall toward the front of the house and winked at his cousin. The oldest of Ruby and Henry's three children, John had been nearly eight when the squalling infant called Samantha had been deposited in his parents' laps. Sam had wanted to be just like John and had followed him around accordingly, which meant she probably had worked a nerve or two. Of course, he'd long since gotten even. Beginning about the time that she'd started dating.

The thought made her take a new look around her. Uncle Henry still held her pinned to his side in a steely, if affectionate, grip, and John and Robbie had casually placed themselves flanking the doorway through which Noah would be forced to enter.

Come into my kitchen, said the big, bullying wolf spiders to the fly, she thought sourly.

"The three of you can just cut it out," she said, restricting her glare to her cousins, but she did lift her uncle's arm off her shoulder and step away from his side. "I'm not sixteen anymore. You have no reason and no right to play Spanish Inquisition when Noah gets here. I can handle my own love life, thank you very much."

"See, that's exactly the problem," Robbie said, running his hand along his jaw and rasping his evening stubble. "You having a love life. That's not something we're all that keen on. Especially not with some guy none of us have ever met."

She rounded on Ruby and Henry's youngest child, the one now barely able to drink. "Don't you even try to play this game with me, Robbie Howell. I changed your diapers, you know, so I sure as hell am not going to start taking orders or advice from you."

"Samantha! Watch your language."

The sting of Ruby's expertly flicked dish towel was familiar but barely made Sam blink. She was working up too good a mad for that. "I'm sorry, Aunt Ruby, but they're being ridiculous. I'm twenty-nine years old. It's time for them to stop treating me like I was just nine."

"You were a lot less trouble when you were nine," Henry growled.

"We're not being ridiculous," John disputed. "We're just looking out for you."

"I can look out for myself."

"We can help."

Briefly Samantha debated the merits of throwing up her hands versus curling them into fists and planting them in her cousins' faces, but she never got to make the final decision—which was leaning heavily toward the fists. The doorbell rang, and before she could even take a step toward the hall, she heard the front door open and someone who sounded like John's wife, Sharon, speaking.

"You must be Noah," she said, her light voice welcoming and cheerful. "I'm Sharon, Sam's cousin-in-law. Come on in. Sam's in the kitchen along with a few of the others."

Sam watched her cousin John's smile turn feral and his fingers flex, and she resorted to the fist anyway. Or at least the elbow, which she promptly jammed into his side.

"Be nice," she hissed, as two sets of footsteps tapped down the hall toward them.

If the welcoming committee surprised Noah, he didn't show it. He swept an efficient gaze around the crowded kitchen, pausing to smile at Sam, before his gaze settled on her uncle. Noah stepped into the room as if her cousins didn't exist and extended his hand to Henry.

"You must be Samantha's uncle," Noah said, his expression relaxed and neutrally friendly. "I'm Noah Baker. It's a pleasure to meet you, Mr. Howell."

Samantha watched as her uncle sized Noah up before clasping his hand in his own. His expression wasn't giving anything away, but she knew Noah had already earned a couple of points. One just from the innate calm and self-possession with which he'd entered the potentially volatile situation and the other from his manner of speech. He'd addressed her uncle as "Mr. Howell" instead of as "Sam's uncle Henry" or, heaven forbid, just "Uncle Henry," a mistake only one of her boyfriends had ever made. After that, Sam had learned to date smarter guys.

Noah had also called her Samantha, instead of Sam, something not many men would have thought of. Everyone called her Sam. That was even what she called herself most of the time, but Uncle Henry had always been quick to point out that her name was Samantha and that anyone who couldn't manage to remember that in a formal situation wasn't showing her the proper respect.

So Uncle Henry had liked that, but that didn't mean she could relax yet. Noah wasn't out of the woods.

"I'd like to say that Samantha has told us a lot about you, Mr. Baker, but I'm afraid that would be a lie. This week is the first we've heard of you."

"I met Samantha about six months ago, sir, through my younger sister. Abby's husband was working with Graham Winters at the time on a diplomatic matter, and she introduced us."

Henry's brows rose. "A diplomatic matter. Is that what you call it when a fiend from the Below tries to take over the world and start a war with the demons that spills over into all of life Above?"

Noah didn't blink. "It's more concise, sir."

That won a chuckle. "I suppose it is."

Samantha tried to break in. "Uncle Henry, I think it's time for Noah and me—"

"Let me introduce you to the family," Henry said, holding out his hand to his wife. She took it and stepped to his side to look up at Noah with a small, polite smile. "This is my wife, Ruby."

"Pleased to meet you, Mrs. Howell." Like a good officer, Noah didn't extend his hand to Ruby, but he shook hers when she offered it. "Samantha speaks of you and your family very warmly."

"Thank you, Mr. Baker," Ruby said. "Oh, but Samantha tells me you're in the military. I should probably be addressing you by your rank, shouldn't I?"

"It's major, ma'am, but it's not necessary. I'd be very happy if you'd all just call me Noah." He smiled. "It makes things a lot easier."

Ruby's smile turned from polite to pleased. "Noah, then."

"And these are Sam's cousins," Henry said, gesturing to the three figures still standing near the door. Sam could hardly believe he'd already called her Sam in front of a date. This was unprecedented! "The one on the right is our oldest son, John. You met his wife, Sharon, at the front door."

Noah nodded to Sam's cousin, but he didn't step forward to offer his hand. He nodded politely to Sharon. "Ma'am."

"And Robert is our youngest," Henry continued. "Our daughter, Caroline, fits in the middle, but she and her husband, Jason, are out back with the kids right now."

"Please give her my regards," Noah said, nodding. "I wouldn't want to interrupt the festivities. It sounds like they're having fun out there."

The whoops and shrieks filtering in from the yard made that an easy guess.

Shaking her head, Sam stepped forward to touch Noah's arm. That was about all the physical contact she was willing to risk in front of this crew, but she wouldn't feel right making him stay to deal with any more of this. "Noah, we should probably get going, shouldn't we?"

"Whenever you're ready," he replied, and when he looked down at her, she could see his eyes twinkling.

Why, the jerk wasn't fazed by any of this! He was perfectly comfortable with her family. It would serve him right if she decided to go upstairs and powder her nose for an hour or two while leaving him to their tender mercies.

"Would you care for a bite to eat or a drink before you leave, Noah?" Ruby offered, smiling up at him.

"No, thank you, ma'am," he refused. "Your kitchen smells amazing, so believe me when I say it's a tough offer to pass up, but I made reservations for Samantha and me at eight, so we should be leaving if we want to get to the restaurant in time."

"Well, we won't keep you, then. You two go and enjoy yourselves."

"Thank you, ma'am." He nodded to Ruby and offered his hand to Henry again. "It was a pleasure to meet you, sir. I hope I'll have the opportunity again soon."

"You be careful," Henry replied brusquely, but Sam

noticed he looked more pleased than intimidating. "Take good care of our girl."

"I intend to, sir."

Placing one hand under Sam's elbow, Noah gently turned her and steered her to the door, pausing only briefly to acknowledge her cousins. "Mrs. Howell, gentlemen, a pleasure." Then they were down the hall and out the front door and heading for the curb.

"I'm parked just down the street," he said, as if nothing unusual had occurred in the history of the world. "The club lent me a car. I had moral objections to picking a woman up for a date and then putting her on the subway."

The hand on her arm moved to the small of her back to guide her along, and Sam cast him a narrow, sideways glance. "So that's it? We're just going to move along and pretend that little episode never even happened?"

He bent his head to give her a look of mild surprise. "What do you mean? I thought it went pretty well."

"It did! That's the thing." She let him help her into the passenger seat, not even really realizing how silly that bit of chivalry was, because with him it seemed completely natural. Of course he would hold her arm while she got in, wait for her to buckle her seat belt, and then close the door behind her. That was just Noah. It certainly wasn't enough to distract her while he circled the car and climbed in behind the wheel. "You might claim that you're human, but only a supernatural force could have managed that scene with my family. What did you do?"

"I was polite," he said, shooting her an amused look

as he pulled out into traffic. "I did get the impression that some of the men you've dated hadn't thought of that."

"That wasn't just polite. Unless you call what a snake charmer does with a cobra 'polite.'" She crossed her arms over her chest and stared out the window, feeling thoroughly off-balance. She'd expected to have to protect Noah, to defend him from her family's tender mercies, and instead they'd practically invited him to sit down to dinner and make himself at home.

"Why would it bother you that your family didn't hate me on sight? Did you want them to?" His eye remained on the traffic, but she could sense his focus on her. "Was dating a rude human supposed to be some sort of slap at them that I failed to cooperate with?"

"Of course not. I love my family and have no desire to deliberately make them unhappy, and I'm not so callous that I'd date anyone just for the sake of some silly statement."

"Then what's got you so on edge?"

A good question. Sam wasn't sure she knew the answer herself. He really had thrown her off balance with her family by fitting in so smoothly, but that was just surprise that would pass soon enough. Honestly, she was glad they'd liked him, for reasons she wasn't quite ready to examine too closely. So what was bothering her came from someplace else entirely, and Sam was pretty sure it was somewhere in the vicinity of Boston, Massachusetts. Like Cambridge. In a microbiology lab.

She sighed and tried forcing her muscles to relax. A few of them even cooperated. "I'm sorry. I guess I am on edge. I'm still worried about Annie. I haven't heard from her since that e-mail on Wednesday."

"I thought it said she wouldn't talk to you again until tomorrow."

"It did, but I don't have to like it."

He smiled. "No, I guess you don't."

Struggling to bring her attention back to the moment, Sam glanced out the window and saw the cables of the Brooklyn Bridge as they passed back into Manhattan. Her curiosity piqued. "So where are we going for dinner?"

"Wherever you want."

"I thought you said you made reservations someplace."

His mouth curved. "I did say that, didn't I?" He shot her a quick look of amusement. "You didn't recognize an exit strategy when you heard one?"

She felt her own lips quirking. "You mean you lied to my aunt and uncle?"

"Are you mad at me?"

"Actually, I'm relieved. If you'd been completely perfect, I'd have had to check under your bed for a pod."

His next glance was still amused but much, much warmer. "Sweetheart, anytime you want to look under, over, or inside my bed, you just say the word. It's entirely at your disposal."

She felt a rush of heat and had to resist the urge to squirm in her seat. "Major Baker, I think you might be flirting with me."

"If you're not certain, I'll just have to try harder."

Sam's memory flashed back to Thursday night and

she wondered what his trying harder might entail. She reached for the button to roll down her window.

Beside her, Noah chuckled. "Feeling warm, Samantha?"

She started to glare at him, then thought better of it. Instead, she reached across the console between them and put her hand on his thigh just below the crease in his hip. She squeezed. "I'm fine," she said, lowering her voice, consciously making it deeper, huskier. "Have you given any thought to what you'd like to have for dinner?"

Her fingers teased the hard muscles beneath them and slid inward to trace the seam running up the inside of his thigh. Suddenly those muscles became even harder.

"I thought I'd let you choose," he ground out, and she noticed his knuckles had gone white around the steering wheel.

Following the seam up and up, she slid her hand between his legs to cup him intimately. She heard him curse, but her attention was focused on what she was doing. Namely, torturing him. It was the least he deserved.

"I know a great little place near the Flatiron," she said absently, and gave him an address. She curled her fingers and gently squeezed. "Small, informal. Very private."

He tore one hand from the wheel and clamped it over hers, stilling her movements. "If you don't stop teasing me, you'll be lucky to eat before lunchtime tomorrow."

She laughed quietly. "Don't be such a baby. I

thought the army was supposed to teach you to test your limits and bear up under physical strain."

"Being tortured by little Lupine witches who don't know any better than to tease hungry soldiers was *not* part of the Ranger Course."

"How disappointing." She shifted her hand to stroke. "Well, I guess you'll just have to tough it out."

The muscle in his jaw jumped, and Sam felt the shift as he stepped on the accelerator. "And you'll just have to do the same when I bend you over our table and fuck you in front of the rest of the patrons."

"You know, I'm pretty sure that's illegal. Not to mention slightly depraved."

"Do you really think I'm in the position to care?"

She pursed her lips to keep from grinning. "I didn't think you minded the position you were in, but if there's another one you'd prefer . . ."

He described one to her, graphically, that had her thighs clenching together and her breath choking to a stop in her throat. Her fingers trembled against him, and she knew he had to feel that. He didn't bother to gloat, just pulled to the curb in front of the address she'd given him and cut the engine.

"This isn't a restaurant," he said, his breathing harsh and uneven. His hand on hers no longer tried to pry her away but pressed her closer as he ground against her.

She shook her head. "No, it isn't. Actually, it's my apartment building. But if you're really hungry, we can find a place around here to eat. There's a good Italian restaurant just a couple of blocks away."

"You have thirty seconds to get wherever you want to be when I take you. Assuming you'd rather it wasn't right here in the car in front of God and all your neighbors."

Sam didn't waste any time arguing. She released her seat belt and burst out of the car, not even bothering to slam the door behind her. Noah's expression had told her he was deadly serious.

As a Lupine, she was fast, but she'd barely turned the key in her lock when Noah appeared behind her and pressed her up against her apartment door. Panting, she got the damned thing open and stumbled inside. She'd probably have landed in a heap halfway across the room if Noah hadn't grabbed her and carried her to the floor right inside the door.

She vaguely heard the sound of the door catching and had just enough presence of mind to be grateful that Noah must have kicked it shut, because she was way too far gone to have thought of it. Her senses had scattered the minute his mouth closed on hers, claiming, possessing, stealing her breath and her thoughts and leaving her nothing but a trembling, aching need. She didn't even grunt when she landed on the hardwood floor, barely softened by the braided cotton rug that covered the entry space. It didn't matter. She was already busy shredding Noah's blue-striped dress shirt into ragged little pieces and scattering them on the carpet around them. She needed to touch him, to feel his smooth, taut skin beneath her hands, her mouth, her body.

But beneath her didn't seem to be where Noah wanted to be just then. Tearing his mouth from hers, he grabbed her hands and twisted, forcing her onto her stomach with himself kneeling above her. She opened her mouth to protest that she wanted to be able to touch him, but the sound died in a whimper when he grabbed the collar of her silky baby-doll top and ripped it in half. His teeth followed the line of the tear, scraping down her spine with furious greed. After that, she didn't think about protests. All she thought about was his mouth, his hands, and his body as he used all three to drive her out of her mind.

His hands clamped down on her hips and yanked them up, bringing her off her belly and onto her knees. She braced her hands against the rug to steady herself, while his fingers darted around, found the fastenings on her jeans, and roughly opened them. The heavy fabric slid away, taking her panties with it, and she had a fleeting thought about the uselessness of wearing sexy underwear around this man, since he never seemed to slow down long enough to see it.

He shoved her jeans down to her knees and left them there, his hands too busy sliding over the smooth, bare skin of her hips and ass to worry about finishing the job. The shreds of her top had already fluttered down to pool around her wrists and hands, and a movement so fast she had honestly missed it had opened her bra and sent it to the floor as well.

Confined by her clothing shackling her wrists and knees, Sam knelt before him and acknowledged helplessly that he'd managed to awake every instinct she had with this position. On her knees, head bowed, hips raised to his touch, she felt every fiber of her Lupine self stirring and purring in pleasure. Every nerve in her body tingled, stretching toward him. The feel of his hands stroking her side, her flanks, reaching beneath her to cup and knead her breasts, had her struggling to breathe through the clenching fist of her arousal. Goddess, if he didn't take her soon, she would die.

When his hand glided over the smooth curve of her ass and followed the crease to the aching need between her legs, she decided she might die anyway. One long, lean finger circled her opening, teasing and testing before it drew back and plunged in deep. She threw up her head and cried out, her back arching and her whole body clenching in pleasure. But it wasn't enough. Not nearly.

"Please," she whimpered, her own voice sounding weak and unfamiliar in her ears. "Now."

She heard a curse as his hand slipped from between her legs, and she couldn't suppress a moan at the loss of his touch. Dimly over the roaring in her ears, she heard the hiss of metal against metal, and then her entire reality condensed to the heart-stopping instant when he plunged full-length inside her.

She screamed. There was no other word for it. The cry tore from her throat, high and wild, and her arms buckled beneath her, sending her shoulders crashing to the floor. The shift lifted her hips higher against him, and the next thrust took him even deeper, bringing another cry from both their mouths. His fingers dug into the flesh of her hips with bruising force, and Sam could have cared less. The only thing that mattered was the rough, steady rhythm of his body sliding deeply and endlessly into hers.

The constriction of her jeans prevented her from parting her legs, and she whimpered in frustration. She felt almost helpless, unable to control the speed or depth or force of his thrusts. All she could do was kneel beneath him and tremble, accepting him and trusting him to drive her closer and closer to the edge of completion.

Since she couldn't spread her legs to urge him on, she had to content herself with arching her back, increasing the tilt of her hips and allowing him another fraction deeper. Breathlessly she realized that allowing had very little to do with it.

He took her as if she belonged to him, and not even in her subconscious mind could she fight the claiming. In her mind and her heart, she *felt* like his.

Suddenly she couldn't bear the separation between them. She levered herself up with her forearms, but Noah was already there. His hands left her hips, and he wrapped his arms around her, lifting her into his embrace. He pressed her back against him until she felt every inch of his smooth, muscled chest along her back. One arm wrapped around her waist, his hand clamped on the opposite hip to hold her steady as he rocked endlessly into her. The other arm circled her body from ribs to shoulder, his forearm nestled between her breasts as he cradled her to him. She felt claimed and protected and cherished, and she lifted her own arms up and back to close around his neck.

The hand on her hip firmed, and he rocked deeper within her, every nudge pushing against her heart. Helpless to move, she did the only thing she could and welcomed him with the warm, tight clasp of her body. She felt the groan rumble up from his chest before it escaped his lips and echoed it with a breathless cry. Her head fell back against his shoulder. As she turned, her lashes parted just far enough to see the taut, intent, absorbed expression on his face. His eyes locked with hers, and their arms tightened around each other in perfect unison.

"Noah," she whispered, her eyes drifting shut as he shifted to rub the faintly stubbled skin of his cheek against hers. It was a prayer, a blessing, a benediction. Her entire world had distilled down to this moment, to this man, and to the way he filled her heart even as he filled her body.

"Samantha." His head bowed, his lips pressing against the smooth, hot skin of her shoulder. He rocked forward and stilled, holding himself high and deep within her. "Samantha mine."

Her heart leapt and her body dissolved and the first words in her heart were the last ones on her lips. "Noah mine."

He shuddered, and she gasped, and they tumbled together headlong over the cliff.

CHAPTER 14

When Noah Baker staked a claim to something, he meant it. Sam figured that out about halfway through the half hour it took to extricate herself from his arms on Sunday afternoon.

Her arguments that she had to be at the club by three for a special function that would last well past eleven that night seemed to make no impression. Only the threat of locking herself into a chastity belt before she came home seemed to get his attention, and then he grumbled the entire time it took for him to follow her into the shower and ensure she used up her entire hot-water supply while getting remarkably little done in the way of bathing. By the end, she had to shampoo and rinse while her teeth chattered and he went whistling into the kitchen to make a pot of coffee.

She found him standing at the counter, sipping from a mug and flipping through her copy of the *Times*. He must have run down to her box and picked it up while she tried to defrost.

He looked up at her entrance, taking in the rosy

sheen of her skin and the determinedly un-seductive black suit, and raised an eyebrow. "You didn't mention you'd be working yesterday."

She didn't answer until she had her own mug of coffee and had gingerly taken a seat at the small table. "It's a fund-raiser for next year's campaign to reelect the Other representative to the president's Committee on Cultural Education. I was going to tell you about it on Friday, but I didn't see you. And somehow I got distracted when you picked me up last night."

He made a humming noise and his lips twitched. "Right. I suppose you're going to tell me I distracted you."

"Ya think?"

"I like to think the distraction was mutual." He set his coffee on the table and leaned down to kiss her, for once more sweet than seductive. "What time did you say you'd be done tonight?"

She shrugged, trying not to let herself get distracted all over again by the powerful grace with which he lowered himself to the chair opposite her. "The party officially runs from six thirty to ten, but by the time people actually clear out and we get things set to rights, I'll probably be looking at somewhere around midnight."

"I wanted to offer a suggestion."

"What kind of a suggestion?"

He laughed. "Nothing indecent, so you can stop looking at me with horrified fascination. Even I have to rest sometimes."

Sam snorted. From what she'd seen so far, those times appeared to be few and far between.

"Since you'll be finishing up late," he continued, "I thought you might want to pack a bag. It's a much shorter commute to walk up the stairs to my suite when the party's over than it is to come all the way back here."

Of course, she wanted to jump up and shout, "*Yes!*" but these things required a bit more consideration than that. She knew perfectly well that Noah found her attractive and he enjoyed sleeping with her, but she wasn't sure he understood what it would mean if she settled down in his bedroom for the night right under Graham's nose. On Thursday, she'd waited until Graham had gone for the night, not just next door but out to dinner with Missy, before she'd snuck upstairs to seduce Noah. Tonight she wouldn't get that chance. As the host of the party, Graham would be there from beginning to end. If she went to Noah's room, Graham would know about it immediately. He might have been forced to acknowledge several years ago that Sam was an adult capable of making her own decisions about relationships, but that didn't mean he wanted to witness them. If he knew she and Noah were sleeping together at the club, he'd take that as a declaration of something a bit more serious than she thought Noah intended.

"I don't know if that's really the best idea."

She liked that he didn't get upset or jump to any conclusions. He just asked, "Why? I thought we were both enjoying ourselves."

"We are. I mean, I am. I just . . . My family was fine with the idea of us dating, but I can assure you they wouldn't have been so calm if they'd known where we ended up last night."

"On the living room floor?"

"And Graham is family, too. He might be more like a third cousin, but he *is* a cousin. And he's the Alpha besides. I'm just not sure that the idea of parading the fact that we're sleeping together under his nose is the best course of action."

"Do you want us to lie to him?"

Noah's tone of voice told her what he thought of that idea. She hurried to shake her head. "No, that isn't what I meant. I'm not saying I'm ashamed that we're involved. That's got nothing to do with it. It's just that . . ." She sighed. "In Graham's mind, I'm under his care on three levels. I'm an employee, I'm pack, and I'm family. It's like a triple whammy of protectiveness. He knows I'm old enough to decide who to date, but to have an affair under his roof would mean something to him that it might not mean to either of us."

He leaned back in his chair, his expression inscrutable. "What would it mean to him?"

"Something more than just an affair. What we do here is out of sight and out of mind. What we do at his club is a different story."

"You make it sound like 'an affair' is a pretty term for getting our rocks off together."

"That's not what I meant. I just meant that to Graham it would mean that this is leading somewhere. An affair is short-term. It has an expiration date. Graham would be thinking about something . . . more permanent."

"What makes you think it's not any more than an affair?"

She froze, one hand on her mug. It took the space of several speeding heartbeats for her to catch her breath. "Is it?"

"Whatever it is, I think it's more than we're going to settle in the next," he glanced at his watch, "fifteen minutes. But as far as I'm concerned, this is already more than an affair. We can talk about how much more tonight." He stood and drained his mug. He even rinsed it out and placed it in the drain rack. "Come on, finish your coffee. I'll drive us back to the club and let you get back to work. That trip to Jersey yesterday put me behind on my paperwork."

She took the hand he held out and let him lift her to her feet. He snagged the mug out of her hand and set it aside; then he reached out and cupped her chin in his palm. He tilted her chin up to face him, holding her gaze for a long moment.

She had to fight the instinctive urge to lower her eyes in recognition of his dominance in their own private hierarchy. She saw his mouth soften, but before she could wonder if his surprising abilities extended to reading her mind, he lowered his head and kissed her thoroughly. For several minutes she thought about nothing at all except the taste of him and the desire to use their kiss to demonstrate how tied up in him she had already become.

When he raised his head, both of them were breathing more heavily and his hazel eyes were heavy lidded and satisfied. He reached down to pat her bottom affectionately. "Go get your bag, or you'll be late."

She reflected, once he'd seated her in the car and

started the engine with her having no recollection of
even leaving her kitchen, that a girl had to be wary of a
man who could scramble her wits so effectively. If she
wasn't careful, her heart would be irrevocably gone
before she even realized.

With great deliberateness, she refrained from doing
a spot check. She'd be better off not knowing.

A s Sam had predicted, the party was still going
at twenty after ten. That was when she slipped
away to her office to check her e-mail. She'd had
her cell phone with her all night in the bag she'd carried with her specifically for that purpose, and Annie
hadn't called. Sam had her fingers crossed that Annie
had been too chicken and had e-mailed instead. She
clicked the send/receive button on her mail program
three times in rapid succession before she gave up
hope. Annie was still nowhere to be seen.

Damn it, if she'd gone to all the trouble of sneaking
away from work for something, it should at least have
been to dart upstairs and spend a few irresistibly frus-
trating minutes sexually harassing Noah before diving
back into the fray. Checking up on her disappearing,
maddening friend did not make an acceptable alternative. Especially when said friend hadn't even had the
courtesy to check in.

Grimly Sam shut down the computer. She'd give
Annie until midnight. After that, she had to tell Graham. And hope he didn't tear her liver out for waiting
so long.

A glance at her watch put the countdown at ninety minutes. Until the go hour, she'd have to continue playing nice, doing her job, coordinating with Richards, supervising the kitchen and waitstaff, and generally pretending her palms didn't itch with the urge to wrap around her best friend's throat and start squeezing.

Itchy palms made Sam think about Noah, whom she'd left sitting at the desk in the living area of his suite, and she indulged in a fit of the grumps that she'd have to leave him there longer than she'd anticipated. She'd told him not to wait up for her, but at the time she hadn't anticipated that she'd have to get through a confrontation with the Alpha before she got to crawl in next to Noah and wake him up.

Assuming there would be enough left of her to crawl.

The buzz of her cell phone startled her from her doom-plagued thoughts. She flipped it open before the vibrations had time to still, but not before she'd glimpsed Annie's name on the caller ID screen.

"It's about frickin' time," Sam barked, not bothering with niceties. She wasn't feeling nice. "I've been waiting to hear from you *all day*! What were you—"

"Sam, I'm in trouble."

The quietly panicked tone in Annie's voice kept Sam from venting her instinctive response. "What do you mean?"

"I'm in the lab, and I think someone followed me here. I think they're trying to break in. I need help."

Cursing, Sam looked down at her snazzy black suit and consigned it to the rag bin. "Five minutes."

Pressing the end button, she bolted for the club's back door and impatiently pounded out the alarm code. She shoved the door open, and by the time it locked shut behind her, she was racing to the lab as fast as her four feet would carry her.

CHAPTER 15

When the secure cell rang, Noah froze. He didn't have a call scheduled, and in his experience, unexpected news usually turned out to be bad news. He punched the send button. "This is one."

"Option C."

"Aw, fuck."

And that's how Option C got its name.

The line went dead, but then, Noah was already stripping as he yanked items out of their storage spots. From the dresser he pulled on a pair of black trousers and a long-sleeved black T-shirt guaranteed to wick away moisture and preserve body heat. The closet yielded a webbed vest already stocked with mission gear and a lethal-looking sidearm in matte black. He spared a wistful thought for the assault rifle he would have carried on an ordinary operation, stomped his feet into well-worn and flexibly soled boots, and headed for the roof.

Making his way soundlessly down the five-story steel fire escape provided something of a challenge, but not enough to slow him down. He had to pause for a minute to be sure no one stirred in the alley behind the club, but he still made it to the designated pay phone in under seven minutes. The unofficial time limit was always fifteen.

He punched in Carter's number. "Who lit the match?"

"A few of our friends from up north, mainly. Jammer sent up the alarm that they had a group out tonight looking like business, but it was Scooter who picked them up. I've had him watching the building where our white-coated friends work. In a remarkable coincidence, something's stirring there tonight, and it looks to be a damned sight bigger than a mouse."

Noah fought back a tidal wave of anger. He hadn't thought Hammond would lose his patience quite this fast. "They send their whole team?"

"Naw. Probably figured they'd only need a couple of bozos with a tranq gun to handle the woman. Who marched into the whole mess about fifteen minutes ago and triggered Scooter's internal alarm system."

Christ. This newsreel just kept getting better and better. "What the hell was the woman planning to do in the lab at eleven on a Sunday night?"

"Can't tell you that, but I can tell you that the B-team seemed pretty excited to see her. Scooter reckons they've got their own eye on the place, but he hasn't spotted it."

"Where are you?"

"On-site. Just me and Scooter."

"I'm on my way. Both of you stay out of sight unless they get inside. If they do, I want you to keep them away from the good doctor. Understood?"

"Damn skippy and passed right along. I'm out."

Had Noah mentioned he'd had a bad feeling about this mission right from the start?

One thing Sam had to give to the jerks skulking around the building that housed Annie's lab: they had the least-in-sight trick down pat. It wasn't easy to stay completely out of sight in Manhattan, no matter what time of day or night, and it had to be even harder for a couple of full-grown men than it was for one largish, dog-like creature.

By the time she got to the building, her tongue was hanging out from the hard run, but she didn't waste time panting. Darting into the alley behind the building, she put her nose to the ground and got to work.

In her wolf form, the scents of the city proved nearly overwhelming, her senses so sharp and tuned in, she could tell what the people walking past on the street had eaten for lunch earlier. She could hear the heartbeats of the ones closest to the mouth of the alley, and the air had taken on a flavor, a taste of humanity and machinery muddled together in a knot of perception. Her vision had sharpened and flattened at the same time, allowing her to see farther in lower light but sacrificing some of the detail her human eyes had perceived. She didn't need detail, though, to know that the two—sniff . . . no, three—men had split up, fanning out from a central point near the back end of the alley where the large Dumpsters would have provided partial concealment.

Loping forward, she heard the soft click of her claws

against the pavement and made a mental note to ask Aunt Ruby to trim them for her next weekend. Too late to worry about it now, though. She'd have to rely on the fact that the sound was so low, the men she trailed were unlikely to hear it over their own breathing.

A loading dock shut off with dark metal doors stretched across the back of the blind alley, providing access into the rear service areas of the lab building. The men had gathered in front of them, had lingered long enough to make plans and for one of them to smoke a cigarette. Looking around, she saw no butts littering the ground, so he'd been smart enough to pack his trash with him. Too bad he'd been too stupid to avoid stinking himself up in the first place. The smoke would make him easier to track, so she pinpointed his trail and began to follow his footsteps across the concrete.

Up.

Growling her displeasure, she found where he'd climbed up the fire escape and halted. He'd drawn the ladder back up after him, probably to cover his tracks, but that made it easier for her to follow if she'd been inclined. Without thumbs, ladder-climbing fell out of her repertoire, but jumping the ten feet to the lowest platform she could handle. She considered the idea, then dismissed it. The stairs up to subsequent levels were manageable but not appealing. If the steady fading of the fumes in the rising air was right, he was headed for the roof, which made him a guard or a lookout, not the point man. She could let him go. For now.

Back to the loading doors. Scent number two struck her as almost subtle after the stink of Camel man, but she didn't find it any pleasanter. Instead of the basically organic if chemically tainted and offensive smell of charred tobacco, number two smelled like stale sweat and anger. She wrinkled her nose and blew out a sneezing breath. No way would she mistake this scent for one belonging to anyone else, but that didn't mean she relished the prospect of following it anywhere.

She paused to check in on number three just to have a frame of reference and paused. Puzzled, she sniffed again. This one smelled . . . different. Not better, just not like anything else she could remember encountering.

There was, at the base of it, the unmistakable meaty, chemical scent of modern human, overlaid with the usual blend of soaps and creams and sprays they liked to layer on. At least, that's what she got on the first sniff. On the second, it was gone, all of it, as if it hadn't existed. Frowning, she tried to wrap her mind around that. Scent didn't disappear and reappear. It wasn't made that way. She sniffed again and smelled something . . . other. Not Other. At least, not precisely. Number three didn't smell like a were or a demon or a changeling. He didn't smell Fae or witchy, and since he smelled at all, he obviously wasn't a vampire. He just didn't smell quite right.

Forgetting all about the stink of number two, she focused on the alien scent of number three and began to trace where it separated from its companions.

With her nose on the trail and her eyes on the ground before her, she cocked her ears to the sides to listen for trouble. Her mind hadn't changed when she shifted, but her brain chemistry had altered, turning down the volume in some places and up in others. As a wolf, she could divide her senses much more easily than as a human; she could sneak and not worry about being snuck up on.

A light breeze ruffled her fur and brought a fresh wave of scent washing in from the western side of the building. On it floated the there-and-gone scent of number three. He'd gone in through the loading bay doors, she realized abruptly; he was already inside.

Retracing her steps deeper into the alley, Sam jumped onto the ledge in front of the doors and sniffed curiously. The scent was here, but the doors remained closed. Biting back a snarl, Sam checked the alley behind her and shifted just long enough to grasp the lever handle and pry the bay door open enough to slip through. She had fur again before the door finished its descent. Considering her choices at that point were either fur or nudity, she'd stick with fur.

Once inside, she caught the scent again and followed it deep into the building's service areas. She'd never been back here before, but her sense of direction kept her from getting too disoriented, and the faint traces of human and not quite human kept her on the trail. The farther inside the building it went, the more she picked up her pace.

Her lack of pockets meant she couldn't carry a cell phone, so she hoped Annie was all right. It had taken Sam longer than the five minutes she'd promised to get this far downtown, but she'd definitely made it in little more than ten. If Annie could hold on another ten, they might be okay.

The slick flooring inside the building slowed Sam's going a fraction, and the polished linoleum failed to hold a scent as tightly as the porous concrete outside, but it didn't take a nose like hers to tell that the scent was getting stronger the deeper she went into the building. When it turned abruptly into a stairwell, she nudged the door open and followed. It was definitely headed up. Toward the lab.

They had too big a head start. She'd have to leave the trail and head straight for Annie.

If luck was on Sam's side, her one enormous advantage might work out in her favor—she knew this building, and they didn't. She could head straight for the lab and not waste time checking wrong turns or empty rooms. Too bad she'd temporarily forfeited the ability to cross her fingers.

She gathered speed as she loped up the concrete steps, the rough treads helping her keep her feet under her. At the landing for the fifth floor, she paused and put her nose to the ground. She couldn't smell any traces of number three in this particular doorway, but that didn't mean he hadn't detoured and taken another stairway. She'd sacrificed that certainty for speed on the way up.

Cautiously she nudged open the swinging door into the corridor and slipped through. Keeping to the shadows wasn't difficult, since most of the building's interior lights had been turned off to conserve power. Even the university was going green these days. She gave thanks for the shadows she could find anyway, since the sight of a large gray-brown timber wolf roaming the halls would have disconcerted anyone she might meet.

Her lips curled away from her teeth as she lifted her nose to scent the air. There was the trace of something off in the air, she thought, but it wasn't strong enough for her to be sure if the men she'd been hunting were inside, or if their scent simply lingered in her nostrils and in the atmosphere of the building. Good HVAC systems made air scenting a hit-or-miss proposition these days. Recirculated air in a large enclosed space could smell of things that hadn't been present for hours or days, which was why she kept her nose to the ground wherever possible. Ground trails never lied.

A rippling shadow caught her eye. Freezing in place, she hunkered down and lifted her nose. A second later, the air currents shifted, and she smelled adrenaline and hostility, their stench masking everything else in the area. Number two was headed toward the lab.

Bristling, she slunk silently along the wall. The man had his back to her and his attention focused on his goal. He wouldn't notice her until she was on top of him. Slowly, carefully, she began to close the distance between them. A hundred feet. Fifty. Twenty. Ten. Her muscles tensed as she gathered herself, drew back. Leapt.

She hit his side, forcing him to spin and face her. He had decent reflexes for a human, she had to give him that much, but he was still a man, not a Lupine. Sam was faster. She jumped again and dropped him. He landed on his back with a grunt and the weight of 150 pounds of wolf on his chest, pinning him down.

Getting between him and his hands, she cut off his reflexive reach for his rifle. Well, he still reached, but he couldn't shoulder, and he definitely couldn't aim. He couldn't even swing the barrel around to get it pointing in her direction. She could smell the stink of sedatives above the bite of powder and knew he carried tranquilizers instead of bullets. He wouldn't get a chance to use them. Fixing her eyes on his, she bared her teeth and snarled.

He snarled back. "Bitch."

Some men were so unoriginal.

She went for his throat, but he'd anticipated that. He dropped the rifle and brought one arm up and over to protect the vulnerable spot. That pissed Sam off, because it hinted that he knew what he was dealing with. Most humans didn't know how to fend off a wolf attack, much less a werewolf attack, but this one had at least some idea.

Still, he didn't know all the tricks. She proved it by taking advantage of the unattended position of his raised forearm and sinking her teeth into the inside of his wrist. If he'd been smart, he'd have shown her the back of his arm where the muscles were thicker and harder. Her fangs sheared easily through the tendons in his wrist, making him scream and rendering his right arm effectively useless. There wasn't time to quibble over being nice. She needed to protect Annie.

He jerked his arms reflexively away, baring his throat. Sam's jaws closed around it and clenched. Fifteen seconds of firm pressure around the trachea and carotid arteries and his struggles dissolved into boneless unconsciousness. As soon as she felt him go limp, she dropped him, not even pausing at the cracking thud of his skull smacking into the hard floor. In the still silence of the nearly deserted building, that scream would travel. She expected to see his pals racing toward her any second.

Grimly she poured on a burst of speed and sped toward the lab. She skidded around the final corner, scrambled to regain her traction, and barreled headfirst into a large, immovable object with the scent of spice and man.

Disbelieving, her head shot up and her eyes locked with Noah's.

A mix of full-out running and creative bumper-hitching got Noah to the lab building in seventeen minutes. He didn't waste a second struggling for his breath, just headed straight for the stairwell. His information on Annie Cryer told him her lab was located on the fifth floor; his instincts told him that was where the B-team was headed. The scream that greeted him when he burst onto the floor confirmed it.

His instincts had said nothing about Sam crashing into him just outside the door.

They'd come from opposite sides of the building and made contact by way of her firm, furry body slamming into his knees at approximately twenty miles an hour. The impact knocked him on his ass, but that was nothing compared to the impact of looking into the eyes of a huge, shaggy timber wolf and seeing his woman staring back at him.

She blinked, a look of consternation creeping into her eyes. Noah felt his jaw clench. "What the hell are you doing here?"

She shook her head, a movement that somehow involved half her body and reminded him of his parents' springer spaniel coming in out of the rain. Not what Noah wanted to think about in connection to the woman who'd spent the last night wet and open beneath him.

She gave a low growl and jerked her head in the direction he'd come from, her eyebrows flexing insistently.

He shook his head. "I just came from there. No one else is over that way."

A twirl of her tail and a soft, low *wuff* assured him no threat was going to sneak up from the way she'd come, either. Ignoring the strange feeling of having had a complete conversation with someone who couldn't speak, he shoved a hand through his short-cropped hair and pushed himself to his feet.

"Then we've lost them," he said, surprised by how much his own voice sounded like a growl. "After the scream I heard coming from up here, anyone with an exit strategy would have exited, and anyone without one would have been here by now." He lowered his chin and glared at her. "What was that scream, anyway?"

She gave a very canine shrug and lifted one paw to scratch at the laboratory door. It opened, and Annie stuck a nervous head out, her eyes widening when she caught sight of him. "Who are you?"

"Noah Baker. Abby's brother." He and Annie might not have met in the six months since he'd known the Silverbacks, but he knew she and Abby had become friends, so he hoped dropping his sister's name would reassure her. He pointed at Sam. "Aren't you going to ask who she is?"

Annie gave him an odd look. "That's Sam. Even if I

hadn't known her since we were babies, I'm the one who called her, so it wouldn't have been that tough to figure out."

"And why, exactly, did you call her?"

Annie's expression went smooth and guarded. "I heard someone trying to break in. I got freaked out."

He stifled the urge to launch a full-scale interrogation and turned his glare back on Sam. "For God's sake, are you going to stay like that all day? Shift back. I have a few things I want to talk to you about."

Sam gave another one of those full-body shakes, accompanied this time by a narrow glare.

"She can't," Annie explained, apparently tipped off by the thunder in Noah's expression. "This isn't like the movies, where her clothes changed into her fur and will magically change back when she shifts again. If she shifts back now, she'll be naked."

"So what? I've already seen it. Shift back."

Annie's eyes went wide, and Sam growled at him. Snarled, really, but he wasn't in the mood to make distinctions.

"I want to talk to you," he repeated.

Sam planted her haunches on the floor, her tail twitching in irritation.

"I think she's saying no," Annie translated, her voice hesitant.

"I know what she's saying. And even if I couldn't tell, after a week of dealing with her god-awful stubbornness, I could have made a good guess." His voice was grim and he never took his eyes off Sam's. "But in the same week, she should have had time to figure out that I can dig my heels in just as deep. I want to talk, and if I have to go knock on Princess Fiona's door to ask her to summon a moon spell to force her change, I'll do it. So she can shift now, or she can make me make her do it and end up pissing me off."

She bared her teeth at him.

"Never let it be said I left you without a choice, Samantha."

Annie looked from him to Sam and back again. "I have sweats in my desk. I'll go grab them."

Sam extended her glare to include her friend and ruffled her fur, but she made no move to stop Annie. When shet set the clothes on the ground in front of Sam, she spared Noah one last killing glance, then smoothly shifted and yanked the sweatshirt over her head.

"Arrogant, hard-nosed, thickheaded son of a bitch," she muttered. When she pulled on the sweatpants, she got creative.

Noah let her run with it. When she was covered and he'd managed to unclench his jaws enough to speak, he asked, "Now who's going to explain to me just what the bloody hell is going on here?"

CHAPTER 76

Sam folded her arms over her chest. "Annie already told you, I'm here because she called me. I think the more interesting question is why the hell are *you* here?"

A muscle jumped in the side of his jaw. "I followed you," he bit out.

She suppressed a start of surprise. "What? Since when?"

"I came downstairs at the club to see how much longer you'd be, but instead of finding you directing the troops, I saw you running for the back door like your tail was on fire. I worried something was wrong, so I followed you."

"You couldn't have." She shook her head. "I'd have spotted you. And there's no way you could have kept up with me anyway."

"Not on foot," he agreed, "but I caught a lift on the bumper of an obligingly speeding delivery van."

Her scowl deepened as she took in his clothing and the pistol holstered at his waist. "You came looking for me at the club loaded for bear?"

"Damn it, I just told you I was worried!"

"You said you were worried when you saw me leave. If you followed me immediately, you had to have been dressed like that before you came downstairs. What the hell aren't you telling me, Noah?"

Annie broke in. "Um, not that I want to get in the middle of this—or, you know, within a good fifty feet of it—but don't you think we should be focusing on the people who were trying to break in here? The ones who sacked my lab?"

For the first time, Sam took a good look around her, and she swore. While she'd been busy scent-trailing the bastards through the building, one of them had already gotten inside the lab and done a quick, thorough, and very messy search.

"Are you all right?" She reached out and grasped Annie's arm. "Were you in here when they did this? Did they hurt you?"

Annie shook her head. "I'm fine. I hid in Gordon's office, but the man out here seemed less interested in me than in . . . whatever he was looking for."

Beside them, Noah snorted. "Let's not be coy, ladies. This isn't exactly a random burglary, and no one breaks into an academic building or a library looking for money and stereo equipment. I think both of you know exactly what he was looking for. The question is, did he find it?"

Sam and Annie exchanged glances. Annie's dropped to her feet.

"Yes."

Sam couldn't stifle the snarl. "I told you the Alpha had to know, and now he doesn't just have a potential mess to clean up; he's got an actual one."

"Sam, I didn't—"

She cut her friend off. "Save it. Right now we need to know who they were and where they went. We can play true confessions once we're back at the club where the Alpha can hear the whole thing. What did they take?"

Annie cast a helpless look around her. "At first glance? I'd say everything."

That earned two muffled curses, one from Sam and one from Noah. "Did you get a look at them?"

"There was just one in here," Annie said. "He had some kind of mask over his face, like a ski mask, and he was dressed—" She broke off and looked at Noah. "He was dressed a lot like you."

Noah didn't bother to answer. His attention seemed focused on the room, his sharp eyes scanning the debris of the search. Restlessly he began to pace along the walls and counters.

"What are you doing?" Sam snapped. As far as she was concerned, that was only the first of a bushelful of questions he had to answer, but at the moment it was the one she settled on.

He ignored it. "What do you smell in here?"

"I don't—"

"Sam, just tell me what you smell."

Grinding her teeth together, she pursed her lips and took a deep breath. Frowned. Then another. "I'm not—" She tried again. "I don't know. There's . . . *something* here, but it's not . . . normal." She looked at Annie. "That guy who did the search. He wasn't a vamp, was he?"

Annie shook her head. "No. I mean, I didn't touch

him, and I was concentrating too hard on staying out of sight to pay much attention to whether he smelled or not, but he was definitely throwing off heat, and he didn't move like a vampire. You know what I mean?"

Sam did. Vampires might not be the equal to shifters, but they had their own kind of grace that would be hard to mistake for a human. But the fact that Sam had been able to see the intruder's heat made it even more certain. Not even a vampire who'd just drunk someone dry could have given off enough of the stuff for Annie to have seen it from her hiding place.

Sam's lips firmed. "I didn't think so."

"Now that you mention it, I'm not entirely sure I know what he was." Annie frowned.

"Me either."

"I do."

Both women turned at the sound of the much deeper voice. Noah paused in his examination of the debris scattered over one counter in particular, and even from across the room his expression looked grim. "He was a soldier."

Noah had known it even before he'd gotten inside, but that didn't make him any happier to have his assumptions confirmed beyond a doubt. The man who'd sacked the lab was definitely a soldier and definitely trained in dealing with Others, or he wouldn't have made it in and out without alerting Sam and Noah to his presence.

Realizing he'd been screwed by his own superiors did nothing to improve Noah's already grim mood.

He cut off the women's questions with a harsh gesture. "Sam is right. We need to get back to the club and get this all hashed out. Whatever you were doing in here, Doc, someone else found it damned interesting. I doubt he's going to wait long to share it, which means that you need to explain it to me, Sam, the Alpha, and the rest of your pack, and somehow I don't think you're going to want to go through that twice. Come on. Let's go."

He nearly fainted when no one argued, but that would have taken away his advantage. Shepherding them out of the lab, he watched while Annie reset the locks and didn't comment. It might be silly to lock up when everything worth locking had already been taken, but he understood the impulse; she needed to take control back, and locking up at least make her feel like she was doing something. And he supposed there might be some equipment in there that hadn't interested the B-team but might prove a little too tempting for a real thief.

Outside, Noah paused and glanced down at Sam's feet. "You can't walk all the way back to the club without shoes. I don't suppose you keep those spare, too?"

Annie shook her head. "Just the sweats. But it wouldn't matter anyway. I'm a size smaller than Sam."

"I'll be fine," Sam protested.

"Don't worry about it. I'll drive us." Annie pulled out a set of keys. "I drove up to Boston, and I haven't turned in the rental yet. I'm parked in the deck next door."

Well, that certainly made everything simpler.

Noah bundled Sam into the back, using the excuse of his longer legs to claim the passenger seat. In reality, he needed any advantage he could get to reclaim some sense of control. The operation had exploded the way he'd been afraid it would, and now the only question was how to deal with the fallout.

He hadn't forgotten Sam's way too perceptive question about his clothes, and he seriously doubted that she had. When they got back to the club and the whole sordid story came out, she'd have a hell of a lot more questions for him, he was sure. He didn't look forward to answering any of them.

He would have to tell her the truth. Tell all of them, and he didn't look forward to that, either. He couldn't think of a single way to make it sound any better. Nothing could change the fact that they'd welcomed him into their community and he'd made a place for himself under false pretenses. He'd taken advantage of them, all of them, and he wouldn't blame them for wanting to kick his ass.

Wanting, hell, they'd do it. The best he could hope for was that they'd stop with the kicking and not follow it through to the end. Any one of them was more than capable of killing him with their bare hands, Sam included, and he wasn't even sure he could marshal the desire to fight back. As far as he was concerned, he deserved everything he got.

At least he could try to explain that things had changed. He'd been betrayed the same as them, and he'd be happy to demonstrate that he intended to make sure whoever was behind it found out what a very bad idea that had been. The challenge would be getting that out before one of them got to his jugular.

He looked at Annie. "Do you have a cell phone?"

"Yes."

"Let me borrow it."

She frowned, but she didn't ask him any questions, just fished the phone from her lab coat pocket and handed it to him. If only her friend could be so accommodating.

"What are you doing?" Sam demanded from the backseat.

Noah ignored her and punched the buttons with his thumb. He felt a slight sense of relief when Missy answered instead of her husband. In as few words as possible, Noah let her know that the three of them were headed in and that they had news that Graham at least should hear, and probably the head of the Council of Others, too. Once again, a woman in Noah's life proved unexpectedly agreeable and assured him without questions that she would take care of it. They would all meet at the club in twenty minutes.

"Why did you do that?" Sam asked when he'd disconnected and handed the phone back to Annie. "You should have let me or Annie call. This is our problem."

He ignored her and pulled Carter's cell from a pocket in his vest. Punching in the preprogrammed number, he waited for the answer. "Clean up on aisle five," he said as soon as he heard Carter's greeting. "I haven't seen it, but I expect a pretty big spill."

"If you didn't see the jar break, who dropped it?"

"Somebody else."

"Is that somebody with an innie or an outie?"

"None of your business," he snapped. "Just send someone with a mop. And make sure the floor is left sparkling."

"What about the back room?" Carter wanted to know if they should handle the lab, too.

"Don't worry about it. It's just a little disorganized. Nothing for you to worry about."

"Ten-four. Anything else?"

He glanced back at Sam's narrowed eyes. "No. But if I don't check in sometime in the next twenty-four hours, you can have my DVD collection."

He clicked off and tucked the phone away.

"And what the hell was that about?" Sam demanded. The words exploded from her as if the strain of holding them back had been the hammer on her trigger. "If you had that in your pocket, why did you need Annie's phone? Noah, I want to know what's going on."

Instead of looking at her, he looked out the window and gauged their location. "In a minute. We're almost there."

He felt her hand grasp her arm and turned. Her eyes met his and she looked less furious than he'd assumed she'd be and more worried. "And when we get inside, you'll tell me whatever it is you're holding back?"

Grimly he looked out the windshield and nodded. "Ready or not."

Here it comes.

CHAPTER 17

Instincts made up a large part of Sam's world; they always had. She'd grown up listening to them, trusting them, considering them one of the most powerful tools she possessed in relating to the world around her and all its challenge and chaos. But they were telling her something now that she absolutely did not want to hear.

She climbed the stairs to the club's second floor behind Annie and with Noah by her elbow. She could feel his presence like a touch, and she knew he was unhappy. Actually, she knew he felt furious and shocked and betrayed and anxious and determined and . . . sorry. She could read it in the set of his jaw and the tension in his muscles; but more than that, she could smell it on him. It muddied his scent and made her own anxiety levels soar. Something was very wrong, and he was keeping it from her. She didn't like that.

Not at all.

She thought her expression might rival his for grimness as they filed into the second-floor library at Vircolac, otherwise known as the War Room. In the last few years it had acquired its reputation as being the place where everyone gathered when something significant was about to happen. It had seen negotiations, fights, rants, and pleadings, Fae royalty and demon police officers. If there was a crisis brewing in the Other world, someone was bound to find out about it in this room and concoct a suitable strategy to deal with it. With any luck, the room's history would rub off tonight.

Noah held the door for her and Annie, then followed them in and shut it behind them. Graham and Missy were already there, Missy in her pajamas and Graham half out of the suit he'd worn to the party earlier. He still had on his trousers and shirt, but his feet were bare and his buttons were mostly undone, leaving his shirt hanging open. He stood beside Missy's chair with his hand on her shoulder and raised an eyebrow at the group's entrance.

"Who died?" he quipped.

"No one you know," Noah answered.

Sam frowned. "No one at all, as far as I know. Unless Noah hasn't even told me everything."

She almost hoped he hadn't, that a body was exactly what he'd been hiding from her.

He just frowned. "We'd better wait for the others."

"Tess and Rafael are right behind us."

The door opened to admit Abby and Rule, who had spoken in his deep, smoky voice. He looked as calm and forbidding as usual, while she wore a distinct expression of worry. She hurried over to her brother and gave him a thorough once-over.

"Are you all right? Are you hurt? What's going on?" she demanded.

He gave her a quick one-armed hug. "I'm fine. We're just waiting for everyone to get here so we don't have to go through a story twice."

"And to torture me," Annie mumbled, just loud enough for Sam to hear.

She squeezed her friend's hand reassuringly.

"This is starting to sound ominous," Graham said, perching on the arm of Missy's chair. "Am I going to like what I'm about to hear?"

Sam noticed that Noah ignored the question. He turned to watch the door and gave a grunt when Tess breezed through in her usual inimitable style.

"This had better be good," Tess grumped. "I had an urgent appointment with a book and some bubble bath that you just made me break." She glanced pointedly at Noah. "Well?"

"Why doesn't everybody sit down?" Missy, peacemaker that she was, waved at the furniture. "I can send Richards for drinks, if anyone wants anything."

"I don't think it's going to be that kind of an announcement," Sam said, but she watched as everyone else settled onto sofas and chairs. And laps. Abby perched in Rule's, and Tess sat so close to Rafe on one end of the sofa that she might as well have been on him. Noah, Sam noticed, didn't sit at all. He placed his back to the fireplace and stood with his arms crossed over his chest.

She hesitated, unsure where she should put herself. Part of her wanted to be with Noah, to stand at his side and acknowledge the fragile relationship they'd spent the last week forging, but another part was afraid. He didn't seem to be asking for anything from her, least of all for her to cuddle with him in a public place. He'd been building up a wall ever since she'd run into him at the lab, and it knocked her off-balance. Her instincts told her that she belonged to him now, belonged with him, but he might as well have been holding up a "BACK OFF" sign. In the past, she would have sat near Missy and Graham, but that didn't feel right anymore, either.

Confused and disliking the feeling, Sam perched on the very edge of a chair on the far side of the fireplace opposite Missy and Graham with Noah standing between them. She didn't like it at all.

"All right," Graham said, fixing his attention on Noah. "We're here, and we're sitting. What's going on?"

She watched Noah turn and look right at Annie, who paled but remained standing still and alone in the middle of the carpet. "The first part isn't my story to tell," he said.

"It's mine." Annie's voice quavered, but she cleared her throat and started again. "I'm the one with something to tell you. Something I should have told you quite a while ago. I offer my apologies, Alpha."

Her eyes dropped to the floor near Graham's feet as she spoke to show her respect for him and his position.

His brow furrowed in a light crease, but he nodded. "Just tell me your story, Annie, including why it is you waited, if it's something I really ought to know."

"At first, I didn't really get what it would mean," she began. "I mean, I knew it was big, but I was thinking in terms of science, not in terms of what people can do with science if they take it over for their own purposes.

If I'd thought about that earlier, I would have told you right away. But I didn't. And by the time I did, the damage was already done, and I kept thinking that if I just waited a little longer, I'd have a way to fix everything, or something would happen and it wouldn't matter anymore."

"Hon, you're not really making much sense," Missy said gently. "You're going to have to explain it to us. What are you talking about?"

"About my work in the lab. About the Lupine genome. I've decoded it."

A few people blinked, but that was the extent of the reaction until Missy smiled. "That's wonderful, Annie. How exciting for you. That's an amazing achievement. I imagine there will be all sorts of new advances in medicine and stuff because of you."

Annie made a noise that would have sounded like a laugh, if she hadn't choked on it. "There's going to be a global Lupine nightmare because of me."

"Why do you—"

"When I decoded the genome, I found certain DNA sequences that could be directly cited as being responsible for the differences in strength, speed, and sensory ability between Lupines and humans. I found them, and I labeled them, and I started a paper on how manipulation of those sequences could be used to create a kind of cell-based therapy that might theoretically give the advantages of Lupine physiology to human subjects."

Sam wasn't sure if the silence in the room had to do with the natural time delay caused when a bunch of laypeople tried to sift through Annie's scientific speech, or if it represented the calm before a very large storm.

Rafe fought through it first. "Are you saying, Annie, that you found a way to turn humans into Lupines?"

"No, there won't be any Hollywood-style wolf men running around biting humans to spawn more of their kind. Humans and Lupines are still two completely different species, and you can't turn one species into another. But even human scientists have found that certain segments of the genetic code from one species can be introduced to another and cause certain adjustments in that subject's physiology or behavior. I couldn't turn humans into Lupines. No one can do that. But I found a way to make humans so much like us in their abilities that it would be hard to tell the difference."

Graham didn't exactly explode, but when he spoke, his voice sounded cold and harsh. "And the reason you didn't tell me about this sooner?"

Annie opened her mouth, hesitated, and closed it again. "I could try and explain again, Alpha, but the truth is . . . because I was stupid."

"I won't argue with that." He gave her a piercing look that had even Sam wriggling uncomfortably and then turned to Noah. "What's your part of this story, then?"

"More recent. Samantha, Annie, and I just came from her laboratory. There was a break-in tonight. Someone stole Annie's data."

Watching Graham's face was like watching a massive glacier descend on the landscape. First everything froze under a thick layer of ice; then the briefest of hairline fractures formed and the whole destructive body came easing forward with its massive, mountain-shearing power. People tended to forget that something slow-moving could carve entire mountain ranges out of the earth.

If they looked at Graham's face, they would never make that mistake again. As soon as Missy saw it, she rose and rested a slim hand in the middle of his chest. As if that would somehow hold him back. He didn't even acknowledge it.

He turned that look on Annie, and Samantha shivered in sympathy. "Are you telling me someone else has all this information? That your arrogance and carelessness has made it possible for anyone to apply the technology you've described? Is that what you're telling me, Annie? Because if it is, I would be perfectly within my rights to rip your throat out, or to run you out of this pack, and you know it."

Samantha saw her friend recoiling, curling in on herself in a bid for self-protection. Instinctively, and perhaps idiotically, Sam couldn't help sticking her own neck out. "It wasn't carelessness, Graham. She didn't leave the stuff sitting out while she threw a cocktail party. Someone broke into the lab."

His gaze swung slowly toward her. "Of all the people in this room, Samantha, you should be the last one opening your mouth," he said so quietly that even Missy looked nervous. "I'm not stupid enough to believe you haven't known about this for longer than the last couple of hours. And somehow in all that time, it never occurred to you to tell me about it."

Samantha didn't step back from the force of his anger, but she did lower her eyes. She wasn't stupid, either. "It occurred to me," she admitted. "But I thought Annie deserved the opportunity to work it out herself."

"Then obviously *thinking* isn't your strong suit."

She clenched her jaw against the urge to talk back. That wouldn't have been stupid; it would have been suicidal. She harbored no illusions that the presence of half a dozen witnesses would hold Graham back. She wasn't even sure if Missy could.

"Before we go placing blame," Noah interrupted, his voice sounding harder than Sam could remember hearing it, "I think we'd be better off figuring out who orchestrated the raid and why."

He stepped forward, and whether it was to distract Graham or to place himself in the Alpha's path, she couldn't be sure. Frankly, they were both equally stupid ideas; and both of them made her stomach flip.

"I think we can all guess the why." Rafe spoke from his position on the sofa, neither rising to his feet nor taking his arm from where it draped on his wife's shoulder, but he sounded tired. After Annie's revelation, he looked tired, too. "The opportunity to become more like us, to gain our strength and abilities, is an idea that has occupied the human collective consciousness for centuries. If Cassidy Quinn were here, I'm sure she would tell you as much. And this . . ." He shook his head. "The idea that they could have all these things without having to pay what they consider our 'price' for our gifts—not have to shift, not have to face the animal inside of them—it must have proved too tempting to bear."

Tess nodded. "It's the how that has me wondering. Somehow I doubt that anything Sam and Annie felt compelled to keep from Graham is something they'd have gone blabbing about to anyone else."

Graham snarled loud enough for the whole room to hear. Missy pressed a second hand to his chest.

"No one is saying they did," she said, but she gave the both of them a stern look. Missy might not be able to rip their throats out as fast as her mate, but she wasn't a pushover. And she was their Luna. Sam felt almost as bad about deceiving her as she did about deceiving Graham. "But whoever broke in must have found out somehow. I'm assuming you didn't get us this worked up about something that started as a random robbery."

Noah shook his head. "A random thief has no reason to break into a secured biology lab, especially when there are at least ten million more financially rewarding targets in Manhattan alone. And if it had been a robbery, they would have taken something worth selling, like the expensive lab equipment or computers. All that looked intact."

Missy sighed. "I didn't think so."

Rafe looked at Noah and raised an elegant eyebrow. "You have a theory, I am guessing."

Noah gave one sharp nod, accompanied by a not-so-subtle shifting away from Sam. She noticed it and frowned. Did he think that he could get her into any more trouble with Graham by describing the break-in in more detail? Her mind refused to focus on any other reason Noah might have for stepping away from her before continuing.

Her mind might refuse, but her instincts were scratching and whining at her subconscious, trying to force exactly that kind of attention. She held firm, but she couldn't stop wrapping her arms around herself, as if the room had suddenly gone cold. She eased from her chair as if she needed to be able to bolt at the slightest notice. Maybe she did.

"I've got more than a theory." Noah stood straight and firm in front of the fireplace, his jaw clenching and unclenching and his scent turning bitter in Sam's nose. "I've got proof. The break-in was the work of the U.S. Army, and the reason it happened was because I failed to bring them the information myself. That was the real reason I came here, not to recruit Lupines for the supernatural program but to get my hands on Annie's research and pass it on to my superiors."

Silence.

For a long moment, nothing happened. Sam heard the words, but it took several slow seconds for them to sink in and untangle themselves into a message that made sense. And even then, they didn't really make sense. She struggled to process them, but her instincts already knew. They sank bonelessly to the floor, raised their muzzles to the moon, and sang out a howl of rage and pain and betrayal, while above them her heart began to shatter.

CHAPTER 18

Hands closed over Sam's shoulders. She didn't know who they belonged to, just that they weren't Noah's, and she was grateful for that. If he had touched her just then, she thought she would have screamed. For a few seconds she thought she might have, but when most of the roaring in her ears subsided, she realized it was only her mind and her heart screaming, not her voice.

"Sam? Samantha. What's wrong? Are you all right?"

The voice belonged to Tess, so Sam assumed the hands probably did, too. They urged her toward the sofa and pressed her down onto it. As soon as her butt hit the cushions, the hands shifted their pressure and began to force her head down toward her knees.

"You're the color of the plaster in here. Put your head down before you keel over."

A hysterical laugh boiled up in Sam's throat and she wanted to tell Tess that forcing the blood flow back to her head was not likely to cure what ailed her just then. She didn't know if anything could. But she couldn't speak. Her voice seemed frozen in the horror of what was happening. Her voice and her heart.

She felt someone sink onto the sofa beside her, felt Annie's hand rubbing her back, and closed her eyes against a fresh wave of pain. How had everything gone so incredibly wrong?

"Tess, what is going on?"

Sam heard Rafe's voice, low and concerned.

"I don't know," his wife answered.

Then Noah's voice, harsh and concerned, talking over the remaining roaring that finally registered in Sam's sluggish brain as the sound of Graham's furious ranting. "What's wrong? Is she all right? Samantha?"

The voice got closer, as if he were going to come to her, to touch her, and Sam recoiled, jerking her head up and pressing herself against the back of the sofa, as if she could scramble into the cushions and get away from him.

Her eyes, wide and panicked, stayed locked on Noah, but in her peripheral vision she could see Tess looking from her to Noah and back again. The witch's eyes narrowed, and she stood, placing herself between the two of them.

"Why don't you tell me what's wrong, Noah?" she said, and her voice sounded hard and more than vaguely threatening. "Why don't you tell me, tell all of us, why the woman you haven't been able to keep your eyes off of for the last six months is taking this news so badly? I mean, I think I can safely say that all of us are shocked, but her reaction seems a little more extreme, don't you think?"

Noah looked as if he was going to ignore Tess. His body shifted as if he would take a step forward, and Sam felt a whimper of protest rip from her tightly seized throat muscles. He heard, and he froze, his jaw clenching until the muscles at the side jumped in protest.

"Samantha, honey, are you okay?" he asked, and she noticed how soft and low he kept his voice. He'd used the same tone when he'd been inside of her, all tender and comforting. She drew harder into herself, wrapping her arms around her knees as if to protect her vulnerable belly from attack. If only she could have protected her heart the same way. But it seemed a little late to try to protect her heart, when it had already stopped and broken apart.

"Does she look okay?" Tess demanded. "What the hell did you do to her?"

"I didn't do anything to her," Noah snapped, turning a large cloud of frustrated anger on the other woman. "I would never hurt her."

"That's a laugh. Look at her. I'd say she looks like you just kicked her in the stomach. Whether or not your boot actually made contact with her skin doesn't have a hell of a lot to do with the matter. You slept with her, didn't you?"

Noah scowled at Tess, wariness creeping into his otherwise hostile expression. "How exactly is that any of your business?"

"It's my business because I'm her friend, you jackass." She took a belligerent step forward.

"We're her friends," Annie echoed, her voice soft but firm.

"I'd say it's the business of everyone in this room at

the moment," Rafe agreed, moving to stand beside his wife. Sam could just manage to see the rest of the room between their rigid bodies. "Everyone here considers Samantha a friend. Some of them consider her to be even more."

"Family," Missy agreed, and she wore an expression Sam had never seen before. She looked almost . . . scary.

"Pack." Graham spit the word out, and he looked as if he'd prefer to be spitting shards of Noah's bones from between his teeth. "Samantha is pack, and she's under my protection, human. So tell me right now why I shouldn't kill you for using her this way."

Sam felt a protest stirring inside her, but she quelled it sternly. She shouldn't want to protect Noah from Graham's anger; she should be cheering the Alpha on while he munched on the man's intestines. Noah had betrayed her; she should hate him, not feel as if the prospect of a lifetime stretching on without him couldn't possibly have meaning.

"I never used her," Noah ground out. "What's between Sam and me has nothing to do with the rest of it."

"Are we supposed to just take your word for it?" Missy glared at him. "You have to admit, it looks awfully suspicious that you gained all of our confidences under false pretenses and then singled out the one person in the world who's closest to Annie and the most likely to know anything about her work. If you ask me, it would be a pretty good strategy to cozy up to Sam, even seduce her, just to see if she'd tell you what she knew."

And she had, Sam thought helplessly. She'd told Noah everything she knew, including a few things she hadn't even understood. And he'd barely had to ask. She'd spilled it all like a leaky pitcher. Goddess, he must have thought he'd hit the lottery.

"You should have just come and talked to me." Annie squeezed Sam's shoulder, then pushed herself to her feet and faced Noah. From the tension in her body, she also possessed a keen awareness of Graham hovering and steaming only a couple of feet away. The fact that she would willingly face down both of them for Sam's sake made her stomach clench. "You should have left Sam out of it. Whatever I might have told her wouldn't have been what you wanted. Sam doesn't know the science. I'm the only one who knows that."

"For Christ's sake, I did *not* get involved with Sam so I could pry information out of her!" Noah barked. "I got involved with her because I can't keep my fucking hands off of her! I can't even look at her without getting a goddamned hard-on. Tess said it herself. I haven't even looked at another woman in six months! Does that sound like a con to you?"

"I don't know what it sounds like, but if you've really wanted her for six months, why did it take till this past week for you to make a move on her?"

Noah rubbed a hand over his head and blew out a frustrated breath. "I haven't been here for six months. Yeah, I've visited and I've spent time here, but I have a job and I have a life away from here."

"I don't think this is the best time to be reminding anyone about your job, ace," Tess snarled.

"What is wrong with you people that you can't see how crazy a man would have to be not to want her for her own damned self?" The words seemed to spill out of him with no thought as to what they really meant. Something in Sam still had enough energy to think wistfully that she wished she could believe them.

"I think the same thing is wrong with us that told you it would be okay for you to betray the trust we showed you in welcoming you into this house," Missy said. "If you lied about your reasons for being here, why shouldn't we think you're lying about this, too?"

"My brother wouldn't do that," Abby said, speaking for the first time since Noah's revelation. She sounded as if she wished she didn't have to speak now. Sam saw her move, rise from her husband's lap and square her shoulders with motions that looked almost painful. "I'm sure that what Noah did, he felt he had good reason for. And I know without a doubt that he wouldn't have deliberately done anything to hurt Sam. He's not that kind of man."

Graham snorted, a sound that might have resembled a laugh if it held the slightest trace of humor. "I'm not sure you know what kind of man your brother is, Abby. I'm beginning to doubt if any of us do."

"That's not fair," she protested. "He's my brother, and if he had to do something like this, I'm sure it was because he felt he had no choice. We at least owe him the courtesy of listening to his reasons for what he did."

"You've got it backwards. After all we've done for him, *he* owes *us,* not the other way around," Graham bit out.

Abby protested, then Annie countered, and Tess and Missy chimed in, with Rafe speaking up to try to keep order. Only Rule kept silent, watching the chaos with his impassive dark eyes. And Noah. Noah didn't speak, either. He just stood with his jaw clenched and his hazel eyes locked on Sam.

She couldn't stand it. She might not have started this mess, but she also hadn't done anything to prevent it from getting to this point. Her mind skittered away from the reality of Noah's betrayal; the wound was too deep for that, too raw, and if she thought about it, she'd never be able to drag herself out of this horrible lethargy, this numbness that had gripped her. She had to shake free and do what she could to fix things. To fix things for the pack. That was all she could do.

Slowly, feeling like an old woman or the victim of a brutal beating, she forced her muscles to unclench and straighten, lifting herself from the sofa with the care of infirmity. An hour ago she'd felt alive and young and vital; now she thought she'd never move freely again. Her heart had shattered, and her body felt like it might be next.

Carefully she opened her mouth. It took two attempts before any sound came out, and even then, her voice sounded strange. Rough and hoarse and painfully slow.

"No one owes anyone," she said, not looking at Noah. She couldn't do it, couldn't stand it. "Talking about debts isn't going to solve anything, and no one here can go back and change anything that's already happened. The best we can do is figure out what to do next."

When she spoke, Noah shifted, his hands reaching for her. She flinched away. If he touched her, her outside would shatter as surely as her inside already had.

"We should talk about who has the information and how we can find them. We have to do it quickly, before they have time to pass it on to anyone else. Everything else can wait. No one's issues are going to just go away. We can afford to move them to the back burner."

"Sam—," Noah started, and his voice sounded almost aching. He must be regretting that she had found out his secret before he'd completed his mission.

She ignored him. "Annie can tell you what's missing, and Noah sounds like he knows who took it. I'm sure the rest of you can figure out what to do about it. This isn't the first crisis the pack and the Council have faced and overcome. I'm sure it won't be the last."

Weariness dragged on her. She wanted nothing more than to find a cool, dark place filled with nothing but silence and curl up there to sleep. Maybe when she woke, she'd even have the strength to lick her wounds. For now, the poison in them made that impossible. Sleep. She would just sleep.

"Don't say that as if you're not going to help with the figuring, Sam," Graham said, his growl less menacing than she had expected, more . . . concerned. "You're already in up to your neck. You don't get to leave just when the water reaches your chin."

She shook her head, her gaze on the floor. Not out of respect, but because she lacked the energy to lift it.

"She needs sleep," Tess said, her tone brooking no arguments. "I'll take her up and tuck her into one of the guest rooms."

"No. I'll take care of her." Noah stepped forward, and Sam issued an instinctive whimper of protest.

"Right now, she wouldn't let you take her to a water

fountain if she'd been six weeks in the desert." Tess sent him an impatient glare and put one arm around Sam's back, turning her toward the door. Sam let herself be led.

Noah shook his head and his eyes blazed furiously. "She's mine, and I'm the one who's upset her. I'll be the one to take care of her."

He reached for her and Sam jerked back, her eyes finally lifting to meet his gaze. She didn't know what he read in her expression, but he lost some of the angry color in his cheeks, and the muscle in the side of his jaw worked like an echo of his heartbeat, jumping in time to the pulse of his anger.

"I don't belong to you," she said clearly, ignoring the small part of her that howled in instinctive protest. A few hours ago, she would have jumped at the chance to be claimed by him. A lot had changed in a few hours.

"You owe it to the Alpha to help get Annie's data back, since you know who took it, and had been planning to do it yourself." She straightened her shoulders and held his gaze with hers. "Help the pack. They still have a use for you. I don't."

CHAPTER 19

For a moment, Noah actually thought he saw his life flashing before his eyes, which was disconcerting enough, but the part that really bothered him was the end. The part where he watched Sam turn and walk beside Tess out of the room, closing the door quietly and firmly behind her.

He knew that Graham stood to one side, growling something suitably threatening and quite possibly plotting all the ways he could think of to rip a human's head off its body, but Noah didn't have time to worry about that. His eyes and all his attention were focused on Sam, on the door she'd just left by.

When he'd made his confession, she had turned paler than the sheets he'd laid her on last night. Her eyes looked like huge pools of liquid honey in her blank face, and he didn't imagine she could look more hurt if he'd blackened one of them for her. Instinctively he had reached for her and felt the brutal stab of rejection when she flinched away. He'd expected her to be furious; he could have dealt with furious. It was wounded that was giving him so much trouble. He wanted to fall to his knees and beg her forgiveness, but he didn't have time for that. None of them did. The damned miserable, worthless mission still dictated every course of action. It still hung over his head like a guillotine blade just waiting for the right moment to fall.

Or maybe it had already fallen and this was just that last moment of clarity before the brain realized the spinal cord had gone missing.

"Samantha," he said, and his voice sounded gruff and weak in his own ears. Too late, of course. She'd already left the room, not even bothering to look back. He supposed it had been too late for a while now. Ever since he'd gotten his orders and walked into her office without bothering to tell her why he was really there.

He hated the way he'd seen her, looking first so shocked as Tess forced her down to the sofa, then almost broken as she'd curled up on it and shrunk back from his touch. She looked like some of the women he'd seen caught in war zones, shocked and traumatized and afraid that every touch could be the one that brought death. He hoped to God she wasn't actually afraid of him. He had never hurt her, and he'd cut his own hands off before he would, but did she know that?

And even if she did, would she still believe it?

"Now I believe it is time for some explanations," Rafe said, slipping smoothly into his accustomed role of peacemaker and voice of reason in a world often ruled by instincts. "Tess will see to Samantha, and as she said, you and Annie know as much, if not more, of the situation as she does. That being the case, I think it would be wise for you to share some of that knowledge with the rest of us. I, for one, find myself fascinated to learn of your transformation. I've never seen a man go so quickly from court favorite to most hated man in the room."

Noah didn't need anyone to remind him of his fall from grace, especially when he knew he probably had a few more feet to go before he hit rock bottom. He felt pretty confident that if Graham Winters had his druthers, the entire length of Noah's intestines would soon be decorating the ornately plastered ceiling. Possibly along with bits of his spleen.

Missy obviously saw the possibility as well, because she had stopped trying to hold her mate back with a couple of small hands and placed herself bodily between him and the rest of the room. If she hadn't been so incredibly precious to him, Noah didn't think even that would have made much difference to Graham.

"You can come into my club, into my *pack,* accept my hospitality, and repay it like this?" the Alpha spat out, as if he'd just been waiting for the green light to let his fury rip. Noah thought he saw a hint of fang peeking between the Lupine's compressed lips. "If my wife and your sister weren't standing right in front of me, I'd rip out your throat and dance on it, you lousy son of a bitch!"

Noah nodded once, Sam's last words still echoing in his ears. "And I'd deserve it."

"You think you can pacify me by admitting your guilt?" Graham laughed, but no one could mistake the sound for amusement. "It's going to take a hell of a lot more than that, human, beginning with blood."

Abby stepped forward, still pale and still looking so

shocked and hurt that Noah wanted to crawl under a rock somewhere. Even worse, he knew that her sense of betrayal couldn't even begin to compare with Sam's. He wouldn't have been surprised if Abby echoed the Alpha's sentiments. He wouldn't have blamed her, either.

"Blood doesn't make anything better," she said, her voice not quite steady. It left jagged little wounds in Noah's hide. Sam's rejection had left them in his heart.

"And if anyone has learned that over the last few years, we have," Rafe agreed. "There has been enough of it spilled by everyone else in this unofficial little war of ours. Let's not go adding to it. If nothing else, I would prefer not to give the humans who call us monsters the satisfaction."

Graham opened his mouth to retort, but Missy cut him off with a glare and a hard smack on the shoulder. "Before you, or anyone, say something I'm going to make them regret, we need to look at this *calmly.*"

"You don't need to play referee, Luna," Annie said, her soft voice still managing to draw everyone's attention. "This is my fault. I'm the one the Alpha is angry with, and I deserve to be punished for my actions. I put the pack in jeopardy. I bear full responsibility for it, and I'm not going to run away from the consequences."

"That's awfully noble of you," Missy snapped, "but from what I can tell, the Alpha is angry with a whole bunch of people right now, and frankly, I'm not all that far behind him. Somehow I don't think you're responsible for the army sending Noah here to spy on us, or for his treatment of Sam, so let's not get carried away.

It seems to me that this situation has plenty of blame to go around."

Annie straightened her shoulders and lifted her gaze as far as the Luna's chin, which Noah assumed proved just how determined about this she was. "That may be true, but in the end, it falls back on me. If I hadn't been conducting this particular set of experiments and following this particular line of research, the humans would have had no reason to send anyone to spy on me."

"That's a big if." Noah tore his gaze from the door through which Sam had disappeared and turned it on Annie. "From what I can tell, they're right about the march of progress. Your work may have given the army a hell of a jump start, but I think they were already working on something similar all on their own."

Annie frowned and opened her mouth as if to demand an explanation, but then she froze. Her eyes widened, and when she spoke, her voice was hushed and revelatory. "Oh, my gosh, you're right. They've been working themselves, and I think they may have gotten almost as far as I have. At least one of the men who raided the lab tonight wasn't quite human."

The room went silent at that, as if everyone in it had stiffened and gone perfectly still. No fabric rustled, and no one coughed or sneezed or even breathed as they digested that information. Noah clenched his teeth and struggled against the urge to head straight out the front of the club so he could find Hammond and strangle the bastard with his bare hands.

"Or at least, not completely human," Annie continued. "I didn't know what it meant until just now, but I smelled something off as soon as I got to the building. I could tell there were three of them. One of them smoked, so I'm not surprised I noticed him, and another smelled really scary, like hostility was billowing off of him. That's the smell that freaked me out enough to call Sam." She shook her head. "But the third one just smelled . . . off. Half the time I couldn't smell him at all."

"But if someone had already figured out a way to combine human and Lupine DNA, shouldn't you have been smelling both those scents? That seems to make more sense than the idea that the two scents would cancel each other out." Missy looked confused.

Annie nodded. "Yes, or at the very least, one of the DNA sequences would take over and you'd smell either human or Lupine. Not smelling anything is just weird. I really didn't smell anything when the guy was in the lab. At the time I thought it was because I was too freaked out from realizing they were coming for the lab, but if Noah is right, an altered human would make almost as much sense. And it would explain a lot."

"I still don't get why they focused on Annie, or even how they knew about her work." Missy frowned.

"It wouldn't have been tough if they knew what they were looking for," Annie admitted, looking uncomfortable. "All genetic experiments have to be registered with the government to be certain they aren't breaking existing laws over cloning and stuff like that. It all gets compiled into a huge national registry that's secure but accessible to people who work in the field or who work for any of the regulatory agencies involved in policing the research. Someone who was looking to find out about any experiments along the lines of what they were interested in could just search the database and they'd hit on my lab. And my name. And if they dug a little deeper, they'd be able to make a good guess about what stage in the work I was at."

"Betrayed by bureaucracy," Rule snorted.

"All right, so now we know Annie's story," Graham said, turning his attention to Noah and making no attempt to look less than murderous. "Let's hear yours."

Noah had no choice and felt almost relieved by that knowledge. He didn't look forward to the reaction of the Others, but it would feel damned good to get the lies off his chest. He'd never been good at the deception, and he'd sure as hell never found peace with it. Not having anything to hide would be a blessing. It was how he preferred to live his life, and he made a vow to himself that he'd never live any other way. He just wished he'd been smart enough not to attempt to live the lies in the first place.

"My team came off a mission three months ago," he said, determined to get this all out as quickly and thoroughly as possible. "We'd been assigned to an anti-terrorism team dealing with a suspected cell in Canada run by a vampire from a sect that never wanted to be Unveiled. He kind of liked it when everyone was afraid of him and viewed him as a killer rather than a regular guy with photosensitivity and an iron deficiency. He wanted to put the cat back into the bag by killing the entire membership of the International Committee on Interspecies Relations and declaring war on humanity. My team took care of it."

He set his jaw and wished all his missions went as smoothly as that one. The team hadn't even broken a sweat. In fact, things had been so easy, he'd managed to get down to New York three or four times for quick visits with Abby. At least, that's what he'd said they were for. In reality, he'd been mooning around hoping to catch glimpses of Sam.

"When we shipped home, we immediately switched on for a ten-week training and resupply rotation. As that was winding up, I received orders to meet with my CO's CO for a one-man deployment." He shifted his stance and clasped his hands together behind his back. He kept his eyes straight ahead. He had no desire to watch Graham flay him with a glance, and he couldn't bear to see Abby looking at him with disappointment. "It was unusual, but orders are orders, so I went. Down to the Pentagon."

Rafe and Rule quirked identical eyebrows, while Graham's scowl morphed into a frown.

Noah just plowed ahead. "I didn't like it, and you can believe that or not, but it's the truth. The only covert operations I've been trained to do are the kind that take place at night behind enemy lines and leave bodies, not bookshelves, behind. I'm a soldier, not a spy."

"Then why didn't they send a spy?"

"You'd have to ask them. All I can guess is that they don't have them ready. The army had a heads-up on the Others, but I have no way of knowing if the intelligence community did. From the flack my team has gotten since the Unveiling, I'm guessing they didn't. So maybe they wanted to send someone in who knew better what he'd be dealing with."

Graham growled, "Good. At least you knew we'd kill you when we found out."

Missy laid a hand on his arm and hissed something at him, and the werewolf subsided. But he still didn't look happy.

"Yeah, I knew." Noah didn't see any point in pretending they all felt civilized over this. "Just like I knew from the beginning that this whole idea sucked, but I had my orders and I carried them out. I tried, anyway, but this whole thing stank from the very beginning."

Rafe's gaze sharpened. "What do you mean?"

"I mean it started off in FUBAR and went downhill from there," Noah snapped. He wanted to be pacing, to work off some of this tension and this angry energy, but he knew the minute he lifted his feet they'd take him up the stairs to Sam's bedside. He didn't think either of them was ready for that. "It was a lousy operation, and I was a lousy choice of operative. I blow things up; subtlety has never appeared on my résumé. But I've dedicated the last fifteen years of my life to the service. I wasn't going to throw all that away by refusing to do my job. So I came here and you all made my life a living hell."

"We bent over backward to help you!" Graham barked.

"That was the fucking problem!" Noah glared right back at him. He didn't care how infrequently that happened to an Alpha Lupine. "If you'd been suspicious bastards, breaking my balls and poking your noses into everything, at least I could have told myself there was a good reason I'd been sent here, but you didn't. Every single goddamned one of you was sweet as frickin' pie. It's been driving me crazy!"

"You want us to apologize for not being on your level of bastard?"

"Yes! Fu— No," Noah shouted, then snapped his mouth shut and grabbed hard at his self-control. "It would make my life easier, but I know perfectly well that's not your job. It made me damned uncomfortable, though. I had a hard time reconciling what I knew about you with what I was hearing from the general."

"The general?" Rafe asked.

"General Elijah Hammond. He's the one I met at the Pentagon, and he's been the one pulling the strings this whole time."

The Felix nodded. "All right. Go on."

Right. 'Cause Noah was really enjoying this. He hadn't realized that baring his soul would be accomplished by tearing bloody strips off his hide one layer at a time.

"I followed my orders," he bit out. "I dug up whatever information I could and tried to find out about this research I was told we needed to get our hands on. I found Annie, followed Sam to her lab tonight, and found out about the break-in. And now we're here. End of story."

"Not by a long shot." Graham shook off his mate's hand and stepped forward. His fists were clenched, but he'd stopped vibrating with rage, at least. "Where does Sam come into all this? When did you concoct your plan to wheedle the information you needed out of her?"

Noah felt himself go cold with renewed anger. "Never. Sam wasn't a part of it, not for one minute, and I suggest you stop insulting her by implying that the only reason I'm interested in her is as a means to an end.

As far as I'm concerned, Sam *is* the end. I wanted her for her. If anything, she was a complication, not a source of information. Do you think it was easy for me to know I was getting in over my head with her while this whole goddamned mission was giving me an ulcer?"

"I've got no idea what was easy or hard for you, human. The only ideas I ever had with your name on them turned out to be wrong, so I'm not taking any chances."

"If Noah says he was serious about his relationship with Sam, then he was," Abby said, her voice growing a little stronger than it had been a few minutes ago. "What reason does he have to lie about it now? He's told us the truth about everything else."

"Has he? Maybe he just thinks that if he doesn't want to have his balls ripped off, he'd better tell me what I want to hear," Graham said, and the threat was low and smooth.

"And maybe you just need to cool it," Missy said, giving Graham the hard stare that few other people would attempt. "Noah could have kept lying to us, but he hasn't. He's the one who came forward. Try and keep that in mind."

"We all might also like to keep in mind that while the fact that Sam has been hurt is an unfortunate event we will return to later," Rafe offered, with a meaningful glance at Noah, "the real problem at present remains the unfortunate loss of Annie's data. That has far-reaching implications for all of us."

"Absolutely," Noah agreed, focusing on the need to do something, to spring into action and make every effort to correct the mess he'd made. "We need to go after the thief and get that information back before it changes hands again."

"And how do you suggest we go about that?" Rafe asked. "If this thief's scent keeps blinking in and out for the Lupines among us, I doubt very seriously that tracking him will be an easy matter. You all confess to having lost him at the lab, and he had been there only moments before. How are we even to know where to start?"

Noah set his teeth. "I know where."

CHAPTER 20

Grimly Noah laid out the rest of the story, telling them all about his contacts with Hammond, the B-team the general had sent in after him, and the members of his own team who had set themselves up in covert surveillance of the team surveying Noah. It didn't do much to keep his mind off Samantha, but it was better than not talking at all. That's when his mind had nothing to do except focus on her. If he kept that up, he'd go crazy.

It also helped to get the whole sordid thing out into the open. Every word spoken lifted another brick from his shoulders. He didn't know if it was a remnant of his Catholic upbringing, but in this case, he could vouch for the fact that confession was good for his soul.

When he'd shrugged the last of his burden off the tip of his tongue, he paused to draw in a deep breath. The weight had disappeared, but the gnawing ache in his chest continued. That wouldn't go away until he'd fixed things with Sam.

"Somehow I doubt this General Hammond would approve of you sharing all of this information with us,"

Rafe said. He steepled his fingers beneath his chin, and his feline green eyes regarded Noah steadily. "I hazard a guess that there will be repercussions."

Noah had already thought of that, thought long and hard, and reached some unexpected conclusions. He had always been a good soldier, from the time he'd entered the service at eighteen. He'd taken to the life as if he'd been born to it. He appreciated order and discipline, and he believed in the concept of a chain of command. He'd seen it in action, had put it into practice himself, and he knew what a good team under good leadership could accomplish. He believed in teamwork, and spending all of his adult life learning how to build and maintain and lead teams had taught him that a small group of dedicated men could move mountains if given the right tools and enough time to work out a strategy. The army had given him all of that, fostering it in him and in the men on his team.

Too bad no one seemed to have passed those lessons on to Hammond.

Now, for the first time, Noah was beginning to see what could go wrong when someone in the chain failed to work by the same principles as everyone else. The entire military system relied on the integrity and ethics of its personnel; as long as everyone played by the same rules, the structure of hierarchy worked with mechanic precision. But when one member of the team or one link in the chain of command went bad, it had to be replaced before the whole thing collapsed under its own weight. When a bad order came from the top, the ripple effect brought the consequences to the men in the field. Noah had been taught from the very beginning that a good soldier followed the rule of law before a bad command. An order was never an excuse to commit a crime, and he stood by that simple concept.

"I'm prepared," he said, unblinking. "Hammond is the one who decided to step over the line here. As far as I'm concerned, he has compromised his command, and his orders are no longer valid. He needs to be dealt with. If I'm going to face a court-martial over that, it's a price I'm more than willing to pay."

Rule watched him, his expression always inscrutable. "You have invested a lot in your career to let it come to an end like this."

"I'm hoping it won't end, but if the alternative is to get screwed for doing my job responsibly, they can take my pension and use it to cover their asses."

Graham glared at him. "You think *you* got screwed?"

Noah fought to keep hold of his temper and mostly succeeded. "Yeah, I got screwed," he said, his voice level. "I come on this deployment reluctantly and with the understanding that getting it done my way would mean I could at least ensure that the damage done to the relationship between the military and the Others was kept to a minimum. I'm not trying to claim that what I've done doesn't suck, but trust me when I tell you, it beats the alternatives."

"I'm all out of trust when it comes to you. Might have something to do with me having a hard time picturing how someone else could have screwed us worse. I don't remember you using any lube."

Noah bared his teeth and called it a smile. "Well, then your imagination sucks, my friend, because the first option involved taking Dr. Cryer into custody by force and to hell with just getting a look at her data."

"And what you did is so much better than that? Let me go ask Sam if she agrees with you—"

"Fuck you, fur ball! Sam can slap me around with a spiked lead pipe if she wants, but you need to keep your nose out of our business!" Noah shot back, feeling his blood begin to boil. "I was trying to keep Annie from being the first American to experience the draft since Vietnam, and since I can see her standing right here, it looks like I did my job. Since I also don't see you filling out missing-persons reports, I'm guessing you aren't out all the Lupines who contributed DNA samples for this research, either. I can tell you for damned certain they would have taken them, too. And now I'm starting to wonder if I shouldn't have left the whole pack of you on your own!"

"There was only one contributor."

At first the soft voice barely registered. Then he heard it but didn't quite get what it was saying. Angry and impatient, Noah turned a scowl on Annie. "What?"

Annie cleared her throat. "I only had one source for the DNA," she repeated. "It made it easier not to get distracted by random mutations in the beginning, and when I needed a control to compare against, I knew I could just use myself."

"You have to tell us who it is," Missy urged, her expression worried as she leaned forward to emphasize her earnestness. "He should make sure they're okay.

Maybe they should even come stay here. At the club. At least until this is settled."

"That's not a problem." Sighing, Annie shifted uncomfortably. "I used Sam."

Noah felt his blood flash right past boiling and imagined it turning to steam and pouring out of his ears.

Graham muttered something obscene. "No wonder neither of you wanted to talk to me about this mess. You were both in it up to your eyeballs."

"Well, that's going to stop," Noah bit out. "It's a damned good thing Sam's already here where I can keep an eye on her, but you should have told me immediately. What if something had happened?"

The look Annie gave him told everyone she thought he was crazy. "The experiment itself never caused her any harm, and even if I had known some military maniacs were after my data, why would I tell you? I don't know you from Adam, and I had no idea Sam did, either. What business was it of yours?"

Clenched teeth barely prevented him from roaring out that everything about Sam was his business now, because Sam was *his*. He didn't think anyone would appreciate that at the moment, Sam included. And the volume he would have likely shouted it at would almost guarantee she'd hear.

"It doesn't do us any good to argue or blame each other or speculate on things that haven't happened." Abby looked expectantly at her brother. "Knowing you, I'm sure you've already thought about what we should do next?"

Noah nodded abruptly and tried to smooth his hackles back down. Spending all this time with werewolves was rubbing off on him. "First, we have to intercept that data before it gets handed off. If we're not already too late."

"The data itself won't do them much good," Annie said. "I encrypted it, and I have the only written key to Sam last weekend. They took everything I had at the lab, but it would take them days, at the very least, to crack my codes."

Caution forced Noah to warn her, "I hope you're right, but I've met some of those code breakers. They're geniuses."

She turned her brown eyes on him, sharp even through the lenses of her glasses, and blinked at him with a peculiar blend of arrogance and innocence. "So am I."

"We need to get Sam down here, then," Graham said. "I want to know where that key is, and I want it safe. If she's hidden it, she can bring it here, and I'll build a nest and sit on the damned thing if I have to."

Missy shook her head. "No. Sam's been through enough tonight. Leave her alone. Wherever she put it, I'm sure it's safe. Sam's smart and capable and she knew how serious this was. She would have acted accordingly. Besides, I refuse to let anyone go running off on a wild hare tonight. We all need rest, and a few of us need time to cool down." She glared pointedly at Graham and Noah. "We can hatch plans in the morning."

Abby frowned. "Can we afford to wait that long?"

"Annie already said it would be days before they could break her code. That's time enough for a few hours of sleep."

"But we don't know if they'll try to break the code themselves, or pass it on to the general right away and let him worry about it."

"They'll wait." Noah was certain of it. "The general doesn't like jobs half-done, and that's what he would consider it if someone handed him a code without a key. They'll be looking for someone to break it."

"That's another lead for us to follow then," Rafe said, his tone signaling a decision had been reached. By him, if no one else. "Missy is correct. If they are not likely to move immediately, we'll be better served by resting and attacking the problem again once we've slept and regrouped."

"I wouldn't delay too long," Noah said, "but a few hours shouldn't hurt."

"Good. Then we shall meet back here tomorrow. Around noon, I would suggest, seeing that it is already well past two."

Graham looked at Noah and opened his mouth as if he'd heard the bell to signal round two, but Missy grabbed him and shoved him toward the door. "That's fine," she said, as she guided her belligerent husband around his target and out of the room. "We'll see every-one tomorrow."

With a murmur about going to fetch his wife, Rafe followed them out, and Annie trailed behind, looking like a misbehaving puppy with her bowed head and shuffling steps. Rule and Abby trailed behind, and Abby paused to hug her brother.

Convulsively his arms closed around her, and he found himself swearing softly into her hair. "God, I messed up so bad, Abby." He shuddered. "I don't know if there's even any way for me to fix it."

Her small hands rubbed up and down his back in the same comforting motions he could remember his mom using all the time when he'd been growing up. "Maybe not," Abby said softly, her tone gentling the words, "but time can handle things that are beyond us mere mortals. You might not be able to make everything better right away, but they will get better. You're a good man, Noah, and after a while, they'll remember that. Especially if you make a point to remember it from now on, too. Keep doing the things you know are right, and I think you'll find that even new friends can handle a challenge."

"I meant with Sam," he choked out, half-laughing, half-sighing. "I like Graham and the rest of them, but I can live with them hating me. I don't think I can live with Sam feeling the same way." He shook his head. "I love her, Ab."

"Oh." Abby fell silent for a moment, then pulled back to stare solemnly up at him. "In that case . . ."

She reached up and threw all her weight into smacking him upside the head.

"Ow!"

"You're lucky it was just coming from me, you giant twit, because I'm pretty sure Sam would have aimed a hell of a lot lower!"

Noah recoiled more in shock than in pain. He hadn't

known his little sister had a violent streak. "I thought you were supposed to be on my side? Where's the sisterly compassion?"

"You don't deserve any," she snapped, her brow furrowed in a ferocious frown. "And I am on your side. That's why I'm so mad at you. You finally find someone who's more important to you than your combat boots, and what do you do? You lie to her and treat her like crap! If you want her to take you back, brother mine, you'd better start practicing your groveling."

"I didn't lie about us. I didn't lie about being attracted to her or about wanting to be with her." Somehow that reasoning had sounded better before he'd said it out loud. Less lame.

"Oh, big gosh-darned deal," Abby said, clearly of the same opinion. "You might not have faked having an erection around her, but how is she supposed to know you didn't fake everything else? It's hard enough for women to trust a man without you coming along and screwing it up like a big old idiot."

Noah felt a lot like he had in the third grade when Sister Mary Eugene had rapped his knuckles with a ruler for throwing spitballs at Freddie Price. He'd known better back then, too.

"I can't go back and undo it," he muttered, shoving his hands in his pockets in case Abby decided to try a ruler of her own. "I admit I screwed up, but there's not a whole hell of a lot else I can do."

She smacked his shoulder instead. "Don't swear at me. And there are still things you can do. Like I said, start with groveling."

He looked over at Rule for some masculine moral support, but the big blond demon just shook his head. "You are on your own here, Noah. As a man and a warrior, I can understand why you felt you had to act as you did. But as a husband, I am afraid I have to agree with Abby's assessment of your behavior. You have acted like an idiot."

"Thanks. That's helpful." Noah ran a hand over his head and hunched his shoulders. "She walked out. She left before I even got a chance to explain." He really hoped that note of bewilderment he heard was only in his imagination. He didn't need his sister and brother-in-law to hear him sounding like such a lovesick puppy. "How can I grovel if she won't even stay in the same room with me?"

Abby gave him a disgusted look and stepped back to her husband's side. His arm dropped over her shoulder to hold her against him. "You're a big boy, No. You'll figure something out. Just make sure it includes the groveling."

He made a face, and Rule grinned. "It comes to all of us," the demon said. "Especially those of us foolish enough to fall in love with women who have minds of their own." He grinned at Abby's narrow-eyed glare. "If you will recall, your own sister had a few things she had to forgive me for before we could move on with our relationship."

"There's a big difference between a little kidnapping and what he did," Abby muttered.

"You did not call it a 'little' anything at the time, sweet," Rule reminded her. "You were furious with me." He looked back at Noah. "Believe me, the groveling does do wonders."

Noah grumbled something and waved them out of the room, watching the door shut behind them. He stood alone in the empty room for a long time, staring sullenly at the floor.

It wasn't that he had anything against groveling, at least not in this situation; he could see where it might be warranted, in Sam's mind at least. But he didn't know if he was strong enough just now to take another rejection from her. He could still feel the blood seeping from the wounds left by the last one. How many cuts could one heart take before it stopped beating altogether?

And did it matter?

He groaned and let his head fall back as he blinked up at the plaster ceiling. He tried to think of anything that would matter if Sam cut him out of her life, but his mind was blank.

How could anyone cause that fundamental a shift in so short a time? he wondered. He'd been perfectly happy before they got involved, so why couldn't he go back to being that way now?

Sighing, he pulled himself back together and straightened his shoulders. He could stand here all night going over this territory in his head, but he knew perfectly well that it wouldn't change anything. Right now, there were three major truths in his world. The first was that he loved Samantha Carstairs. The second was that he would do whatever it took to make her listen to him, and the third was that he was willing to do whatever it took to make her forgive him, whether that involved groveling, begging, pleading, or public acts of humiliation. He didn't care. No matter what it required, he would win his woman back.

He just really hoped she wouldn't put him in the hospital first.

CHAPTER 27

Staring up at the ceiling of the guest room Tess had tucked her into, Sam wondered idly where this feeling had gotten the name of a broken heart. She'd been thinking about it for an hour at least, and she still hadn't come up with a good explanation. Why call it a broken heart when she felt like every last part of her had shattered into a million fragile pieces?

Tess had been incredibly sweet, clearly demonstrating that her sharp-tongued, tough-cookie exterior hid a gooey marshmallow center. She'd wanted to draw Sam a bath but had accepted the refusal easily and instead commandeered a nightgown from somewhere while Sam made mechanical use of the club's toiletries to wash her face and brush her teeth.

Like a toddler, Sam had allowed the other woman to help her out of her borrowed sweats and into the borrowed gown, then tuck her into the big, soft bed. Tess had even brushed the snarls from Sam's hair and sat beside her, talking about nothing in a calm, soothing voice until she had pretended to go to sleep in order to make her stop.

It wasn't that Sam didn't appreciate the inordinate amount of care that her friend was taking of her; it was just that her nerves were so raw, she needed to be completely alone to make them stop screaming in pain. The silence at least didn't demand anything. It didn't try to sympathize with her or make her feel better or tell her that everything would be all right. It just settled, heavy and still around her, and gave her time to scab over.

She wished it wouldn't take so long.

Maybe she was spoiled by the Lupine ability to heal wounds by shifting between forms, or by the fact that even without shifting, they healed fast enough to be regarded as something a half step down from a miracle by most humans. Either way, she found herself impatient with her inability to heal the cracks in her heart. Apparently, that was one area where being Other didn't convey much of a benefit.

Her eyes grew dry with staring, and she blinked reflexively. She hadn't cried. She wasn't sure what that meant, the fact that she had reacted with this terrible numb silence instead of the raging, flowing tears she had half-expected. It couldn't be because she didn't feel it deeply enough; it had gone right through her, but maybe it had to circle around again before the tears could come.

She winced at the thought. Goddess, she hoped not.

With Tess gone and the room silent and empty, it got harder to keep her mind from replaying the scene in the library. She kept seeing Noah's face, kept hearing him say those words and tell her that the connection they had forged had been all window dressing on his side. Just a pretty costume to make those around him believe he had no purpose other than the lie he had fed them. It would loop over and over in her mind until her stomach twisted with nausea, and only then could she force herself to think about something else.

Unfortunately, that something usually ended up being about Noah, too. About the way he smelled and tasted and the way he felt when he was buried so far inside her she could feel him nudge her heart. A few minutes of that and the pain and longing became so overwhelming that the only way to quell them was to think about his betrayal. And then the cycle started all over again.

Damn it, she felt like she was on some kind of fiendish hamster wheel, condemned to the eternal torment of loving and hating Noah all at once. Forever.

Slowly, she rolled over away from the bedroom door. Her body felt stiff and sore and old, as if she'd been beaten or been in a car wreck or had some kind of major surgery, only she couldn't find a position or a way of moving that eased her particular pain. Not when there was that little voice inside of her whispering that she didn't really hate Noah.

She tried to shut it up, but it persisted, soft and wheedling and unbearably honest. She only wished she hated him.

It would be easier, she thought, if she could work up some kind of righteous anger, or get offended, or convince herself that he was really a scumbag with no redeeming virtues. The problem was that she knew that wasn't true.

Noah Baker was a good man.

She'd seen that in him from the first moment she'd met him. On that day, he'd dropped everything and traveled more than five hundred miles from his base in North Carolina to the center of Manhattan on the basis of a one-word distress call from his sister. Even before he'd known what the situation was, he'd been prepared to mow people down if they threatened Abby. He was fiercely protective and fiercely loyal. Those had been two of the first things Sam had learned about him, followed by his possession of a wicked sense of humor and the fact that he had a hell of a head in a crisis and courage to spare.

For a long time, she'd also thought of him as being as honest as bedrock.

Maybe she would have to revise that last one.

"Samantha."

She heard him whispering to her and squeezed her eyes shut against the leap of her heart. Even now, after everything that had happened, just the memory of her name on his lips could bring every nerve in her body to high alert and send her broken heart speeding in excitement. Goddess, she was one sick puppy.

"Samantha."

The voice came again, no longer a whisper, and she jerked around, clutching the blankets to her chest. Noah stood at the foot of the bed, frowning, a tall figure in the darkness of the room.

"We need to talk," he said.

"How did you get in here?" she demanded. "I didn't hear you. I thought I locked the door."

"You did. I picked it."

She stared at him. "You picked the lock? You broke into my bedroom?"

He didn't even twitch. "I told you, we need to talk."

Sam felt the first flare of white-hot anger and nearly wept with relief. "I have absolutely nothing to say to you. Get out."

"No." He stepped forward and she felt the bed shake a little as his knees bumped into the mattress. "If you don't want to talk, then you can just listen, and I'll do the talking."

"What makes you think I have any interest in anything you have to say?" she snapped, shoving aside the blankets and scrambling to her knees. She no longer felt the least bit cold. Her anger was blazing hot, driving away that horrible icy emptiness inside her and filling the space with a seething mix of hurt and anger. She concentrated on the anger. "From what I can tell, most of the things I've ever heard from you have been lies, so why should I want to hear more of them?"

"I didn't lie to you," he growled, and she could see his hands clench into fists at his sides. At least she had that much of an advantage over him. In the dark, she could see him relatively clearly, but he had to be half-blind. "I may not have always told you the truth, but I didn't lie."

She scoffed. "Don't split hairs with me. You know damned good and well that you lied through your ever-loving teeth. You admitted it downstairs to everyone else. Why not admit it to me?"

"Because the things I lied about had to do with the people in that room downstairs; they had nothing to do with you and me."

His voice sounded strained and harsh, as if he spoke through clenched teeth. Like he had any right to be angry. She was the one with all the righteous wrath here.

"It feels like they had to do with me. Or wasn't I supposed to care that you were only making up to me to try to get information about my pack and my friends?"

"That's a lie!" He gave a strangled roar, as if he wanted to shout but knew better than to bring this little visit to the attention of anyone else in the club. "What is between us has *nothing* to do with my orders. Every single thing that happened between us was true! All of it. And you know it, too. Don't think I'm going to let you deny it just because you're in a snit."

"A snit? A *snit*?" Man, the man couldn't dig himself down any faster if she'd handed him a shovel. "You think that my reaction when I find out that the man I'm f—I'm having an affair with is only using me is to have a *snit*? I'm furious! I could kill you for this! You *used me,* Noah!"

He shook his head and shifted to come around the side of the bed. "No. No, I absolutely did not. I never used you." She backed away from him, but it was hard to move on her knees across a soft bed while she was still wrapped in the twisted folds of an ankle-length nightgown. "Do you think I had orders to sleep with you? Do you think it was actually helpful to my mission that I became so obsessed with you I spent more time thinking about how to get you under me than I did about how to accomplish my objective? Is that what you think, sweetheart?"

"I am not your sweetheart."

"Oh, you sure as hell are," he growled, and reached for her. She twisted away and barely managed to elude his grip, scrambling to the far corner of the bed. "And I'll tell you what else you are," he continued, sidling along the edge of the mattress toward her. "You're my woman. I told you so last night, and nothing that's happened tonight has changed that. The devil himself wouldn't change that, sweetheart, so you'd better find a way to get used to it."

"You arrogant son of a bitch," she hissed. "Do you honestly think there's an icicle's chance in hell that I'll let you lay so much as a hand on me after what you did? You can play at being the big, bad wolf all you want, Noah Baker, but I'm a bigger and badder wolf than you'll ever be. Do you really think I'll let a human get away with what you did to me and then acknowledge him as my mate?" She forced a bitter, taunting laugh. "You need to find another flavor of crack to smoke, my friend, because it is never, *never* going to happen."

She might as well have dressed in scarlet and yelled, "Olé!" His roar this time wasn't strangled or stifled or even remotely muffled, and it barely gave her enough warning to throw herself bodily for the other end of the bed.

He reached for her, and she scrambled away, but he was fast, so much faster than she expected a human to be. His large, rough hand closed over her ankle and held tight, tugging her inexorably back toward him. Her free foot lashed out and caught him in the shoulder. He grunted but didn't loosen his hold. She hadn't hit him hard enough. Damn it, she didn't want to hurt him! Not really. Not permanently. As angry as she was, she was acutely aware of the difference in their strength. She could kill him with her bare hands, but even if he deserved it, she didn't want that on her conscience. At least one of them should have a clean one.

She squirmed and tried to tear her leg out of his grip, but the man clung like a barnacle. Or an octopus, considering his other hand was sliding down her leg looking for something else to grasp. "Let go!"

He didn't bother answering, just found her other ankle and grasped tight. She kicked both legs, but he held on and began to slowly reel her in toward him.

Her heart raced, and she had a shameful moment of doubt over whether that was from anger or excitement. She couldn't deny either emotion, as hard as she tried. He'd lied to her, so she had every right to be mad, but even now, all he had to do was be in the same room with her and her body went haywire with the need to join itself to his. In her life, no other man had ever come close to making her feel like this, and it had to be him? Worse than that, it had to be now when the only thing in her mind should be the desire to punish him for the way he'd treated her? What the hell was wrong with her?

He dragged her closer, making the bedspread and her nightgown catch and bunch beneath her. Every inch she moved across the mattress, her nightgown moved a half inch higher on her legs. She noticed it when she felt the first stirring of a breeze on her overheated skin, and of course, the minute she noticed it, Noah noticed it as well.

His eyes gleamed in the darkness, and she felt them running over her like a caress, lingering on her increasingly bare skin. She expected him to yank, to drag her fast against him and bring her half-naked into his grip as soon as possible, but his steady, even pulling never altered. He brought her to him inch by inch, forcing her to make a decision about whether or not to fight his touch.

Damn him! Couldn't he leave her with a little dignity?

Her struggles were getting weaker, not because she was tiring but because her body had begun to acknowledge what she herself preferred not to think about. No matter what he may have done, this man was hers. Her mate. Her lover. Her fated partner. Hers for the rest of their lives. The knowledge made it difficult to contemplate shortening either one of those lives.

Cursing, she poured one last burst of energy into her escape attempt, twisting and bucking and ending up facedown in the tangled bedding, and all the while Noah held calmly on. Sam's heart just wasn't in it. And worse than that, he had to know it. He knew as well as she did that if she had truly wanted to escape, nothing he did could have stopped her, short of silver chains or enough sedative to knock her completely unconscious. So if she stayed, he would know it was because she didn't want to leave.

Biting back curses and the tears that finally threatened to spill over, she buried her face in the coverlet and muffled her own frustrated scream.

His hands slid up her legs, hands still grasping, but now he caressed as much as captured. He covered her with his body, pinning her beneath his weight, and she felt him nuzzle through the tangle of her hair to press a kiss to the hollow just below her ear.

Damn him to hell and back.

"Shh," he murmured, his tongue darting out to smooth the sensitive skin. "Hush, baby. It's all right, sweetheart. It's okay. I'm sorry. I'm so sorry, Samantha. Hush, baby. God, I'm sorry."

She didn't realize until she heard Noah that her scream had turned into a sob. She lay beneath him, her body shaking not with anger or frustration but with the harsh, wracking tremors of weeping.

He covered her like a living blanket, all heat and strength and disconcerting tenderness. She had never felt so safe, so protected. So cherished. And she wanted to kill him for it.

"I hate you," she choked out, tasting the salt of her own tears. "I hate you for what you did to me, Noah Baker. You deserve to be strung up by your balls and left out for the crows to feed on."

"I know I do, honey. I know." He pressed more kisses to her neck and the space just behind her ear, and his hands ran in long, soothing strokes down her sides. "I'm a bastard. Hush, baby. God, please don't cry, sweetheart. I'm not worth it. I'm so not worth it."

A laugh tore from her throat, swollen and heavy with tears. "You think I don't know that, you son of a bitch? I'm too goddamned good for you, and it's about frickin' time you realized it, too."

His sigh tickled her skin and sent her hair fluttering

against her cheek. "You don't have to tell me, sweetheart. I've known that since the first time I met you."

She struggled for breath, but the sobs were powerful and had been denied for too long. He held her through all of them, his body warming and sheltering her, his hands calming and soothing. It seemed both impossible and completely natural that the man who had broken her heart would be the only one in the world who might be capable of putting it back together again. It was yet another black mark to put on his record, because in no way, shape, or form was that even remotely fair.

"Shh. I'm sorry, baby. I swear to God, I'm sorry. Aw, baby, hush. You're gonna make yourself sick. Samantha, baby, please."

She heard him, listened intently to every word, but there was nothing she could do to stop the storm of emotion. All she could do was ride it out and feel her throat growing tight and raw from weeping. If it made him miserable to hear her crying, well, that was just gravy. He deserved to suffer, damn it, and she had no intention of doing anything to make this easier on him.

Gradually, though, the tempest wore itself out. Her sobs faded to shuddering breaths, and her red, aching eyes refused to produce any more tears. They felt as if they'd nearly swollen shut, and she knew her skin would be red and blotchy and stained with salt. She knew perfectly well that she must look like shit, but she had no intention of worrying about it. Let Noah take a good look. He was the one who had caused it; he could live with the consequences.

Her entire body went limp, sinking deep into the mattress, pressed there by Noah's warm weight. She shifted a little and turned her head so her cheek wouldn't be lying in the puddle she'd made on the smooth sheets. She still had to fight to breathe after so long with her chest painfully clenched, but even that was easing. With a long sigh, she closed her eyes and knew it wouldn't be long before she slipped into sleep. She still had a lot to say to the man on top of her, but it could wait. She'd never be able to muster the energy now.

His fingertips touched her skin, and she felt him softly brush the damp and tangled strands of her hair away from her face. He tucked them behind her ear, then slid his hand under the loose mass of her hair and lifted it aside, laying it on her other shoulder. The air felt cold on her flushed, wet cheek, but then his breath warmed it, and his lips, as he brushed tender kisses over her skin. His tongue darted out, tasting her tears, warm and tender as a mother with her cub.

She sighed again and felt sleep creep over her. She'd ridden a roller coaster tonight, and exhaustion hung heavy upon her. Vaguely she felt Noah slip his arms beneath her and hug her tight against his chest. Carefully he rolled to his side and brought her along with him, nestling her back to his chest, cradling her bottom against his groin. She felt the hard length of him pressing against her, but he didn't even acknowledge the erection. He cuddled her close, her head on his bicep, his other arm keeping her against him, his hand splayed protectively over her stomach.

"Go to sleep, sweetheart," he whispered, and she felt his stubbled cheek press against hers. "I'll take care of you."

And it seemed the most natural thing in the world that he would.

The last thing she remembered before she drifted off to sleep was the indisputable feeling of being home and the soft soundless whisper of his voice telling her he loved her.

CHAPTER 22

She woke him with a kiss, but the moment his eyes slitted open, she punched him right in the gut.

"Oof!"

She didn't say anything, just turned her back on him and headed for the bathroom. When he heard the shower turn on, he felt himself relax. If she'd been gone when he woke up, or if she'd grabbed her clothes and ditched him the second his eyes were open, he'd have worried. The kiss had reassured him, but the sound of her making herself at home in his room at the club was even better.

Turning his head, he glanced at the bedside clock. Nine forty-seven. They had plenty of time before they needed to be back downstairs.

He levered himself off the mattress and walked across the carpet, one hand rubbing his stomach. She'd pulled her punch, no question, but what she'd given him hadn't exactly been a symbolic tap. He felt like he'd been hit. Hard. Thankfully, she'd aimed the impact so it hadn't encountered any vital organs. His spleen was still intact, and not even his ego was bruised. She could use him as human punching bag, if it meant she'd stay around. He'd realized last night that when it came to Sam, he had no pride. He'd do whatever it took to keep her.

Steam wafted over the top of the shower doors as he stepped into the bathroom. Through the patterned glass, he could see the pale peach of her skin. She stood beneath the spray with her face turned up to the water, her hair slicked back and heavy with moisture. His presence didn't cause her to turn, but he knew very well she was aware of him. It counted as damned near impossible to sneak up on a werewolf. The only reason he'd managed it last night was because she'd been so upset, so tuned inward, that she hadn't been paying even cursory attention to the things around her.

She didn't look over when he slid the door open and stepped into the shower behind her, just kept her eyes on the slick tiles covering the enclosure walls. He wouldn't have argued if she'd turned around and wrapped her arms around him in welcome, but she hadn't kicked him out, either. Noah would take what he could get.

Since she hadn't touched him, he did the honors and touched her, wrapping his arms around her and tugging her close, relishing the feel of her wet, naked body pressed full-length against his. She didn't melt the way she had before, but she didn't rip his arms off, either. He could live with that.

They stood in silence for a few minutes until Noah

broke it. "If you want me to apologize again, in daylight and to your face, I've got no problem with that."

Her hands hung at her sides, not touching him and not pushing him away. "Do you think the number of times you apologize really makes a difference? It doesn't make what you did suck any less."

"No, it doesn't." He rested his chin on her shoulder and looked at the tile in front of them that seemed to have her so fascinated. "We both know well enough that there's nothing I can do to change it. Trust me, in this case, hindsight is better than twenty-twenty. But it's still hindsight."

"So do you want me to just go on and pretend it never happened?"

"I don't, because that would be a lie. I don't want any more lies between us. If I can help it, there won't be any more lies within fifty feet of us, ever again."

"That's quite an about-face."

"Actually, it isn't. Or if it is, it's the second one, 'cause all it's done is bring me back where I started. I've always hated lies, and whether you blame Mom and Dad or the Church or my own stubborn hide for that, I don't suppose it makes a difference. What does matter is that I realize that the one time I let myself think that lies were okay because the end justified the means is the time I almost ruined everything that really mattered. You can bet your ass that I won't make the same mistake twice."

She made a little noncommittal humming sound, but her hands lifted to clasp his wrists where they lay against her stomach, and she wasn't trying to pull them away. "You won't, huh?"

"Not a chance."

She was silent for a minute, leaving the sound of the water to fill the air around them. "I think you should tell me what's on the list of yours, the one where you put the things that, quote, 'really matter.'"

He lifted his head so he could look at her. Her expression was neutral, carefully so, but he could feel her attention fixed on him.

"It's pretty short," he said, just as carefully. "My country is still on it, because I'm a soldier, and I've been one too long to think that one man's actions negate the greater good, but it's not in the top spot."

"One item doesn't make a list."

"My friends are on it, too. Provided I have any left after this little incident. I can't blame any of them for wanting nothing more to do with me." She hummed, but she was listening, her face turning just a little, not to face him, but moving closer to it. "My family, too. Abby and my parents. They mean a lot. Of course, the good thing about them is that they love me no matter what, even when I do something monumentally stupid."

"How generous of them."

"Oh, they'll make me pay," he assured her, beginning to smile. "I hesitate to even think what penance Abby is thinking up for me right now. She hit me, you know. Last night. She smacked me upside the head and told me I was a 'big old idiot' and 'a giant twit.' She also told me I should grovel."

"I've always admired your sister's intelligence and talents of perception."

At that point, he actually let out a chuckle, and he

couldn't stop his arms from tightening in an affectionate squeeze.

"Is that the whole list?" she asked carefully.

He shook his head. "Oh no. I haven't gotten to the top yet. That's the space occupied by my woman, and I'd be an even bigger fool than my sister called me if I let my own bad decisions ruin what I have with her."

"I'm sure that when you meet her, she'll be happy to hear it."

"Well?" Grasping her chin, he gently turned her head until their eyes met and he looked into those sticky honey pools. "Are you happy?"

For a long minute, she didn't answer him. She looked into his eyes, searching his expression, while he waited on pins and needles. He had reason to be cautiously optimistic, since she was here and wasn't fighting to get away, and there had been that kiss this morning . . .

But he wanted to hear her say that. He needed to hear her say it. Only when she'd admitted it to both of them did he think he'd be able to really breathe again.

Finally, she pursed her lips and raised an eyebrow. "I'm still waiting for my groveling."

Giving a shout of laughter, a sound replete with joy and relief, he turned her around, sank to his knees, and buried his face in her stomach. "Sweetheart, I will grovel every day of our lives, if that's what it takes. Just let me run out and buy some knee pads."

She ran her hands over his short-cropped hair, smoothing away beads of water. "No one said this was supposed to be comfortable for you."

"Oh, I'm not thinking about comfort," he said, and lifted his head to flash her a grin he figured probably rated its own wattage label. "I'm thinking in terms of staying power. I blow a kneecap and I won't be able to grovel. This is all for your benefit, babe."

She smiled at him, and his heart nearly stopped. Gods, he hadn't even realized it until then, but if she'd never smiled at him again, he'd have died. The expression had become like oxygen to him, a non-negotiable necessity.

Her hands ran down to the sides of his face, cupping it and keeping it turned up to her. Her eyes narrowed in a mock glare, but he could see the sparkle had come back into them and he knew everything would be okay.

"And don't you forget it!" Her voice rumbled with a playful growl, but all Noah could do was kneel in front of her wearing a shit-eating grin and being happy about it.

"Yes, ma'am," he said, and turned his lips to her stomach.

His arms wrapped around her hips and held her to him in a possessive embrace. Finally, with her in his arms and her hands stroking and kneading his shoulders, he felt the pieces of his universe settle back into their proper places.

He didn't know how long they stayed like that, but he did know he should be grateful for the club's generous hot-water system. He almost thought he could have stayed that way forever as long as the water didn't turn cold, but then he took a deep breath and filled his senses with the scent of Sam and soap and clean, damp skin and he realized maybe he didn't want to stay *exactly* like this.

Turning his head, he placed a kiss to the spot on her tummy that barely, gently curved. Her skin was soft against his lips, soft and warm and tempting. His tongue darted out to taste, dragging through beads of water, and he felt her draw in a breath of surprise. Surprise and something else. He repeated the caress and got the same response.

Oh yes. Surprise and desire.

He felt his mouth curve and tried it a third time. Her fingers tightened on his shoulders, no longer kneading but holding on. He loosened his grip around her, not moving away but giving his hands the opportunity to roam over her damp skin. They went immediately to her bottom, drawn like magnets to the soft, giving, fascinatingly rounded flesh. He stroked, kneaded, and felt the curious tightening and softening that signaled her arousal.

Fingers curved, cupped, then slipped down to tease the backs of her thighs and make her shiver against him. He liked that so much he did it again, savoring her involuntary reaction to his touch. He slid his hands inward, fingers gripping between her thighs and gently parting them. She shifted eagerly, widening her stance, a soft moan breaking from her lips as he slid his mouth slowly down the curve of her belly to the warm welcome below.

The first touch of his tongue tightened her like a bowstring. He flicked the nub of her clitoris with teasing pressure and heard her breath hitch in her throat.

He caught the sweet scent of her growing stronger and wondered if she was wet, if already her body had begun to prepare itself for him.

Fingers biting into her thighs, he dipped his head and prepared to find out.

His tongue slid into hot, flowing cream, thick and sweet and scalding to his senses. He explored the slick folds, teased the entrance to her body, and felt his powers of self-control fraying. She felt and smelled and tasted like heaven and he needed to be inside her more than he'd ever needed anything in his life.

Her nails bit into his shoulders and he shuddered helplessly. He wanted her like a house on fire, but more than that he wanted to give her pleasure. He wanted to show her that she meant more to him than the pleasure he gained in the hot clasp of her body. And damn it, he wanted to make her crave him. He wanted to give her so much pleasure that she would feel his touch all the time, even when they were apart. He wanted her to ache when he wasn't inside her and to dissolve when he was. He wanted her to be as much at the mercy of her desire as he was.

One hand moved, grasping her leg just above the knee and lifting it over his shoulder. It left her open to him, balanced on one foot, completely at his mercy when he wasn't sure if he had any.

He feasted on her, devoured her like the last meal of a starving man, so intent on consuming her that the entire world faded away and there were only the two of them in the close confines of the shower, water beating down on his head and the sweet, wild taste of her coating his tongue.

"Ah . . . Noah . . . ," he heard her whimper, and the sound of it was like a fist around his cock. And around his heart.

His hand released her leg, leaving it draped over his shoulder, and his fingers slid up the curve of her thigh, teased her soft folds, then shifted and parted her. He heard her moaning, felt her tremble, and slid a finger into her snug opening.

She cried out, arching into his touch, into his mouth, then nearly jerking away when he gently captured her clit between his teeth and flicked the tip of his tongue repeatedly over the little bundle of nerves. Her grip on his shoulders turned almost painful, but he couldn't have cared less. His finger thrust, stroked, then withdrew, and two returned, pressing high and hard inside her.

He heard her incoherent cries, felt her trembling like a live wire beneath his hands and mouth, teetering on the edge of orgasm. He wanted to feel her go over.

Curving his fingers into a hook, he rasped the tips over her inner walls and felt her clench around him. She cried out, meaningless, incoherent sounds, but he knew what she needed. He played with her clit, torturing it with alternating hard and soft touches while his fingers thrust back and forth within her swollen passage. He found the spot that made her scream and ruthlessly worked it, fingertips pressing and scraping over and over until her entire body tensed and then dissolved in his arms.

She was sobbing, struggling for breath, her inner muscles still rippling with her climax when he withdrew, but he couldn't wait another second. In one smooth motion he rose, turned, lifted and pinned her against the tile wall. His mouth came down on hers, hard and possessive, and his hands brooked no argument as they slipped between her thighs, catching her knees in his elbows and holding her spread wide and helpless before him.

He lifted his head only because he could feel her struggling for breath, but he had no power to slow down, let alone stop. Shifting her weight, he fitted himself to her entrance and thrust ruthlessly inside her.

God, she felt like heaven.

His head fell back against his shoulders and he had to grit his teeth against the instinct to come. He didn't want it to end this soon. He needed the balm of her body wrapped around his cock, accepting and pleasuring him. He needed to feel the connection, to know she was with him, and to imprint himself like a brand on her flesh.

He heard her whimper, and his eyes shot open to lock on her face. "Am I hurting you?" he growled, and he hoped she could understand his harsh, rasping voice, because he barely could.

She shook her head. "No. Goddess, no." She was panting, her breath sawing in and out of her lungs as if she'd just run a four-minute mile in two minutes. "I just . . ." She broke off. Whimpered. "How can I need you again this soon?"

If she expected a verbal answer, she had a lot to learn about men in general and about him in particular. At least him when he was buried hilt deep in her sweet, tight little body.

He braced his hands against the tile beside her ribs and flexed his hips, stroking himself with her clinging flesh. Already he felt his balls drawn tight against his body and he knew he had only seconds before he came. He was determined to savor every single one.

In her present position, she couldn't move, couldn't distract him, so he took shameless advantage, holding her still and tight against the cold tile as he began to thrust hard and rhythmically within her. She fit him like a glove and squeezed him like a fist, and he was surprised the top of his head hadn't blown off the minute he'd gotten inside her.

Every thrust took him deep. He felt himself nudge her womb and had a wild, primitive thought of making her pregnant. Before Sam, any such thought would have filled him with horror, but in that moment it filled him with lust. He imagined her belly round with pregnancy, imagined his child suckling at her breast, imagined a part of him joined forever with a part of her, and his last hold on control snapped like a rubber band.

He slammed into her, over and over, trying to get to the heart of her, forcing her to open for him so that he could spill his seed at the very mouth of her womb. He felt her hands clutching at his upper arms, heard her frantic, breathless cries in his ear, and he knew that if his cock didn't explode, his head would. No one could survive this kind of pleasure for long. Certainly not him.

"Noah!"

He heard Sam scream, saw her throw back her head, and felt her buck wildly in his arms. Her body clenched hard around him, milking him, squeezing him with powerful contractions, and he gave one last, mighty thrust, driving to the very heart of her and spilling himself with a rough, ragged groan of perfect completion.

CHAPTER 23

S am felt extraordinarily . . . clean.

She'd seen her face in the mirror while she dried her hair after their incredibly long and thorough shower, and she knew she glowed. Part of it was a blush she wasn't sure would ever fade, but the rest was something more. Something she still didn't want to examine too closely for fear it might melt out of existence.

Noah hadn't stopped touching her all morning. Even after they'd made love so completely she thought it might be months before either of them mustered up the energy for another round, he'd constantly had his hands on her. He'd washed and dried her so tenderly, then combed the tangles from her hair and stood close while she dried it. He'd been the one to dress her and had held her hand while they ate from the tray he'd asked the kitchen to send up. He'd kept his hand at the small of her back as they walked down to the second floor to meet the others in the War Room, and now he'd folded his long frame into the corner of the sofa and hauled her up against his side, his fingers playing with the bare strip of skin that the too-wide neckline of her sweatshirt kept revealing.

"I see you still have all your parts," Tess said, strolling into the room ahead of her husband. She gave Noah a quick once-over and cast Sam a curious glance. "Are you sure that was the best decision?"

"Leave them alone, my love," Rafe scolded mildly, placing a hand on his wife's back to guide her to the love seat at a right angle to the sofa. "Whatever decisions have been made, they are their decisions."

"Oh, I know." Tess settled herself on the cushions and crossed her legs. "But that doesn't mean I can't make suggestions."

"I have a few suggestions myself." Graham and Missy entered as well, with Abby and Rule trailing right behind. The Alpha looked calmer than he had last night but not significantly happier. "Care to hear them?"

"Not really," Sam said, catching his eyes just long enough to gain his attention before she shifted her gaze to his chest. "I think I can guess what they would involve."

"Really? Frankly, I've been surprised by the depths of my own creativity."

Missy hushed him and leaned down to brush a kiss over Sam's cheek. "Ignore him. It's what I do. Are you okay?" She glanced from Sam to Noah and back again, and her brow wore a furrow of concern.

"A little bruised, but yeah, I'm okay," Sam answered, reaching out to squeeze the Luna's hand. "Thank you."

"If you need anything, you let me know, understand?"

Sam smiled. Missy might have grown up human, but she'd also been born with a maternal instinct ten miles wide. She'd taken to her role as pack Luna with impressive skill and enthusiasm. "I understand."

Satisfied, Missy grabbed her husband's hand and towed him to the farthest chair in the room and toppled him down onto it. Then she crawled onto his lap as if she could pin him in place. Like all mothers, Missy believed in the saying about better safe than sorry.

Abby moved to gaze down at her and Sam with her hands on her hips and a scowl on her face. "I'm not sure whether to be relieved she didn't hurt you or disappointed," she said, her gaze roaming her brother much as Tess's had. "Now he's going to think he got away with that junk."

Noah snorted beside Sam and she just grinned. "I wouldn't say that," she corrected, pasting an innocent expression on her face. "He got a stern talking-to, but he's already made great progress with his groveling lessons."

She jumped a little when his hand slipped down to pinch her bottom, but she was still grinning.

"I'll show you exactly how much progress I've made the next time I get you in a shower," he growled into her ear, keeping his voice low. But he'd obviously forgotten he sat in a room full of Others.

"I'm gonna kill him," Graham announced, bracing his hands on the arms of his chair and preparing to rise. "Did you hear that? You have to let me kill him."

"Stay right where you are," Missy ordered. "There will be no killing. I thought I made that clear to everyone last night. Don't make me go over it again."

"Even though we missed it? Sorry we're late." Fiona Walker stepped in with her big Lupine husband right behind her. "I have to say, though, after we missed the excitement last night, it seems pretty unfair of you all to start without us this morning."

"We haven't started anything," Rafe assured her.

"No, we were just discussing killing Noah," Tess informed her cheerfully.

"Oh, right." Fiona turned her eyes on the human man, and from the way they narrowed, Sam guessed someone had filled Fiona in on the whole story to date. "Need any help?"

"No one needs to kill Noah," Sam announced, torn between amusement and exasperation. "I'm the only one with a right to, and I'm more than capable of handling it myself if I felt the need. So you can all just back off and drop it, okay?"

Noah squeezed her hand and shook his head. "They've got nearly as much right to be mad at me as you do, sweetheart. I lied to them, too."

"I'm glad to hear you admit it," Graham growled. "But I still don't think a pretty apology is enough reason to let you live."

"Enough, already!" Missy shouted, rolling her eyes. "You know perfectly well that you don't really want to kill Noah. You like him too much for that. You're just pissed that your famous Spidey sense didn't tell you he was up to no good from the very beginning. Everyone here knows that if you'd been in his position, you'd have been hard-pressed to do anything differently than he did. If you thought the pack depended on your actions the way he thought his country did, you'd have done the same damned thing, so spare me the righteous-indignation crap. I don't want to hear it."

Sam had never heard anyone talk to the Alpha that way, not even the Luna. It astounded Sam that he did nothing more drastic than turn his head and glare at his mouthy mate. "Who asked you?"

Noah gave a half laugh. "Listen, I appreciate both the willingness of some of you to defend me and the desire of the rest of you to rip out my spleen, but we have more important things to be arguing about. We took all morning off to rest and regroup. Now we need to get back to business and find Annie's missing data."

Abby frowned and looked around the room. "Where is Annie? She knew we were meeting back here at noon."

"Was she supposed to join us?" Fiona asked. "Tobias and I passed her as we were walking into the club. She was just leaving and she looked like she was in a hurry. I assumed she wasn't needed or she would have been coming, not going."

Sam heard Graham swear and felt Noah's fingers squeezing hers.

"Did she say where she was going?" Noah demanded.

Tobias shook his head. "She didn't say much of anything. She walked right into me, mumbled some kind of apology, and said she had something important she had to go take care of."

"What?"

"We didn't stop to play twenty questions. Fiona and I were late, so we came right upstairs. Annie left through the front door. Maybe she told someone else her plans?"

Noah swore and pushed himself from the sofa. Graham just swore.

"Is she really stupid enough to go off and try to recover that data on her own?" Noah demanded.

"Watch who you're calling stupid, human," Graham snarled. He set Missy firmly to the side and glowered as he rose to his feet. "Sam, where do you think that idiot has gone?"

Ignoring the irony, Sam shook her head. "I don't know. I knew she felt really guilty about all of this, but I had no clue she was going to go off half-cocked and try to fix things all by herself. That's crazy."

"Especially since she doesn't even have all the facts," Noah agreed. "If she'd come down here first, I could have told her that I have a good idea where to start looking for information."

"What do you mean?"

"I mean that if the people who took the data are who we think and are working for Hammond, then we should start by checking out their safe house. I told you last night that my team had located it and was keeping it under surveillance. If we want answers, that's where we need to start."

Graham grunted. "I forgot about that, but you're right. We should check it out. But we can't just leave Annie to her own devices. We need to find her."

"I can track her," Sam said, already heading toward the door. "Fiona and Tobe just saw her. She can't be more than ten minutes ahead of me. I'll pick up her trail in the entry hall and I'll have her back here within the hour."

Noah snagged her upper arm. "No way," he said. "I

want you with me. You're not the only one in this city with a good nose. Someone else can go after Annie."

"She's my friend," Sam protested. "Do you expect me to just sit here while she wanders into a dangerous situation?"

"Of course not. Like I said, you're coming with me. The most dangerous situation will be where the B-team is, and that's where we're headed. The faster we get the data back, the faster we can make everyone else lose interest in Annie."

Sam didn't like it, but she could see his point. "Fine, then let's go now."

"I'll get a tracker on Annie," Graham said. "And I'll send up a howl. If we have the whole pack out looking for her, she won't get very far."

"I'll send a few trackers back to the lab, too," Tobias offered. "It's a logical place to look for her, and if she's not there, maybe we can pick up something else from the goons who broke in last night. They might not all be hiding out in some safe house."

"I doubt they will be," Noah said. "The house will be more like a base of operations. They won't leave it unguarded, but they won't all be hanging out there all day. You never know. You may stumble onto something. If you do, let the rest of us know immediately."

"Will do." Tobias gave a casual salute and towed his wife toward the door. "You can come. Rule said Sam and Annie smelled something weird about one of the men at the lab. Maybe you've got some voodoo we can use to figure out what the problem was."

Missy looked at her husband. "I'll stay here and help you direct the troops, of course, but I don't like the idea of Sam and Noah walking into a vipers' nest all by themselves."

"Tess and I will tag along," Rafe suggested. "There's more than strength in numbers. We can cover more ground and gather more information with four than with two."

Sam felt Noah's hesitation, but within seconds he was nodding. He knew enough about the werejaguar and his witchy wife to know they wouldn't slow him down and could very well prove to be useful. "Fine."

"What about us?" Abby asked, clutching Rule's hand tightly enough to turn her knuckles white. He didn't even seem to feel it. "I can't just sit here and worry while everyone else is gone. It'll drive me demented."

"There's no need for you to put yourself in danger," Noah said, and Sam heard the tenderness in his voice. "The rest of us can handle it."

"And I can handle taking care of my wife," Rule told him. "The two of us will find another way to be useful. No one has suggested cutting off the head of this particular beast. If your general is orchestrating all of this, he should be dealt with as well."

Noah's protest was instant and emphatic. "No way. I don't want Abby within ten city blocks of that man. Besides, there's no reason to suppose he's even in Manhattan. He can orchestrate a war from D.C., so he can certainly manage one operation."

"Yes, but I believe this one might be of particular concern to the general. You did mention he had paid your progress an unusual amount of attention since your mission began."

"I don't care. It's bad enough I know I can't keep Sam out of the middle of it. There's no reason Abby needs to get involved, too."

Sam grabbed his hand. "I'm glad you realize the part about me, but you need to give both your sister and her husband a little credit. You know perfectly well she's a smart, tough, capable woman who can look after herself. And more than that, you know Rule would never let her face any real danger. So give that protective streak of yours a rest. She really would go crazy with nothing to do."

"Absolutely," Abby agreed, shooting Sam a grateful glance. "And no one is saying we're going to go knock on his door and make a citizen's arrest, but if we can find out where he is, we can keep an eye on him and give you a heads-up if it's necessary."

Abby rubbed her hands together almost gleefully. If anyone could find out if the general was in town, Sam realized, it was Abby Baker. She worked as a professional researcher for a local television station and the things she could dig up in five minutes of computer time made Sam's head spin.

"Thanks," she said, and smiled at her lover's sister, a woman who'd been a friend for a while, and now felt more like family.

"Good," Missy said. "I'm glad everything is settled. Now let's get moving. We've got some work to do."

CHAPTER 24

The safe house looked no different from a dozen other row houses on the same block. Its red sandstone exterior looked warm and almost inviting in the late afternoon sun, and the green-painted stoop was neat and nondescript. No one lurked around outside, and with the shades drawn over the windows, it was impossible to tell if anyone lingered inside, either. Noah had to assume they did. He knew he wouldn't leave his base unattended in the middle of a city after the incident at the lab the other night. Someone obviously knew the B-team was in the city, so if Noah had been its leader, he'd have left a guard posted at the base 24-7.

He glanced down at Sam, saw concentration furrowing her brow. He didn't know what else to call it, even though it was currently covered with fur, so he stuck to "brow." Or maybe he should use "forehead."

She had insisted on accompanying him in wolf form since her sense of smell was so much better this way. To make them less conspicuous, she'd produced a collar and leash with a breakaway catch in case she got tangled up in something or needed to make a fast escape. When she'd handed it to him, it had been accompanied by a warning glance so fierce he hadn't even tried to crack a joke, and he'd been very careful to keep the leash slack between them the whole time. Tess and Rafe hadn't seemed to find anything all that odd about the arrangement. Tess had just accepted the backpack full of clothes Sam had handed her in case she needed to shift back to human, and shrugged into the straps. Then the four of them had set out for the safe house, Tess and Rafe looking like nothing more than a couple of lovers out for a stroll a couple of blocks ahead of Noah and his dog.

To him, Sam looked exactly like a wolf, with her dense gray-brown fur, pointy ears, and huge golden eyes, but he'd discovered as they made their way along the street that no one else had given her a second glance. Maybe it was the leash and collar, but people seemed to dismiss her as nothing more than an oversized mutt. Maybe some kind of Siberian husky cross. He pitied them for their ignorance and hoped none of them ever did anything to deserve meeting a Lupine in a bad mood.

Sam seemed to sense his gaze on her, because she looked up and gave him a canine nod. There was someone in the house all right.

"How many?" he asked softly.

Her head jerked once, then went still.

Just one.

Noah looked around casually and spotted Tess and Rafe on the other side of the street, leaning against a wall a few houses up. They looked as if they were absorbed in each other, but Noah knew they were both waiting for a signal from him.

He glanced back at Sam.

"Is he in the front of the house?"

She nodded again.

"Armed?" Noah had to assume he was, but it didn't hurt to ask.

Another nod.

Noah gave one of his own, along with a stifled curse. "Okay. Looks like you're circling around back."

This was the part of the plan Noah hated. He'd argued like the devil against it, but he'd lost; and worse, he'd known the others were right. The safe house was in a residential neighborhood in the middle of a residential block. There weren't any convenient alleys to slither down, no easy access to the back of the building. And it was the middle of the day. If he or any of the others had tried to break into the house, front or back, someone would have noticed. But no one would notice a stray dog slinking through the neighboring yards and up to the safe house's back door.

Grimly Noah leaned down to unhook the leash from Sam's collar. He cupped her muzzle in his hand and forced her to look at him. "If you get hurt, I'm going to kill you," he warned solemnly, trying not to wince at the humor and excitement in her eyes.

She had warned him that adrenaline affected her differently in this form. The anticipation of the chase was stronger and tended to drown out even common sense sometimes. He knew all that, but that didn't mean he liked it.

Muttering something dire, he bent his head and

pressed a kiss to the fur between her ears. "Be careful," he growled, and she turned to swipe her tongue over his cheek before she bounded off for the end of the block.

She had fifteen minutes before he charged in like the First Cavalry Division. He'd be counting every last one.

S am felt every second of her allotted fifteen minutes ticking away. She wanted to rush, and she did for the first few minutes, but once she got onto the property behind the safe house, she forced herself to slow down and take her time. It galled, but no matter how her animal instincts wanted her to go straight for the throat, her human mind knew that would be a bad idea. The neighbors who caught glimpses of her might be willing to write her off as a stray dog prowling through the city, but the man inside the house would know better. He'd have training and would know that the last thing he wanted to find would be a wolf at his door.

Belly low to the ground, she prowled along the perimeter of the property where the weeds had been allowed to grow into bushes. The foliage helped conceal her, and she crouched among the fronds and branches for a moment, her eyes surveying the back of the house. The bright sun contrasted with the darkness inside the house, making the windows little more than rectangular black cutouts. Someone would have to walk up close to them before Sam could see, and right now she couldn't see anything.

Cautiously she crept forward. Noah had warned her

about the security the B-team might have put in place, so she watched her steps. They wouldn't use booby traps, nothing that might pose a risk to a neighbor or a kid taking a shortcut, but that didn't mean they wouldn't have tried to protect themselves against a sneak attack. Sam kept her nose peeled and could detect faint traces of men in the yard, but nothing very strong. She didn't think they spent a lot of time out here, definitely not enough to have rigged up any elaborate early-warning systems.

The scents got stronger as she approached the back door. She could smell the acrid smoke stench of Camel man, the one who had played lookout on the roof of the lab building, and had a clear picture of him standing by the back door puffing away. She investigated the ground where his scent was strongest, but there were no butts littering the ground there. Apparently, even at his own base he was careful about his bad habits.

She sniffed along the base of the house, paying close attention to the basement windows, but the B-team wasn't composed entirely of idiots. She could see the little white sensors on the sill and knew an alarm would sound if someone tried to open the window. They hadn't made this easy for her.

Wishing she could wear a watch in this form, Sam sank to her haunches and estimated almost half of her fifteen minutes had passed. She had to find a way inside soon or admit defeat and head back to the street before Noah came barging in after her, guns blazing. He'd do it, too, she was certain. If he thought she was in danger, he wouldn't hesitate to cause the biggest and most ill-advised ruckus this side of a Britney Spears concert.

Sam stared at the back door and considered her options. She had a good feeling that the back door wouldn't be wired while someone was in the house. If at least one of them smoked, they would have gotten used to leaving it unalarmed for the sake of convenience. And men usually felt they didn't need alarms to protect them, only to protect their things when they were away from home. So she could probably get the back door open without making herself known, because she also felt pretty confident about her earlier assessment that the man inside the house was near the front, not in the back. If she shifted forms, she could open the door, slip inside, and shift back before anyone knew she was there.

Probably.

She didn't like the idea, and she was damned certain that if Noah had heard it, he wouldn't have liked it, either. In fact, he probably would have pitched a wild fit and chained her to something solid until she came to her senses. The problem was that, as bad as the idea might be, she really didn't think she had many options.

Five minutes left.

Biting the bullet, Sam slunk up to the back door, threw herself into the shift, and slipped through as soon as she had the thumbs to do it. Immediately she shifted back and took a moment and a couple of deep breaths to allow the dizziness of the lightning-speed transformation to fade.

She had entered the kitchen, and the half-round table and three chairs against the back wall offered her a small measure of concealment while she surveyed the situation. She could smell the sharp tang of gun oil and the sour odor of metal mixed with the smells of men and food. The place was a far cry from immaculate, but it wasn't messy. Everything was in its place, even if it could have stood a thorough dusting and definitely an airing out. Over the other smells she scented blood, and curiosity drove her into the doorway.

She could hear the low murmur of a television set and, when she concentrated, the steady, even breathing of a man, both coming from the front room. Taking special care not to make a sound, she ghosted down the tiny excuse for a hall and peeked around the corner and into a dim living room. The drawn shades cut off the late afternoon sunshine, and the television provided the only artificial illumination. The man, stretched out in a recliner chair with his eyes closed and his hand clasped protectively over a black remote control, hadn't bothered to light a lamp. Or maybe, she thought, noting with satisfaction the sling around his neck and the bandages wrapped around his right wrist, he hadn't been able to. The lamp was on his wounded right side.

Mr. Anger Management himself, and from the looks of it, he was sound asleep. That must have been why she hadn't recognized his scent as being the one inside the house. While he was unconscious, his anger would be in hibernation mode. A testosterone lull.

Moving carefully forward, Sam sniffed the air and caught a faintly bitter aroma. She had to fight back a feral grin. Poor little soldier was taking painkillers for the boo-boo she'd given him. He was definitely down for the count, and by her estimate she had about three minutes left to signal Noah that everything was under control.

No time to be delicate. Shifting to human form, she grabbed the lamp off the table beside the soldier and brought it down hard just above his temple. She saw him jerk, then settle back into unconsciousness. Now he wouldn't wake up accidentally.

She sprinted for the front door and took a moment to examine it for alarms. She saw the sensors mounted in the top corner and swore. She had like ninety second left. Apparently, she should remove delicacy from her repertoire altogether. Reaching up, she pinched the sensors together and yanked, keeping them in perfect contact with each other but removing them from the door completely. Then she pulled open the door and stuck her head out.

"Noah! Come in!"

He was across the street and up the steps in two seconds flat, and when he pushed his way inside, he looked down at her naked body and scowled.

"Why are you naked?"

She rolled her eyes. "Because I'm not wearing any clothes." He looked like a thundercloud, black and threatening. "I had to shift so I could knock him unconscious," she explained. "But don't worry. He already had his eyes closed. He didn't get a free show."

"And neither will De Santos," Noah barked, shoving her back toward the kitchen. "Stay in there until Tess gets here with your clothes!"

Sam thought he was being a little ridiculous, but she went anyway. She knew Rafe wouldn't have cared that she was naked, since he was way too wrapped up in his wife for any other woman's body to make an impression, but she understood that humans had hang-ups about that kind of thing. To her, skin was skin, but apparently to Noah, her skin was his.

The door slicked shut behind the other couple and she heard voices for a second before Noah shoved her backpack into the room and braced his body against the door. She just shook her head and pulled on the clothes Tess had brought her before yanking the door open and rejoining them in the other room.

She noticed that Noah looked her over, as if to assure himself that she hadn't forgotten and left a breast hanging out or something.

Tess looked at her and grinned. "I counted forty-four seconds to spare. Nice work, girl."

"Forty-one," Noah grumped.

Sam shook her head, but she still reached out to squeeze his hand. "The key there is not the number, baby; it's the words 'to spare.'"

Rafe ripped a piece of duct tape off a roll and placed it over the unconscious soldier's mouth. His hands and feet had already been taped together. "Either way, I say we get down to business," Rafe said, straightening. "Noah, why don't you tell us what exactly we're looking for?"

"Anything and everything," he answered. "Annie's data, though I have a feeling that's not going to be here. It would be too valuable to leave with one guard. I think they've probably taken it to a rendezvous point to try to work out the code and prep for the handoff. But it can't hurt to look. I'll be looking for a logbook with the mission records, and I want Sam to sniff

around to see what she can find out about how many
are on the team. You can, Tess, just keep your eyes
open for anything interesting."

Tess pursed her lips. "Well, that's nicely specific."
But she didn't protest; she just followed Rafe up the
stairs to the second floor and prepared to be interested.

Sam turned to look at Noah. "I'll do what I can, but
if I shift back to Lupine now, I'll be naked again, so
you'll have to make do with this nose."

He grunted and headed for the back room. "That's
fine. It's still better than mine, and we're not trying to
track anyone. We're just looking for clues."

He stalked out without even smiling at her, grumpy
bastard. He really had no sense of humor about her being naked in front of other people. Sheesh.

While he rooted around in what she figured was a
back bedroom, she ignored the unconscious man in
the armchair and put her nose to work. It took concentration to separate out the scents, to peel back the lay-
ers and uncover how many there were and where
they were strongest, how long ago they had last been
here, and which ones had distinctive markers, like
Camel man's cigarettes or Mr. Anger Management's
rage issues.

She thought she counted seven in all, five more in
addition to those two, but it was hard to tell. One she
thought might belong to the third man at the lab, but
here, too, his scent kept blipping in and out. It was as if
he was here one minute and gone the next with no fading trail to indicate either how he'd entered or how he'd
left. She wanted to be certain she was smelling the
same man, but she detected two other scents that were

distinctly separate from his and yet shared that elusive ephemeral quality.

If she focused too hard on those three, it would drive her crazy. Better to pay attention to the odors that made sense and find out what she could about the others along the way.

That philosophy carried her into the back bedroom where Noah had the beds pushed back against the walls and the drawers out of the dressers. If there was anything interesting in there, he would find it.

Sniffing again, she followed her nose up the stairs to the landing flanked by doors on either side. Both stood open, and she could hear Tess and Rafe moving around in opposite rooms. Sam looked in on Rafe and saw him conducting a search nearly as thorough as Noah's, so she crossed the hall and joined Tess.

The witch sat on the end of one of the three beds in the room, the one that wasn't part of a bunk set, and she looked up when Sam entered.

"You have an unusual searching technique," Sam said, sitting next to her.

"There's nothing interesting in here." Tess shrugged, turning her sharp blue eyes on her friend. "At least, there wasn't until you came in."

Sam glanced at her, then looked away. "You've known me for years. You know I'm not really all that interesting."

"You weren't before, but Noah makes you absolutely fascinating. Trust me. Are you going to tell me why you're pretending he hasn't hurt you?"

"I'm not pretending that. He did hurt me, and he knows he hurt me. He apologized for it. I think my friends need to work on remembering that I'm the one who decides whether or not to accept that apology."

Tess nodded, but her eyes were bright and shrewd. "Oh, I know it is, honey. I just want to make sure you've accepted it for the right reasons. And at the right time. It never hurts to make them sweat a little."

Stifling a laugh, Sam smiled at her. "Trust me, he sweated."

"All right, then." Tess nodded decisively and pushed herself off the bed. "Now that that's settled, let's go see how my own walking, talking headache is doing."

Rafe looked up with a frown when they entered. "You've finished already?"

"Efficiency, thy name is woman," Tess quipped, sweeping a glance around the room that looked a lot like the one across the hall, only this one had just two single beds, no bunks. "There was nothing interesting in there anyway. Now, in here, I'd love to see what you find." Her head shot around and she stared hard at the head of one of the beds, the one farthest from the door. "There. Right there. Behind the bed."

Sam looked at her, surprised. "Behind the bed? Tess, the headboard pushes right up against the wall. What do you think they could have back there?"

"Right *there*," she repeated forcefully.

Rafe was already pushing the piece of furniture aside. "It does not do to argue with my wife."

Folding her arms over her chest, Sam tried not to snort an "I told you so" as soon as the blank white wall was revealed. Tess wasn't listening to her anyway.

Stepping forward, the blonde tucked a couple of stray curls behind her ears and slipped into the space where the head of the bed had been. She laid her hands on the dingy, cracked wall and closed her eyes.

A minute later they popped open and she grinned at her husband. "Go get Noah, and when you come back, bring me a lead pencil and a key that doesn't fit anything."

Again, Rafe didn't ask questions, just nodded and headed for the stairs. Tess nodded in satisfaction. "I've trained him well."

"I still don't see anything back there, Tess," Sam said, trying not to sound skeptical.

"You will."

The men returned in under two minutes. Noah had an unfriendly look on his face as he dropped a slim black notebook onto the end of the bed. Rafe didn't say anything; he just handed the requested items to his wife. "The key is one of the ones on my ring I cannot identify. It probably opens something, but I haven't used it in so long that I can't remember what it is for."

"That will do."

"What did you find?" Noah demanded, looking around. "I don't see anything."

"Sheesh, would you people have a little patience, please?" Tess turned back to the wall and frowned. "Crap, I should have asked for a piece of string, too."

Rafe looked around and his gaze settled on the blinds at the window. Sam saw him reach out and his hand flash, a claw slicing through the drawstrings like butter. He handed his wife the string a moment later, held in a perfectly human hand. "Will this work?"

She stretched up to kiss his cheek. "Perfect."

Sam felt Noah step up to her shoulder, and they both

watched, impatient and fascinated, as Tess tied one end
of the string to the key and the other end around the
pencil. Then she found the center point and let both objects dangle from the ends. Pressing the string to the
wall with the tip of one perfectly manicured finger, she
muttered a few words that Sam didn't quite catch, and
the key and the pencil began to move.

Sam felt the crackling energy of magic fill the air. She
watched the key move down the wall until it stopped
with its top lodged in the seam between the baseboard
and the drywall. When it stopped, the pencil spun in
seven perfect circles, scribbled something on the paint,
and then went limp on the end of its string.

Tess hummed with satisfaction. "There you go. Pull
the baseboard back, love, and let's see what we have."

Rafe hunkered down and did as she instructed, carefully prying the baseboard away to reveal an opening
into the wall.

"What's inside?" Sam asked, leaning forward in fascination.

Peering into the hole, Rafe shook his head. "It looks
empty. It's not very deep."

"Oh, there's something there, all right," Tess assured him. "You just haven't found it yet."

The Felix reached down and felt inside the opening,
shaking his head. Then he turned his hand and felt the
inside of the wall just above the top of the entrance and
he froze. "I feel some kind of button," he muttered.

They all heard the click when he pressed it and a
mechanical whir as the wall seemed to shift, the cracks
that ran down it now looking less like the work of some
bad construction workers and more like deliberate

camouflage. A section of drywall, irregularly shaped and about two feet across and three feet high, popped out a half an inch as if on springs. Carefully Rafe grasped the edges and lifted it away. There, tucked into the wall behind it, was a small brown refrigerator, like the kind kept in dorm rooms around the world.

Sam blinked. "A fridge? What? Were they midnight snackers?"

"I doubt it." Noah urged her aside and stepped forward to open the small insulated door. Inside there was no light, but they didn't need one to see the neatly stacked medical vials and the sterilely wrapped syringes. Noah picked up a small, clear vial about the size of his thumb and examined the contents. The glass was unlabeled. There was no telling what was inside.

"Okay, somehow I doubt that these guys are either insulin-dependent diabetics or hide-the-stash-in-the-wall junkies."

Noah shook his head. "They're not. This is something else."

Sam saw the grim lines of his face and frowned. He clearly didn't like this latest discovery, but what was he thinking about that she couldn't see? She wracked her brain and a terrifying thought occurred to her.

"Oh, my goddess," she breathed, her eyes widening. "You don't think the military is already giving the members of this team Lupine DNA, do you? How would that be possible? If their research isn't as far along as Annie's, it should be *im*possible."

"I don't know," he said, sounding about as happy as he looked. "Yeah, it should be impossible, but who knows what Hammond neglected to tell me? Maybe he lied and the military program is further along than we thought."

"I doubt it," Rafe said. "If that were true, the general would not need Annie or her research enough to risk so much with the break-in at her laboratory."

"Doubts are great, but I want to be sure." Noah grabbed a second vial and handed them both to Tess. "Take one of these with you and head back to the club. If the others have found Annie, maybe she can identify what's inside. And if not, give the other vial to Fiona. If science can't do it, Fae magic might."

Tess nodded. "Right. I'm proud of myself just for finding the damned things, but magicking out their chemical composition is slightly beyond me."

"Call me as soon as you find anything out." Sam had given him her cell phone earlier.

"Where will you be?" Rafe asked.

Noah picked up the notebook from where he'd laid it on entering the room. "We'll be down at the Chelsea piers," he said. "I found their logbook, not quite as well hidden as their stash. They have a warehouse down there, apparently, that they use for rendezvous and for moving things in and out. At first I thought it was supplies, but now I think it's more of that stuff." He jerked his chin to indicate the vials in Tess's hand.

"Does it say what the stuff is?"

"It might, but if it does, I can't read it. It looks like math to me, which means it might as well be Greek."

"If Annie's back, she can tackle that, too," Tess suggested.

Sam frowned. "I hope that logbook has an address, because I'm not sure I can trace them by scent. At least three of them are doing that on-again, off-again thing the one at the lab did the other night. I can't track something I can't smell."

"Shit. Three of them?"

She nodded. "I think so. It's hard to tell when the scent keeps blipping in and out. Why?"

He paused, then shook his head. "The book. I got the impression that whatever the stuff in the vials is, it's being given to three of the seven men on the team."

Sam felt her stomach clench in a very unpleasant way. "You mean that whatever is in the vials might be what's disguising their scents? Holy crap."

Rafe put it more succinctly. "We will rush these samples back to Annie and Fiona. As soon as one of them has news, we will call."

"Good."

All four of them started at the sound of a cell phone beeping. Rafe frowned and looked down at his pocket. "I think that is mine." He flipped open the handset. "Yes?"

He had turned away slightly, the instinctive reaction of a private man who had large demands on his time, but Sam still noticed the second his expression went taut and forbidding.

"What?" she demanded. "What is it?"

"Annie left a voice message for Missy. She called the house instead of the club, so Missy didn't pick up and she didn't answer right away."

"Is she okay?"

He nodded reluctantly. "She was when she left the message. Missy says it was time-stamped at three thirty-one P.M."

Sam looked at the alarm clock next to the untouched bed. "That's only a little over an hour ago," she said, wishing she felt more relieved, but Rafe's face hadn't softened. "She should still be fine."

"So we can all hope," the Felix said.

"Rafael." Tess spoke softly, her pretty face frowning as she laid a hand on his sleeve and looked up at him. "What's wrong? What did Annie's voice mail say?"

He sighed and placed his hand over his wife's, but his eyes, bright and worried, were on Sam. "She wanted to warn the rest of us to be careful," he said slowly. "She has a theory about what the military has really been up to and she thinks it might tie into these soldiers with the lack of scent."

Noah froze and laid a hand on Sam's shoulder. "What?"

"She thinks they have been engineering DNA, but not Lupine DNA. They have been using vampires."

The perfect sense of it came crashing down on Sam's head and rendered her momentarily speechless. They had been injecting human soldiers with vampire DNA. How and where they got it would be something they looked into later, but for now it explained why their scent sometimes seemed to disappear and then reappear again later. If the injections had a temporary effect, like a drug that wore off once the human immune system recognized and began attacking the foreign material, their scents would naturally seem to flicker in and out, just like she and Annie had sensed.

Tess was the first to speak. "But if they have been conducting their own experiments with vampire DNA and done it successfully, why did they come after Annie? Her research is on Lupines."

"Graham and Missy have been working on that, and they have two different theories. The first is that military thinks Annie's research has gone even further than theirs and that if they apply her techniques to what they've already managed, they can give themselves a huge leg forward."

"And the other reason?"

"That's the one where they don't care how far Annie got. They just want to destroy her data, but more than that, they want to use it to lure her into a trap. If they just destroy the data, they still have to worry that she'll re-create what she's already done. With her mind I doubt it would take long."

"It wouldn't," Sam agreed over the pitching and roiling in her stomach.

"Which is why we're pretty sure they're going to try to kill her."

CHAPTER 25

S am watched the room spin crazily around her and shook her head to clear it. "What did you say?" she demanded hoarsely.

Rafe shook his head. "I'm sorry, Samantha, but it makes the most sense. Noah himself said he suspected that the military had their own scientists working on the same type of research Annie was pursuing. It doesn't make any sense for them to steal her data unless their intent was not to use it themselves, but to make sure no one else could."

Sam understood and it made sense, but she couldn't stifle the instinctive urge to deny it, to stuff it in the closet with the skeletons and pretend it didn't exist.

"That's . . . We can't—" She broke off and cleared her throat. "We can't just leave her to it, then. We have to find her. Is the pack out looking for her?"

Rafe nodded. "Graham has every available tracker on it, Sam. We're going to find her."

"Yeah, but will it be in time?" She turned to Noah. "We have to find that warehouse. If that's where they do their dirty work, it's probably where they'll take Annie."

"Sweetheart, we don't even know for sure if they have her."

"If they do, this is our best chance to keep them from harming her, and if they don't, then maybe we can stop them before they find her." She squared her jaw, biting painfully against the anxiety that threatened to spill over. "Please."

Noah exchanged glances with Rafe, then nodded. "All right," he agreed. "We'll find the warehouse. Don't worry, baby; Annie will be safe. We'll make sure of it."

She shivered and leaned against his solid warmth. "Goddess, I hope so."

So did Noah. He hoped like hell he could keep his promise. He'd taken a vow never to lie to Sam again, so he didn't want to turn his promise into one.

They had detoured by the club only long enough to consult with Graham and Missy and for Noah to change his clothes. He dressed again in his mission clothes, checked his utility vest, and hoped like hell he wouldn't need anything that was inside of it.

Sam's first words once they got through the front door had been to ask the others if they had heard anything new about Annie. They hadn't, of course, and Noah had seen the worry on Sam's face. He remembered their phone conversation from earlier in the week, remembered how she'd told him she and Annie had been friends their whole lives, and he knew it would be devastating to Sam to lose her. He would make it a point to prevent that from happening.

He had left Sam in the front hall, talking quietly and intently with Missy and Graham, and when he jogged back down the stairs, that's where he found them.

"Graham is sending a couple of men with us," Sam told Noah, her hand reaching out toward him even before he joined the small group. She must have read the hesitation in his eyes, because she took his hand and squeezed. "Just Tobias and Rule. You know they both know how to handle themselves, and it's on the understanding that you'll be giving the orders."

The two men peeled away from the wall where they'd been standing and approached.

"It's your party," Tobias told Noah, "but you're already outnumbered. It doesn't make any sense to go in there with just the two of you. Think of us as the brute squad."

Rule nodded. "Seven against two are not bad odds, but seven against four are even better."

Noah knew when he had to give in; when someone else had a point was usually a good time.

"Fine." He nodded. "How fast can you be ready?"

Tobias grinned. "My wife is in the other room. As soon as I give her a kiss."

He looked at Rule, who shrugged. "I would say the same thing, but I have been reminded recently that my wife is also your sister and you probably do not want to hear me say things like that."

Noah chuckled. "Go ahead. Both of you. I'll avert my eyes."

The two men disappeared into the other room, and Noah sent Sam an inquiring look. "How did they convince Fiona and Abby not to come?"

"Fiona and Abby know that too many bodies could get in the way, and this isn't really their problem."

What Sam left unspoken was that she considered it hers.

"Don't worry," Noah said, his voice gruff as he rubbed a thumb along the plane of her cheekbone. "I'm not going to tell you to stay here. She's your friend, and it's your pack. I get that."

She blinked up at him for a long moment; then her mouth curved. "Good. I'll give you one thing, Noah Baker. You sure are a fast learner."

The sound of traffic spilled over the piers, amplified by the water of the Hudson. Sam could hear the bustle, the voices and activity, at the Chelsea Piers Sports & Entertainment Complex just north of them, but where they were, the area seemed almost eerily quiet.

She could sense the three men ranged around her, each one of them throwing off insane amounts of heat in the chilly evening air.

The sun had nearly set, and the shadows were lengthening, which was good for them. In their black clothing, they would blend in better with the shadows, and at least three of them had vision to let them see in pitch-blackness. Somehow, she didn't think Noah's human eyes would slow him down any.

He crouched a few steps in front of them with Sam at his back and Tobias and Rule slightly farther back at the rear. They were hunkered down just inside an abandoned storage shed with a good view of the warehouse farther out on the pier. It looked like an airplane hangar, and Sam thought she'd heard of it being used as a bus depot at one point, but these days it was supposed to be abandoned. She supposed it would be if the infamous B-team hadn't set up shop inside.

She felt impatience rising inside her and struggled to beat it down. She had agreed to play by Noah's rules as a condition of her coming along, and if Rule and Tobias smelled this calm, she supposed they had to approve of his approach, but damn it, she wished he'd hurry up and signal them to move. Even the silence, as wise as she knew it to be, was driving her crazy. She could hear the conversations of couples in cars driving by, but she heard not a peep out of her companions. They had agreed to it beforehand and brushed up on the military sign language Noah planned to use. Each of the men carried a cell phone, and each hoped he wouldn't have to use it.

The sun seemed to take forever to set, but finally the sky began to dim rapidly and twilight turned into early evening. When the light around them descended to an inky charcoal, she saw Noah shift and smelled the sudden tension in his body. Thank the moon, he was nearly ready.

She had shifted her weight, ready to spring into action, when the sound of an approaching car caught her attention. Lots of traffic had flowed past the end of the pier, but this was the first time a vehicle had peeled away from the rest and approached the chain-link fence that surrounded the property to discourage vagrants, scavengers, and curiosity seekers. Turning, she focused her attention on the sound and saw it had Tobias's interest engaged as well. Noah glanced back and saw their distraction. Sam signaled him to wait.

She saw when he heard it, too. By that point the car had paused, someone had gotten out to open the gate, and the car had pulled through onto the property. As it approached, Noah eased closer to the shed's entrance and watched as the car came into view.

It was a dark SUV, indistinguishable from thousands of others owned by New Yorkers crazy enough not to care about parking and gas mileage and car thieves. It had tinted windows and New York plates that had been smeared with mud and debris to make the numbers illegible. As they watched, the two front doors opened and two men got out. The driver moved back and opened the rear door, reaching for something inside. When he stepped back, Sam could see Annie's limp figure hanging trussed and unconscious over his shoulder.

Sam nearly went for his throat then and there.

Noah stopped her. The hard pressure of his hand on her shoulder reminded her of his presence and brought her back to reality. In the dark, his eyes met hers and he silently urged her to remember her promise.

Gritting her teeth, she sank back into her crouch and forced herself to wait silently. It was one of the hardest things she'd ever done. She wanted to move, to tear the man carrying Annie limb from bloody limb; she wanted to scream at him. She wanted to ask Noah a million questions and demand that he do something right *now*. But all she could do was sit and wait while the man carried Annie toward the warehouse with the passenger trailing behind, his fist closed tight around a big, black pistol.

When they disappeared inside the building, Noah finally rose from his crouch and waved them forward. They moved as a unit, quiet and efficient, keeping down and keeping to the shadows as they crossed the open lot and circled around to the back of the massive structure. Sam felt her heart beating in her throat, sped on by the rush of adrenaline coursing through her. She concentrated so hard on keeping herself contained, holding herself back from tearing straight through the building's metal walls, that she almost choked on the smoke before it registered.

Frantically she hooked her fingers in the back of Noah's vest and hauled him to a stop, signaling both the men behind her to freeze as well. When Noah turned back to look at her, she tugged his head down and pressed her mouth right up against his ear.

"There's someone standing out back by the rear entrance." She spoke in a low, toneless voice, less audible than a whisper. "Smoking. I can smell it."

Noah looked down at her, searching her face for confirmation. She nodded. His expression twisted as if the struggle to stifle his curse was almost too much for him. He managed it, though, and lifted his hand so the men could see it as well. Plan B.

With sharp nods, Tobias and Rule drifted away,

stalking back toward the front of the building and the door the late arrivals had used earlier. Sam took a deep breath, shucked out of her jeans to keep the cloth from ripping, and shifted. She saw Noah blink at the transformation, his eyes watching the whole thing, and that was apparently all it took for him to accept that the woman beside him had just turned into a four-legged carnivore.

Goddess, she loved him.

She stropped herself against his leg once, then ghosted past him toward the building's rear entrance. When she got close enough, she would hunker down and watch until the guard was distracted or looking the other way, and she would take him down as quickly and quietly as possible to let Noah slip past them and into the building.

That was the way it was supposed to work.

It might have, too, if she hadn't startled a small black shape also crouched in the shadow of the building. The feral cat, probably hunting mice in their hidey-holes beneath the building, took one look at the approaching wolf and let out a yowl that probably echoed in Yonkers. Mentally cursing, Sam gave up on keeping quiet and dug her claws into the cracked pavement, pouring on a burst of speed.

She rounded the corner at the same time as Camel man, knocking both him and herself off-balance. She went spinning through the pool of light cast by the guard's dropped flashlight, and he careened off the tin wall with a booming clatter. In the distance, she heard Noah's hissed curse and saw him running flat out toward them. At the same time, footsteps sounded inside and the rear door opened, two more soldiers spilling out, their weapons already in hand.

Sam howled a protest and launched herself at the one with his gun pointing at the corner Noah would round any minute. Her paws slammed into the soldier's chest and her teeth sank deep into the muscle of his shoulder. With a mighty shake, she dislocated the joint and followed the screaming man to the ground.

The clamor distracted the third guard, who looked toward Sam just long enough for Noah to clear the side of the building and bring the butt of his own pistol down on the back of the man's skull. He sank into a heap, but the original guard had regained his balance and was taking aim at Noah's head.

With a snarl, Sam charged the guard, knowing already that she wouldn't be fast enough. She felt her heart lodge in her throat as she saw his hand tighten around the trigger, and knew that it stopped the instant the report sounded in the cool night air.

Noah, though, kept standing.

The bloom of ugly red that she had expected to see on him materialized in the middle of the guard's chest instead, and he toppled to the ground just as she made impact. She followed him down and rolled away, scrambling to her feet just as the back door swung open again. Noah turned, his gun still raised from the shot he'd just fired, and watched as the figure in the doorway beckoned them in.

"I can't say I was expecting you, Major, but perhaps I should have been. Please, come inside. After you drop your weapons, of course."

She saw Noah's jaw tighten and smelled the wave of hatred that flooded through him.

"General Hammond," he said, and slowly crouched to lay his pistol on the ground.

CHAPTER 26

Noah laid his weapon down and rose slowly, his hands spread out by his shoulders. His mind raced through a dozen scenarios in which he relieved the general of the gun he held and shoved it up his ass, but every single one of them involved an unacceptable risk to Sam.

"Very good," the general said. He wasn't a particularly tall man, maybe five-nine or five-ten, but his posture and bearing made him appear taller. He carried himself with authority, and with his barrel chest and crisply tailored uniform, his dark gray hair and his ruddy complexion, he carried it well.

"Now, come inside." He gestured with his head, not the barrel of the gun. The cautious son of a bitch. "And be sure to bring your companion."

Noah didn't even glance down at Sam. He could feel her pressing against his leg, her fur tickling his fingertips. He nudged her in ahead of him. If they had to be on the wrong end of this bastard's sights, Noah could at least make sure the bullet had to go through him to reach Samantha.

He heard her toenails click against the building's concrete floors, the sound echoing in the cavernous space. A few bare fluorescent bulbs dropped down from the ceiling, barely cutting through the thick darkness. The warehouse had no windows, just three-story walls and a metal-girdered roof lost somewhere in the black space above them. Inside, near the center of the open space, he saw a handful of tables set up. A couple looked as if they held complex computer and communications equipment. A microscope sat on another, and a third was covered with weapons, ammunition, and other debris of military life.

A bench along the wall held a lumpy pile of fabric that Noah realized was Annie. Her hair hung over her face, concealing her features, but he didn't see any blood or any obvious wounds. With luck they had only drugged her or knocked her unconscious.

He saw three soldiers seated at the fourth table, though when the general approached, they rose. Beside him, Noah felt Sam stiffen, her hackles rising along her back.

"At ease, men." The general sounded almost jovial, as if something had put him in a very good mood. "Major, I'd like you to meet the pride of the new Paranormal Regiment Special Ops team. These three men represent the future of our operation. Every one of them has proved his ability to successfully tolerate the introduction of vampire DNA into his system and to make full use of the resulting extraordinary abilities. I would offer to have them give you a demonstration of those abilities, but I'm afraid that their last doses have already worn off and the serum is back at their headquarters. But trust me when I tell you that these men are going to revolutionize warfare."

Noah heard the gloating, arrogant tone and wanted to scream. Hammond made it sound as if he'd created these men, like some kind of sculptor molding them from clay. He had no idea what he was doing, what this nightmare meant for the Others. Worse than that, he didn't care.

"Tonight is our lucky night, gentlemen. All of our problems are gathered here in this room just waiting for us to deal with them once and for all. What could be better?"

A soldier with a clean-shaven head and a neck as thick around as a tree trunk looked at them and frowned. "Sir, where are Manning, Burcher, and Katz?"

The general sighed. "Burcher and Katz are outside, if you want to go collect them, but I'm afraid Manning is no longer with us. Major Baker here shot him."

All three men turned to look at Noah with hatred in their eyes. He didn't doubt they all had plans for exactly how they'd like to kill him. Too bad Hammond seemed intent on spoiling their fun.

"We heard the bullet," the bald soldier said. "It's gonna bring the police down here eventually. Even in this neighborhood, people love to report gunshots."

Hammond shrugged. "Then we'll just have to work fast." He reached out and grabbed Sam by the scruff of the neck, shaking her so hard that her front feet lifted from the floor. "Where are the rest of Dr. Cryer's notes, Ms. Carstairs?"

Noah shouted a protest and took an instinctive step forward, only to earn himself a rifle butt in the stomach.

The soldier who gave it to him, a narrow-eyed redhead with an incongruous faceful of freckles, looked as if he couldn't wait to do it again.

"I'm going to have to ask you to control yourself, Major. I would hate to have to kill you prematurely. I have a few questions to ask you before I shoot you. You've spent a great deal of time with the werewolves. I want to know exactly what parts of them we need to copy to take our work to the next level." Hammond shook Sam again, then dropped her so abruptly, her legs splayed out beneath her, sending her crashing to the floor.

She never made a sound, but Noah could see the light of murder in her eyes.

"I suggest you find yourself a human tongue and tell me, Ms. Carstairs. We've already learned from Dr. Cryer that she gave certain documents pertaining to her research to you for safekeeping. The only reason either of you is still alive is because I need those documents. If that work were to be published, it would end up in the hands of all the wrong people. My program is the very cutting-edge application of interspecies gene transplantation, and I'm not going to be upstaged because some little girl in a lab coat thought she could cure her people of fleas. So tell me where they are before I have to resort to less civilized methods."

Sam bared her teeth in a snarl. If she'd had fingers, Noah felt pretty sure she'd have given the general one of them. The middle one.

Hammond sighed and looked at his soldiers. "Go wake our other guest, Farley. It seems Ms. Carstairs has decided to be stubborn. Not a very good decision, I'm afraid."

Baldy crossed over to the bench near the wall and roughly hauled Annie to her feet. When her legs didn't respond quickly enough to hold her up, he shook her roughly back to consciousness. Then he half-dragged, half-shoved her back toward the others.

She'd been drugged, Noah decided, taking in her dazed expression and the blank, foggy look in her eyes. She was having to fight to stay conscious, and shivers wracked her in spite of the comfortable temperature inside the building.

"Sergeant, let's start with the doctor's fingers, I think."

Hammond kept his eyes on Sam while he said it, so he saw when she sat back on her haunches and bared her teeth. He also saw when she stretched and shimmered and shifted right in front of them.

Noah swore a blue streak. Sam was stark raving naked, and judging by the expressions on the faces of the other soldiers, he wasn't the only one who had noticed. Only Sam seemed oblivious. She stood as naturally as if she'd worn full body armor, her head up and shoulders back and pale skin almost glowing in the harsh, uneven glow of the overhead lights.

"Don't touch her," she growled, sounding just as feral as she'd looked when she'd been covered in bristling fur. "Don't you lay a single fucking hand on her, or I'll chew it off. No matter which shape I happen to be wearing."

"That's not a very cooperative attitude," the general scolded, his eyes raking over Sam's bare body in a way that made Noah want to rip them out and feed them to him. "I would think you would want to play nicely, Ms. Carstairs, in order to protect your friend."

"I'd rather give birth to kittens than play anything with you, Hammond. So let Annie go, and then maybe we'll have something to talk about."

Hammond chuckled. "I'm afraid that's not the way this works, my dear. You see, while I have you and your friend here, I hold all the power; and while I hold the power, I make the rules."

"I was never much good at following the rules."

The general's dark eyes narrowed. "Now might be a very good time for you to learn."

"Eh, I'm not that ambitious."

"Her fingers, gentlemen."

Noah saw Sam's face pale and her eyes shoot daggers at his former commander.

"Fine," she snapped, her eyes darting between Annie's dazed form and the figure of evil in front of her. "I'll tell you what you want to know, but you'll have to repeat the question. I'm afraid it slipped my mind."

The general's eyes narrowed, but he maintained his cheerful smile. "Very well, I'll repeat it once," he said. "But if you have trouble remembering it again, I'll assume it has something to do with me, and I'll let one of my men ask you. Alone."

Noah was afraid his jaw would snap in half from the pressure he was putting on it. He had it clenched so tightly, he figured he'd have molars in his sinus cavity before the night was over.

Sam, though, didn't flinch. She faced the monster with dignity and disgust and waited for the question.

"Where are the rest of Dr. Cryer's notes?"

Sam shrugged. "I brought them to the Alpha for safekeeping."

Hammond glared at her. "You're lying. Farley, start with the right hand. Dr. Cryer already informed us that neither of you told Winters about her work until last night, and she gave you those papers a week ago."

"I'm not lying," Sam snapped, her voice tense and convincing. "I couldn't think of any place safer to put them than on the other side of the Alpha. But I didn't give them to him personally. I brought them to his office and put them in his safe."

She had her eyes fixed on Annie, still swaying where she stood, but at least all of her fingers were whole. For now.

Noah swore silently and wondered how long Tobias and Rule were going to wait before they came to the rescue.

"All right, if that's true, then you'll need to retrieve them for me."

"Let Annie and Noah and me out of here, and I'll go fetch them lickety-split."

Hammond laughed through a sneer. "What a novel idea! But I have a better one. You can call Winters and instruct him to bring the papers here. He'll come alone to the gate, and Banks and McCray here will escort him inside. If he attempts anything heroic, I will kill him myself and then let you watch while I take my anger out on the lovely doctor. How does that sound?"

"Like the plan of a man who's going to spend all of eternity roasting in a fiery hell."

"How quaint. Farley, bring me a secure cell."

Noah interrupted. "That's not necessary. I have one right here in my pocket."

The general shook his head. "I'm sorry, Major, but

I'm afraid the phone I sent you is a fairly long way from being secure. But then, how else was I supposed to keep track of you? Farley's cell will do very nicely."

Shit.

Noah knew damned good and well the phone wasn't secure. That's why he'd wanted Sam on it. He'd asked Carter to have Jammer locate the cell frequency and find a way to listen in. If his team heard the call Sam was about to make, they'd be all over this place like white on rice in fifteen minutes flat. All Noah would have to do would be to stall Hammond that long.

Helplessly Noah's gaze strayed to Sam and found her staring at him intently. Her honey gold eyes seemed to hold a message for him, and when she nodded her head infinitesimally, he had to force his muscles to relax enough to return the gesture. She had something in mind, and at this point, all he could do was trust her.

S am's hands were itching for the chance to get on that phone—any phone—and she had to fight hard to keep from letting her excitement show. She had a plan. She couldn't be certain it was a very good plan, but it might give them a chance, and at this point a chance was all she needed. Annie looked ready to collapse at any second, and she needed to get out of here as soon as possible. Goddess knew what they had done to her, but Sam would worry about that later. She would worry about revenge later, after the people she loved were safe.

She could feel Noah vibrating with rage across the five feet separating them, but even if she hadn't felt it, she would have smelled it. It poured off him in waves, sharp and acrid and smoky. She knew exactly how badly he wanted to wrap his hands around the general's throat and squeeze; she knew how badly he wanted to find a blanket to wrap around her to cover her nudity; and she was so proud of him for his control. Any move on his part would have brought the general's fury down on Annie's head, and it was for her sake that Noah was reining in his murderous fury.

Sam didn't like the feel of the soldiers' gazes on her body any more than he did, but she ignored them because she knew reacting with embarrassment or shame was exactly what they wanted. She wouldn't give them even that much satisfaction.

Ignoring them completely, she held out her hand for the phone. "Do you want to write that down for me, or do you think I'm smart enough to remember all that?"

"Oh, I think you're definitely smart enough to realize what will happen to your friend if you forget, Ms. Carstairs." The general stepped closer to Annie and wrapped his fingers around her elbow. The gun he kept trained on Noah. "Go ahead. Place the call."

Sam's fingers flew over the buttons, and she fought to keep them steady as she raised the phone to her ear. She heard the line open, but the person on the other end didn't answer.

"Graham," she said, trying to keep from sounding excited or worried or anything other than wary. "This is Sam."

"Shit."

"I'm fine. Listen, I need you to do me a favor. I put

some things in your safe the other day, and I need them back. I need you to bring them to me."

Rule growled into the phone, "We know you ran into trouble in back. Did you take any of them out?"

"Yes. A sheet of loose paper and a notebook. They're in the third drawer. They're Annie's."

She felt the general watching her and sent up a quick and heartfelt prayer that she could get make this happen without anyone dying.

"So you took out three, which means there are three more in there with you. And Annie as well. Is she hurt?"

"No, don't be silly. I'm fine. I promise."

Rule muttered a curse in a language Sam was just as happy she didn't understand. "More than three? Sam, what is wrong? Is their boss there as well?"

Hammond tightened his grip on Annie, making her whimper. "Tell him to bring the documents here and wait by the gate. The men will meet him outside."

"Yes. I really need you to bring me those papers. I'm on the piers, the abandoned pier just south of Chelsea. If you bring them here, come to the fence and wait by the gate. Two people will meet you there and get the documents from you. Once you get here everything will be fine."

Sam heard a murmur as Rule and Tobias briefly conferred; then Rule growled, "Two more minutes, Samantha. Hold on that long, and I promise everything will be okay."

Then the line went dead in her ear. She kept talking.

"No, that's it. Just remember to come by yourself and stay out by the gate till someone comes for you. If you do that, we'll be just fine. But hurry, okay?"

She let a little quiver enter her voice at the end and saw the general's satisfaction at the sound. He wanted her to be frightened. The bastard got off on it. Sam couldn't wait to see if he liked being on the wrong end of his petty little threats.

"Good," Hammond said, and his grip loosened a tiny bit around Annie's arm. Sam could see the blood rushing back where his knuckles had been white. "At this time of night, it should take Winters about twenty minutes to get here. Add another two minutes to open his safe and gather the papers, and I estimate we have twenty-two more minutes to enjoy each other's company. However shall we pass the time?"

Sam stared at him with an expression of unmasked loathing, but her real attention was focused on the far side of the room, the front of the building and the two men she could sense just outside the door. In another minute they would be inside. She wanted to warn Noah, but there was nothing she could say without alerting Hammond to the impending attack, so she settled for sending him a look filled with every ounce of love she had for him and hoped it was enough.

That was when the room exploded.

CHAPTER 27

Three things registered for Noah all at once. The first was that Sam loved him. That was obvious from the look she gave him just before the front door to the building burst in and a six-foot, four-inch demon launched through with a five-foot sword in one hand and a hound of hell at his heels.

Noah assumed the hound was actually Tobias, but knowing that didn't take away from the impressive entrance.

The second thing to register was that Hammond and his three goons had been taken by surprise by the invasion, and the third was that Sam had not. In the instant the door parted from its frame, she was already in the air, throwing herself at Annie, knocking her free of the general's grip and carrying her to the floor. A shot rang out, but Noah couldn't see if it hit. Sam was already rolling herself and Annie several feet away before tucking the other woman underneath a table. Then Sam sprang to her feet and launched herself back into the fray, this time on four feet.

Noah barely had time to process revelation number

three before he found himself in action, his instincts automatically taking over to guide his muscles in the necessary movements. He heard two more shots, but he didn't have time to look for them. One leg swept out and caught the redheaded soldier directly in the left kneecap. The soldier's legs buckled and he collapsed on a scream, his hands cupping protectively around his injury. Noah snatched up the rifle the soldier dropped and turned immediately toward Hammond.

Out of the corner of his eye, Noah could see soldier number three pinned to the floor beneath a snarling, snapping Tobias, and Baldy was currently working on keeping his head attached to his neck. The way Rule swung that sword of his, the poor bastard wouldn't be able to manage it much longer.

Noah's eyes locked on Samantha and he felt his heart go cold. A crease in her side bled heavily, the red liquid staining and matting her thick fur. She lay half on her side, her front feet planted on the concrete, and she struggled to right herself. Hammond had his arms outstretched, one eye squinted as he peered down at them with Samantha directly in his pistol's sights.

Noah didn't even hesitate. He didn't think about his career or his future or the prospect of a court-martial or a murder trial. He just lifted the rifle to his shoulder and squeezed the trigger.

Hammond's body jerked in shock, his arms shaking, his shot going wild and pinging through the metal wall of the warehouse somewhere to the right. He dropped to his knees, then collapsed facedown on the concrete.

Noah threw down the rifle and sprinted to Sam's side, gathering her up in his arms, not caring about the blood or the fur or the tail. All he cared about was Sam and knowing that she would be all right.

"Sam! Samantha, honey, I'm so sorry. God! He hurt you." Noah heard his voice trembling as he ripped his T-shirt off over his head and pressed it to the wound in her side. All he could think about was stopping the bleeding. Stop the bleeding and get her to a hospital, and God, please let her be okay. "I'm so sorry, baby. Let me help. I'll apply pressure and then we'll call an ambulance and get you in for some stitches. You're going to be okay. I promise."

He felt a ripple as she shifted in his arms, and when he looked down, her very human face was smiling up at him.

"I know I will," she said, tugging at the hand he had pressing the T-shirt to her side. "Noah, it's all right. You can let go. I'm not bleeding anymore. See?"

She pushed his trembling hand away and he looked down at the red, puckered skin on her side. The open wound from the bullet crease was gone, partially healed over as if it had happened weeks ago instead of only a few minutes.

He moaned and squeezed his eyes shut, burying his face in her neck. "Oh, my God, I almost died!" He fought to catch his breath, to force the memory of seeing her wounded from his mind, but he knew even then that the picture would never leave him. "I saw you bleeding and I almost died. You can't ever do that to me again, baby. Promise you'll never scare me like that again."

She wrapped her arms around him and stroked her hands up and down his trembling back. "I'm certainly not planning to get shot again," she told him, sounding almost amused. "It hurt like hell!"

As he choked back a cry, his arms tightened around her until she squeaked and pressed against his shoulders to give herself room to breathe. "Don't even joke about it!" he scolded fiercely. "I love you! God, I love you so much. Do you have any idea what it would have done to me to lose you? *Do you?*"

He felt her hand cup his cheek and urge him to look at her. Through the glitter of tears, he saw that her eyes were warm and golden and loving, as sweet as summer honey.

"I think it would have done the same thing to you that it would have done to me," she told him, her voice achingly tender. "It would have killed me."

She brushed her lips against his and he clutched her to him as if he would never let her go.

When she whispered to him that she loved him, he knew he never would.

EPILOGUE

I t had been exactly one month since the incident at the piers, and Sam knew she loved Noah even more now than she had that night when he'd cradled her against him and told her he loved her. But if he didn't stop treating her with kid gloves, she swore to the moon she was going to kill him.

For four weeks he'd been all sweet kisses and gentle caresses, tender embraces and whispered words of love. At first, she'd understood. He'd had a shock, seeing her shot like that, and even though she'd healed a hell of a lot faster than any human, it had still been a couple of days before the last twinges had left her side. She'd thought it was very sweet of him to be so solicitous, so careful and undemanding of her. But she'd had enough of it three and a half weeks ago. She wanted the old Noah back, the one who threw her to her living room floor and took her until she screamed his name.

And damn it, she was going to get him back if it killed her.

She set the stage carefully, beginning with the timing. Noah had gotten the letter officially informing him of the U.S. Army's decision to clear him of any and all wrongdoing in the death of General Elijah Edward Hammond just yesterday. They'd been expecting it, but it had still been a relief for Noah to see it in black-and-white. Tobias and Rule had been very helpful in offering testimony to the investigation committee, as well as in cleaning up the mess they'd left on the pier. They had stuck around while Noah carried Sam back to the club to assure himself she didn't have any further injuries, so by the time the police arrived, and the MPs shortly after that, the three soldiers Hammond had used in his experiment had been more than ready to testify as well in return for the lighter sentences of life in prison.

Now that the whole mess was behind them, she figured it would be a good time for Noah to concentrate on the really important things. Like bringing her to a mind-blowing orgasm or three.

She had left the office early, never mind the usual Friday end-of-the-week chaos, and had rushed home to prepare. She had cold cooked meats, beer, and snacks in the fridge, candles glowing in strategic parts of the apartment, and she was wearing the kind of thing she'd once despaired of Noah ever getting to see, since he used to be so eager to get her clothes off, he never even bothered to look at what was underneath.

Tonight, she wanted him to look. And touch. And hopefully drool.

She heard his key in the lock and posed herself in the bedroom doorway, clearly visible when he opened the door.

"Sam? Where are you, sweetheart?"

"Over here," she purred, and watched as the keys fell from his hands and the blood rushed from his head to pool someplace farther south.

"Holy Christ," he groaned, stumbling back against the apartment door and knocking it shut. "You're trying to kill me."

"Absolutely not." She grinned and walked slowly toward him, loving the way his eyes locked on the sway of her hips as if a tow truck couldn't have pulled them away. "Why would I want to kill you when I'm not nearly done with you yet?"

Wrapping her arms around him, she pressed herself up against his starchy uniform and kissed him until she guessed his eyes had crossed. She knew for sure that hers had.

"God," he whispered against her lips, and she felt his hands on her hips, felt the tiny tremor that shook them. "You're driving me crazy," he said. "I don't think I can hold back anymore. I want you so bad, I think I might die from it."

But still he didn't make a move to lower her to the entry carpet. Of which she had some very fond memories. "Well, then quit wasting time and *do* something about it!" she shouted. "Who the heck asked you to hold back? I'm pretty certain it wasn't me, since I've spent the last month fantasizing about what it would be like the next time you pinned me up against the shower wall. Only you haven't done any pinning."

Her voice sounded accusing, but damn it, she was frustrated, and it was all his fault.

She felt those trembling hands lift and stroke the hair back from her face. His hazel eyes gazed down at her, searching her expression. "Baby, are you sure?" he asked. "I know you had a rough time. I don't want to scare you."

"Scare me?" she laughed. "The only thing I'm scared of right now is that you've decided you don't want me anymore. Yeah, what happened on the piers sucked, but I wasn't hurt and I wasn't traumatized. It was a bad day, but you know what? I've had bad days before, and I'll have bad days again. If you're going to act like I'm made of glass every time I do, I swear to the moon, I'll bean you over the head with something."

This time Noah laughed and his arms tightened around her. "I think I get the picture."

"Good!" She pulled back to look at him. "I'm a strong woman, Noah. I can handle more than you might think. And besides that, I have you. I have a mate who loves me almost as much as I love him. With you to remind me how lucky I am, what could possibly get me down?"

She felt his hands firm, dragging over her hips, her back, her bottom, and setting every single one of her nerve endings on fire.

"Oh, I don't know," he murmured, and his eyes glinted wickedly as he began slowly lowering her to the floor. "Sometimes I think down is a pretty good place to be."

Sam grinned and dragged his mouth down to hers. "I'll make you a deal. I'll stay down as long as you keep it up. How does that sound?"

He laughed against her mouth and slid his hands

inside the tiny panties that this time she knew he'd at least noticed.

"You," he whispered, sliding his fingers deep inside her and making her eyes roll back in her head, "have got yourself a deal."

Read on for an excerpt from the next book by
Christine Warren

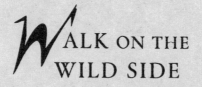

WALK ON THE
WILD SIDE

Now available from St. Martin's Paperbacks

Dear God, it hurt. Everything hurt.

Kitty lay in the darkness, struggling to tear her mind from the biting intensity of the pain long enough to figure out where it was coming from. Her hip, she thought, the right one, and her right leg as well, but that made no sense because she seemed to be lying on them. Why would she lie on her hip when it hurt so badly?

In fact, the whole right side of her body felt like someone had put it in a vise and squeezed until she began to come apart. Her head throbbed, too, making it harder to think clearly, and it felt as if a herd of elephants had recently danced across her chest. Just breathing made her wonder if a few of them hadn't returned for an encore. If she wanted to find out, she would have to open her eyes.

She didn't want to.

The dark was full of pain, but something told her the light would be worse. If there was any light. Frowning into the blackness, she realized she couldn't quite remember where she was, or how she had gotten there, or why everything hurt. Maybe there was no light.

Instead of opening her eyes, she listened as hard as

her aching head would allow. She heard a rough, hard rasping sound first, close by and erratically rhythmic. For a long moment she concentrated, listening for a pattern, a clue, a source. It was when she tried to inhale and heard the sound stutter into a ragged moan that she recognized her own breathing. She listened harder.

Crickets, tree frogs, cicadas. The nighttime chorus seemed eerily close, almost on top of her. She heard a rustling, intermittent and uneven, and realized that the wind was shaking the branches of a nearby tree. Was she outdoors? No, she couldn't smell grass or earth or the autumn night sky, and she knew it was autumn somehow. All she could smell was stale cigarette smoke and the pungent slap of gasoline.

Gasoline.

Car.

Driving.

Driving with Misty.

Driving with Misty the back way from Dalton.

Driving fast. Too fast. Fighting.

Headlights. Cell phone. Empty road. Deer. Brakes. Screaming. Skidding. Flipping. Screaming. Rolling-FallingScreamingThudding—

Silence.

Panic grabbed her by the neck, shaking away the last fog of unconsciousness. Eyes flying open, Kitty whipped her head around to look at the driver's seat. She saw the limp wreckage of the airbag hanging down toward her. Saw the equally limp form of her mother Misty dangling into the air above her, held in place by her seatbelt, her pale, freckled face the color of blackboard chalk. Saw the odd drop in one shoulder.

Smelled gasoline and the thick, charred scent of the end-of-the-season wildfires that still smoldered in the foothills of the Smokies.

Her heart tripped, stumbled, then righted itself and bolted toward an invisible finish line. She had to get out of there, had to get her mother out of there before a stray spark finished what the wreck had started.

The car had run off the road and down a hillside, landing on the passenger side with Kitty smashed up against the crumpled door. The driver's side pointed to the sky, the window smashed out and the door dented where it must have hit the guard rail or a tree or a boulder on the way down. The roof had partially collapsed, pressing them down against their seats. There wouldn't be much room to maneuver, and the only way out appeared to be through the driver's-side window.

She didn't waste time looking for her cell phone. She remembered holding it, remembered it flying out of her hand just before the impact when she'd tried to brace herself against the seat. If it was still in the car, there was no telling where it had fallen. She'd have to get herself and Misty out, and if she managed that, she could worry about finding it afterward.

Waiting for a rescue would be a waste of time as well, even if the smell of gas and smoke weren't already making her nervous. Someone would come along eventually, but on the back country road they'd been travelling, passersby were few and far between. Besides, at night they might not notice the skid marks, and even if they did, she had no way of knowing if the truck would be seen from the side of the road. She couldn't wait.

Gritting her teeth against the pain already threaten-

ing to overwhelm her and the surge she expected moving to cause, she reached around for her seatbelt and
pressed the release button.

Nothing happened.

Cursing, staring at her mother's limp form, she
pressed again, jamming the button as hard as her trembling fingers could manage, but the belt held firm. The
locking mechanism must have been damaged in the
wreck. If the truck hadn't been nearly as old as she
was, she might have wasted a few minutes trying to
find an emergency release near where the shoulder belt
connected to the frame behind the door, but it would be
useless. She'd have to find another way to free herself.

Carefully, she grasped the belt between her breasts
with her left hand, the only one that seemed to be
working, and pulled. It had locked in place, leaving her
precious little wiggling room. She pulled as much
slack as she could manage and ducked her head, unable to stop the whimper that escaped as her entire
body protested the movement.

Forcing her shoulders forward and the belt back, she
managed to free herself from the shoulder harness after what felt like slow, painful hours. Her fingers
slipped from the hard fabric weave and she heard the
rapid-fire clicking of the belt retracting and a dull snap
as it thudded against the back of the seat. She bent over
her knees, fighting back simultaneous surges of nausea
and dizziness. She couldn't afford to quit now.

Her breathing sounded like some kind of power
tool, loud and harsh and rasping in the unnatural still-
ness. She listened hard over the chaos in her head and
finally heard Misty's, uneven and much too weak.

As soon as the nausea faded, she sucked in a breath, ignoring the sharp, stabbing pain the movement caused in her side, and gripped the lap belt. She pulled and found herself whimpering again when the restraint offered no give. She yanked harder, but the fabric stayed in place across her belly. God, this could not be happening.

Her brain scrambled for some alternative solution even as her hands clenched, and she poured all her strength into another pull. Misty moaned, the sound barely more than a pain exhalation, and Kitty felt the fear inside her rising. The smell of smoke and gas intensified, the air thickening, and she could have sworn she heard the faint, distant crackle of flames.

God. If she didn't get them out of the wreck, they were going to die there, in a broken-down old truck on the side of a deserted back country road during a week-long vacation to visit her granddad. All because of a damned stupid deer that hadn't had the sense to run at the first sign of headlights.

Kitty did not plan to go out that way.

Her heart, already racing, sped even faster, and the dizziness she'd felt before returned with a vengeance. This time, she didn't bother to put her head down and wait for it to pass. No time. She might pass out, but so long as she did it after she made it out of the truck, she couldn't care less.

She heard Misty shift and gasp, heard the gasp turn into a cough. A series of coughs, breathless and much too quiet. Smoke was definitely blowing at them now, and if the wind was pushing the smoke toward them, the fire wouldn't be too far behind.

Swearing, she pulled and yanked and tugged, but the seatbelt wouldn't move. It had locked in place over her hips, blocking her escape. If she couldn't make it move, she'd have to move around it. Holding it in her left hand, she began another slithering attempt to ease herself out of her seat. The pain clawed at her, but she ignored it. It wasn't going to go away any more than the fire, and unlike the fire, the pain wasn't going to kill her. In fact, it was almost nice to be reassured that she hadn't died.

She braced her left foot against the floorboard and tried to lever herself up in the seat. The belt slipped an inch off her belly and onto the tops of her thighs, then stopped to grip even more tightly, trapping her. Damn it, she couldn't be trapped. She had to get them out of there.

The right side of her body screamed in protest at the slightest movement, and she couldn't seem to control most of it. She would have worried about paralysis if it hadn't hurt so damned badly. But even if she could feel it, she couldn't move it. No more than an inch or so, and that with concentrated, sweat-inducing effort. It wasn't going to lend her any power in escaping; more likely, she'd be dragging it behind her. If she managed to escape at all.

Misty coughed again, the sound even weaker, and Kitty redoubled her efforts to escape. God had gotten His chance to kill her in the initial wreck; if He hadn't done it then, she figured she'd been meant to get out of there. She didn't intend to give Him or the devil a second chance.

Determination, though, wasn't getting the job done.

No matter how she wriggled and pulled and tore and pushed, the belt and her body refused to budge. She felt her heart speed up, racing, until the sound of its pounding echoed in her ears. Her breathing became rapid, shallow pants that barely drew in enough oxygen to keep her conscious. Or maybe she wasn't getting enough. Her vision had begun to blur. Blinking against a haze she assumed had to be smoke, she peered at the mangled interior of the truck and made a helpless sound of protest as it started to melt and twist around her.

Her body seemed to melt and twist as well. It didn't hurt, precisely, but it frightened her, the way she had suddenly become something out of a Dali painting. She guessed that if she looked into a mirror, she would see her own features running down the surface of her face. See her limbs twisting in ways nature had never intended them to twist. See her insides and her outsides rearranging themselves into something she instinctively guessed she would never recognize.

She heard Misty cry out, but the sound seemed to come from a great distance. Everything seemed to be more distant than it had been a moment ago, as if she'd been plucked out of her skin and set back down in a slightly different place than she'd occupied before. Her mind had gone quiet and blank of all thoughts but those of escape.

She reached out one more time to push the belt away from her and blinked in shock when the thick fabric shredded in front of her eyes as if a scalpel had sliced through the tough webbing. How the hell had that happened?

Did it really matter?

Resolving not to bother asking questions, Kitty tugged her legs out from under the confining lap belt, tumbling forward into the center console when the task seemed to take a good several inches of leg less than it should have. She bumped skull-first into Misty and shook her head to clear it. Actually, it had felt like she'd gone nose first, nose and mouth at the same time, which was ridiculous. Her nose was perfectly average, not big enough to precede her into a room, and no one had ever accused her of having bee-stung model lips. Her forehead must have made contact first. She was just disoriented.

Her vision still hadn't cleared. She felt almost as if she were looking through a haze of smoke at an old black and white television set. Her color perception seemed off, probably from the smoke, but her depth perception was all screwed up as well. Nothing seemed quite where she thought it should be. She reached out for Misty, and her hands caught nothing but air. She couldn't even seem to reach her mother, let alone grasp her under the arms like she had planned so she could haul them both to safety.

Misty cried out, an honest-to-God scream this time, and Kitty could read the terror clearly on her face. The older woman stared at her daughter as if she didn't even recognize her, and Kitty felt a stab of pain that had nothing to do with her battered right side. In fact, her right side felt a lot less battered now than it had just a couple of minutes ago. Getting free of that seatbelt had been like a miracle cure. It must have been cutting into a nerve or something. That had to have been why she hadn't been able to move before.

Dismissing the inconvenient curiosity, Kitty reached out again, and again missed her mother's body. Frustration welled up inside her, and she suppressed the need to roar her displeasure. The smoke was definitely thickening now. It obscured her vision and filled her lungs, and the need to get out of danger urged her on like a pair of razor-sharp spurs in her sides. She had no time left for mistakes. She had to do this *now*.

She reached for Misty one last time, completely unprepared for her mother's small fist to come smashing down on the side of her face in an astonishingly forceful blow.

For a second, Kitty stared out the half-empty wasteland of shattered glass where the truck's windshield used to be. That's what she'd found herself looking at when her mother's punch sent her head swinging away from the unexpected momentum. She blinked, her mind reeling, her brain scrambling to make sense of an attack from the woman who had given birth to her, who she was currently trying to save from a painful and undignified death beside a deserted country highway.

That was when something inside Kitty Jane Sugarman snapped and shifted and settled down into a place it had never been before. That was when she opened her mouth, let out a spine-chilling yowl, clamped her strong, animal jaws around the back of her mother's neck, and dragged the other woman bodily out of the ruined truck and up to the apron at the side of the asphalt roadway. Then she settled down on her furry haunches, her tail twitching behind her, and stared at her human mother through wide, green, feline eyes.